Readers love
JEFF ERNO

My Dumb Jock

"This *"jock and nerd fall in love"* series is one of the best I've read and has always held a special place in my heart…"

—My Fiction Nook

Teacher's Pet

"Very well-written story with amazing details…"

—MM Good Book Reviews

"If you like a fast-paced roller-coaster ride which moves in lots of directions at once, throwing you off the track, you may enjoy this murder mystery. Thanks, Jeff, for an entertaining story."

—Rainbow Book Reviews

Glitter

"I found this book well written with a distinctive plot. The main characters and the secondary characters were realistic. I loved the ending because it was not who I expected. I had a hard time putting this book down."

—Hearts on Fire Reviews

By JEFF ERNO

Published by DREAMSPINNER PRESS
www.dreamspinnerpress.com

Slim Chance

Jeff Erno

DREAMSPINNER
PRESS

Published by

DREAMSPINNER PRESS

5032 Capital Circle SW, Suite 2, PMB# 279, Tallahassee, FL 32305-7886 USA
www.dreamspinnerpress.com

Slim Chance
© 2017 Jeff Erno.

Cover Art
© 2017 L.C. Chase.
http://www.lcchase.com
Cover content is for illustrative purposes only and any person depicted on the cover is a model.

ISBN: 978-1-63533-546-0
Digital ISBN: 978-1-63533-547-7
Library of Congress Control Number: 2016920371
Published June 2017
v. 1.0

Printed in the United States of America
∞
This paper meets the requirements of
ANSI/NISO Z39.48-1992 (Permanence of Paper).

There is no real beauty without some slight imperfection.
    —James Salter

CHAPTER ONE

AN EXASPERATED sigh followed by what sounded like hyperventilation caught Oliver Paxton's attention. He rushed around his cubicle divider to check on his coworker.

"Are you okay? I'm calling 9-1-1."

"No, no!" Ben gasped for breath and frantically waved his arms. "I'm... okay...."

At his weight, getting down on his knees wasn't exactly easy, but Oliver placed his hands against the desk and carefully lowered himself, then knelt beside Ben's chair. "Are you sure, man? You can hardly breathe."

Ben pointed to the computer screen. "I... I can't figure... I can't figure this out. Have deadline."

Oliver glanced at the computer, then back at Ben. They'd met, and Oliver knew the guy's name, but he knew nothing about him.

"Wait." Oliver looked back at the screen. "Dude, you just missed one of the commands. Here." He reached in front of Ben and typed rapidly on the keyboard to complete the code.

"W-wow." Ben leaned in, staring wide-eyed at the screen. "Y-you fixed it! How'd... how'd you know?"

Oliver shrugged. "Guess I just remembered that code. I see how you missed it, though. Common mistake." He smiled as he looked into Ben's dark brown eyes. The tension drained from his coworker's face as Ben returned his smile.

"I kind of panicked there. I... well, this is my first job. I knew if I didn't meet this deadline, I'd probably get fired. I've been stuck at this stage of the programming for the past three hours."

"Really? Well, you're almost done. Let's just bang it out real quick."

Ben shook his head emphatically. "Uh... no, you've done enough. I'm fine now."

"Don't be silly. Two heads are better than one, right? And I'm sure I'll need your help one day, probably sooner than later." He winked before turning his attention once again to the monitor. He started keying in the codes while Ben got up and offered Oliver his chair. Ben then pulled over another chair from a neighboring cubicle. A half hour later, they'd finished the coding.

"I guess they weren't lying when they said you were smart."

"Who?" Oliver turned to Ben, smiling. "Someone told you I'm smart?" Oliver had graduated top of his class with a degree in computer science. He'd landed a job as an IT specialist for the insurance firm where he now worked, and Ben had started in the same department about a month later.

"A few people, actually. Head of your class...."

Oliver waved his hand dismissively. "Well, don't believe everything you hear. I do know about computers, but so do a lot of people. They're kind of my passion, which is why I'm also a gamer."

"I think most people in our profession are... uh...."

The guy wasn't having another panic attack, was he? Oliver placed his hand on Ben's shoulder. "You all right?"

"S-sorry. I used to... uh... st-stutter real bad. Still do sometimes when I'm... uh... nervous."

"Well, you totally don't have to be nervous around me. I'm not your boss or anything." He laughed. "And yeah, I agree with you. Pretty much anyone who goes into computer programming has got to love computers, or they're in the wrong profession. Are you a gamer?"

With a slow nod, Ben looked over and smiled. "Most people call me Benjy. My friends, I mean... and family. And yeah, I do, um, I mean I *am* a gamer."

"Cool. Well, I hope we can be friends, Benjy."

"You play, um... Overwatch?"

"Only all the fucking time." Oliver raised his eyebrows as Benjy's grin broadened. "What do you think of the latest patch notes?"

"Oh my God. They, like, totally nerfed my character. It sucks, man. I mean, they diminished his healing bubble, like weakened it. I was so pissed."

"I hear ya, man. Happened to a lot of characters."

OLIVER STOOD perfectly still, emulating a statue, but as the seconds ticked by, he found it increasingly difficult to resist the urge to raise his hand to adjust the collar of the tuxedo shirt. Finding dress shirts that didn't choke him had become challenging in recent years, and though he had a wardrobe full of nice clothes, few of them fit other than what he special ordered from a plus-size distributor. Over the previous decade, his neck size had increased along with the rest of him, and for some reason, clothing manufacturers didn't seem to understand that plus-sized people also had large necks.

The tailor had offered him the largest neck size available for his particular shirt, which meant it was also the longest. This created another dilemma, one with which Oliver was all too familiar. He didn't need a dress shirt that hung down far enough to be used as a nightshirt as well. When he put it on, before even trying to tuck it in, the shirt extended to his knees. It would've been perfect had he been a mere eight or nine inches taller.

Fortunately the size sixty-two tuxedo jacket successfully concealed his torso. Though he wouldn't characterize the suit as "slimming," it certainly concealed some obvious effects of his portliness.

For months he'd been determined to lose as much weight as possible prior to the wedding. He couldn't say no to his best friend, Amanda, when she asked him to stand up for her. Though a bride usually chooses bridesmaids as attendants, Amanda insisted her gay best friend also be her best man. Sure, it was an unconventional choice, but then Amanda was an unconventional friend. She reveled in her rebellious acts and enjoyed shocking people.

If shock value had been her only reason for choosing Oliver, he certainly wouldn't have accepted the nod. But she truly was his closest friend. They'd been besties since grade school, back when she'd taught him all the cool jump-rope games and they'd played "Down Down Baby, Down by the Roller Coaster" at recess. His coming out didn't surprise her in the least. In fact, she laughed, stating it had taken him long enough to admit what she'd suspected all along.

Back then, back in the third and fourth grade when they'd first started hanging out together, he'd been thin... well, relatively. He'd never been a beanpole, but at least prior to middle school, he'd been close to "normal" size. He didn't really start putting on weight until he hit puberty. Fortunately the only physical fitness requirement for high school was freshman phys ed. After getting that out of the way, he no longer had to worry about embarrassing himself by trying to run or perform calisthenics in front of an audience of peers.

That certainly didn't provide any immunity from teasing and bullying, though. As his girth continued to expand, so too did their taunts and jeers. The endless stream of name-calling and teasing became so commonplace, he learned to laugh it off. Some of his classmates even mockingly nicknamed him "Slim." It was easier to be the brunt of a joke when he was in on it, going along with the degradation. The name-calling didn't seem so hurtful that way but more like endearing monikers.

Amanda wasn't exactly Twiggy herself. Though she didn't compare to Oliver's size, she wouldn't have been welcomed with open arms onto the cheerleading squad. Oliver didn't consider her fat, though she often referred to herself as "overweight." For girls, the standard seemed to be even more unforgiving. At least with guys, there was a range. You could be anywhere between skinny and husky and still be accepted as normal. You had to pretty much be excessively obese to be labeled "fat," and that's precisely what he was.

At five-foot-ten, he weighed two hundred eighty-three pounds the day he graduated. Four years later, when he received his bachelor's degree, he was another forty-five pounds heavier. At twenty-four, Oliver could see no light at the end of the tunnel when it came to his weight battle. He feared by the time he hit his thirties and forties, he'd be an eligible contestant for *Biggest Loser*, or even worse, *My 600-lb Life*.

Staring at his reflection in the full-length oval mirror, Oliver wanted to vomit. He turned slightly to view himself in profile, trying to imagine how he'd look in the wedding photos. His absurd attempt to suck in his gut made no difference whatsoever, so he balled his hands into fists and gritted his teeth, resisting the urge to punch the mirror.

"You look awesome."

He turned to Benjy and rolled his eyes. "Please, don't mock me. I know I look like the Goodyear Blimp."

"I'm not mocking. You really do…. You look amazing. That suit really suits you."

"It's a tuxedo, and my gut's too huge for me to even wear the cummerbund."

"It's okay. You don't need it." Benjy stepped closer and reached out to pat Oliver on the shoulder. Of course a guy Benjy's size wouldn't understand the humiliation Oliver felt. If Benjy weighed a hundred thirty pounds while soaking wet, Oliver would be surprised.

"Two of you could fit into this tuxedo. I'm so disgustingly fat. My face looks like a pig." He glared angrily at his reflection.

"I wish you wouldn't put yourself down like that, Ollie. You know, you carry your weight well. It's hardly noticeable."

"And I wish you'd stop saying such stupid things you know aren't true! I know what you think of me. I know what everyone thinks. I'm a fucking whale!"

The tailor, who'd finished taking measurements, stood on the other side of Benjy. He cleared his throat as he raised his chin. "Well, I think I have everything I need here. You can change at your leisure and leave the tuxedo hanging in the dressing room. We'll have the alterations complete by Friday." He turned and exited as briskly as he spoke, then made his way back behind the counter.

Oliver sighed. He looked into Benjy's face and registered his crestfallen expression. Suddenly he felt like an ass. "I'm sorry, man. I didn't mean to snap at you."

"No, it's cool. Don't worry about it." Benjy smiled. "I get how stressful it is. I… uh, I couldn't imagine having to stand up in front of all those people like that. I'd probably, um, faint or something."

Actually, Benjy wasn't exaggerating. He probably would literally faint. He didn't do well in crowds, and he didn't handle stress like a normal person.

From the day they'd first met at work, they shared a passion for online gaming, their gaming conversations never stopped—their secret language. And interestingly, this common interest also served as a shield. Oliver enjoyed a comfort level with Benjy and could always communicate through gaming, no matter what was happening on the job, in his nonexistent romantic life, or at home. Even when Oliver felt frustrated, or lonely, or like the fattest, ugliest man on the planet, he could always talk to Benjy about video games.

But at times, Oliver wondered if he and Benjy would even be friends were they not coworkers and fellow gamers. Otherwise, they were nothing alike. Benjy was short and skinny, while Oliver was a big chubby dude. Benjy was shy, while Oliver had always been more outspoken. Benjy, at twenty-four, had just leased his first apartment, which he kept immaculately clean. In every way neat and tidy, he represented the opposite lifestyle Oliver embraced.

Oliver, though not a slob, had no propensity for tidiness. He lived and worked amid a swirl of controlled, manageable chaos. His rented two-bedroom home certainly wasn't filthy, but he found comfort within the mounds of clutter that surrounded him. Things might not appear organized to outsiders, but he always knew where to find everything he needed.

But since he graduated college, now nearly fifty pounds heavier than he was his freshman year, most of his friendships had dropped off. In high school he'd always managed to insert himself into the group, participating in a range of extracurricular activities. Band, drama, and even the production of a school yearbook and a monthly newspaper had captured his interest and allowed him to interact with other students. Of course, they often regarded him as the token fat kid, but he was one of them nonetheless. As an adult, all that had changed. In the real world as a twentysomething, size seemed to matter even more than it had back in high school.

So how was it he'd gotten to this point? How had he allowed himself to grow to this size? Along the way, he'd known it was happening. As his pants and shirt sizes increased and his clothes no longer fit, he couldn't deny he'd grown. It became more difficult for him to slide behind the wheel of his car, and he couldn't explain away his ever-widening girth. As it became more difficult to dress himself, bathe, and even wipe himself in the bathroom, he could no longer make excuses.

And yet… he did. He always had excuses, and often they were valid. Other guys his age ate just as much as he did, often more, and they didn't turn into orcas. With both of his parents being overweight, undoubtedly there was a genetic component. He had really low metabolism. He might even have a thyroid problem or something.

The cruel, baseless assumptions people made about fat people infuriated him. He wasn't lazy. Far from it. He didn't binge eat. He didn't subsist solely on fast food. He wasn't a filthy slob. Just because he was overweight, people assumed things about him, that because he was less attractive physically, he was less of a person. He was less intelligent, less motivated, less personable.

And in some cases, the assumptions became self-fulfilling prophecies. He did find himself at times receding into himself, pulling away from others. At times the fat jokes became too much to bear. The snide remarks and cursory glances cut into his soul, bruised him. He fought the natural tendency to think of himself the way he knew others viewed him. And with each passing day, he felt himself losing the battle.

Now decked out in the fanciest duds he'd ever worn, staring at his reflection in the full-length oval mirror, he raised his chin to examine the roll of fat encasing his neck. He held out his arms, taking in the puffiness of his bloated hands. He turned again to the right to view his profile and glared angrily at his distended belly. This wasn't who he wanted to be, not now at the age of twenty-four and not ever.

"I hate you," he whispered.

Benjy took a step closer to him, perhaps fearing the comment was directed at him. "Ollie, please… please don't say that."

"It's true, Benjy. Look at me. Look at what I've become. I'm a big fat slob. A pig. I'm nothing but a disgusting hog."

"You're not disgusting to me."

His eyes now misty, Oliver turned to Benjy. "You say I'm not disgusting to you, meaning I obviously am to everyone else."

"No! Ollie, you're putting words in my mouth. You're not disgusting. You're… *imperfect*. You're a normal person who doesn't happen to have an underwear model's body. You're not an athlete or a movie star, though. You're a computer programmer and my best friend. I see you for who you are, who I know you to be. Smart, funny, and the best friend—"

"Benjy, stop! You're not helping."

Benjy sighed and shook his head. "I just wish you could see yourself as I see you. As Amanda sees you."

"I have to do something about myself. I can't go on like this."

"Okay." Benjy stared up at him, his eyes wide and perhaps a bit misty as well. "I'll do anything I can to help."

CHAPTER TWO

OLIVER NEARLY lost it when the bride looked up at him from the aisle, smiling proudly. Stunning in her flowing, white gown, Amanda about took his breath away—almost as gorgeous as her groom. Tyler, a marketing systems analyst, had met Amanda in college. With his blond hair and brilliant blue eyes, he made an excellent Ken to Amanda's Barbie. The day Ollie met him, he had to confess to his best friend how utterly consumed with jealousy he was, yet equally happy for her. Tyler and Amanda were the consummate heterosexual couple, head over heels in love, and sure to realize every piece of the American dream. Oliver could see their future clearly, like looking into a crystal ball. They'd buy a home in the suburbs with a white picket fence, have two or three kids, and live happily ever after.

His own future, far murkier, didn't seem so optimistic. But today wasn't about him. Today was about his bestie and her wedding. At the reception, Oliver stood at the attendants' table and raised his crystal goblet, tapping the side with his silver spoon to capture everyone's attention. He placed the spoon down, waiting for the murmurs to quiet, before speaking. He reached up to his neck, slid one finger behind the collar of his dress shirt, and wiggled it a bit for comfort. Actually, it already felt somewhat looser than it had two weeks prior at the tuxedo fitting. He'd started his new diet but hadn't yet dared step on a scale to check his progress.

As all eyes turned to him, he cleared his throat. "I know this isn't really typical, having two best men at a wedding, one for the bride and one for the groom. Then again, Amanda and I are not typical best friends.

"Back in third grade, when we met, Amanda recruited me to play the dad in a game of house on the school playground. She, of course, was Mom." He looked at Tyler. "So I already have experience being married to this lady, and let me tell ya, you're in for a hell of a ride." The audience chuckled.

"Amanda works as a chef, ya know. Already landed herself a position at one of those fancy-schmancy upper-class restaurants. I know you probably can't tell by looking at me, but I know a thing or two about food… and Amanda's been feeding me all my life."

His gaze locked on Amanda's, and though she still maintained the sweet, ever-broadening smile, he detected a hint of sadness in her eyes. After clearing his throat, he continued. "In all seriousness, I've known this gal since elementary school, and she's my dearest friend. She's one of the kindest, most compassionate, and accepting people on the planet. When she and Tyler met five years ago, she made a special trip up north to the college I was attending, just to introduce him, and I have to say, I immediately approved. They're an amazing couple, and they're sure to head into a spectacular future together… decades of happiness and prosperity.

"I'd just add one word of caution to the groom, though. Tyler, don't let her overfeed you. You don't want to look like this in five years." He held out both arms, displaying himself as the example. "Did I mention Amanda and I were in band together? People have often asked me, what was your favorite instrument? 'Oh, that's easy,' I told 'em. 'The lunch bell.'"

The crowd burst into laughter as the bride's smile waned just a bit. "But, hey, this isn't my fault. I've been fat since I was a kid. This whole obesity thing could have been avoided, though… if they'd have just sent an ice cream truck into our neighborhood every day. What? You don't get it? Not just an ordinary ice cream truck. No, an ice cream truck that never stops."

This time the laughter was accompanied by a smattering of moans. "Oh, I know, I'm killing you. But this tuxedo's killing *me*. These things are designed more for people who are in shape. Wait, I'm in shape. Aren't I? Isn't *round* a shape?"

Oliver knew a lot of fat jokes. He'd heard them all and could go on for hours, but as he looked up once more to Amanda, her smile had become a grimace. He might have taken the self-deprecation a bit too far this time. Not only had he hurt himself but also his best friend. He just smiled, though, laughing it off as he raised his glass for the toast.

"To the bride and groom. I love you, Amanda. I love you, Tyler. Here's to a wonderful future."

Later, during their dance, Amanda held him close, pressing her cheek against his. "You look magnificent in that tuxedo, baby."

"For a beached whale, ya mean?"

"Ollie, stop it." She pulled back and stared straight into his eyes. "For anyone. I'm telling you, you look amazing, and if you'd quit feeling sorry for yourself, you might just meet someone. You know, like really *meet* someone, as in a date. Half the guests here are gay."

Oliver laughed and leaned in to kiss her cheek. "No, because even if what you say is true… even if I do look good in this tux, I also know what I look like underneath it."

"Honey, please stop putting yourself down." The tone of her voice pierced Oliver's heart. She needed him to stop belittling himself… for his own sake.

"I'm sorry. You're right. This is your day. It's not about me."

"No, that's not what I mean." She pulled back again, this time holding him by the shoulders. "I mean you need to quit judging yourself through this lens. You are more than a fat person. In fact, I don't even like that term, because you're not really all that overweight."

Oliver had to laugh, though mirthlessly. "Amanda, I'm at least a hundred seventy pounds overweight. Google it if you don't believe me."

"So what? I love you just the way you are, and there's someone out there… some equally amazing guy, who is going to feel exactly the same way."

"A chubby chaser."

"Maybe, but so what?"

He brushed a thumb against her cheek. "Amanda… baby… can we not have this discussion here, on the dance floor—on *your* dance floor during *your* dance?"

She nodded and released a frustrated sigh. "Fine, then learn to take a fucking compliment. You look amazing. Period."

Nodding slowly, he closed his eyes. When he opened them, Amanda was staring into his face, tears streaming down her cheeks. "Thank you," he whispered, and once more kissed her on the cheek before stepping aside to allow one of the groomsmen to cut in.

OLIVER'S DETERMINATION to lose weight felt drastically different this time. He'd previously made numerous attempts, some serious and some fleeting and half-assed. Some lasted days or possibly even weeks, some merely hours. Every time he made the slightest progress by taking off a few pounds, he'd then turn around and gain it all back and then some.

This time, however, he decided to stick with it no matter what. Going for a complete lifestyle change, he hauled his industrial-sized trash can from the garage into the center of his kitchen and began tossing shit into it from his cupboards.

"Ollie, those are my favorite!" Benjy sat on a stool at the bar separating the kitchen and dining area. "Marshmallow cream chocolate graham-cracker cookies, and they're not even open!"

"Take 'em if you want 'em." Oliver didn't even turn around but continued tossing items over his shoulder into the huge plastic tub. "Six-pack of Snickers bars, Cheez-Its, Fig Newtons… no wait, those are fat-free."

"I'll take the Pop-Tarts if you're gonna just toss 'em."

Oliver grabbed the family-size box and handed it to Benjy. "You want this box of Cap'n Crunch too?"

He made a face and shook his head. "No, thanks. I hate how they get soggy when you put milk on 'em."

"Oh my God, that's the best part. Sugary goodness melting against your tongue." Oliver's mouth watered thinking about it. But he'd stuck to his diet for almost a month now, and he should have done the kitchen cleanout a long time ago. He was finally getting used to his low-fat, low-calorie diet. That meant very little sugar, and he'd discovered the longer he went without it, the easier it became to resist.

"I think the diet's working, Ollie. I can see it in your face. It looks so much thinner." Benjy's unfailing optimism annoyed Oliver at times. He didn't need to hear about his face getting thinner. He didn't fucking care about his face! He needed to shed some massive pounds from his humongous, grotesque body.

"My pants feel looser, actually." Oliver kept his temper in check. Benjy meant well, after all. "But I don't want to weigh myself yet, not until my one-month anniversary."

"That's a good idea. I've heard people say you shouldn't weigh yourself too often when dieting."

Just what the hell would that beanpole know about dieting? Maybe Oliver should just ask him to leave.

"You wanna play Overwatch when we're done here?" Benjy asked. "That new guy from Virginia texted me this morning, asked if we wanted to join his team."

"We've already got our own team, and no, I don't want to play. I have to work out."

"You mean like at a gym? I could go with you if you want."

"I don't go to a gym, and I don't want an audience." At this point, he no longer even tried to conceal the edge in his voice. "I think you should just leave. You're not any help here."

Benjy laughed, obviously thinking Oliver was kidding. But when Oliver turned around and glared at him, the smile drained from Benjy's face. "Oh, okay. I'm sorry, man. I can—"

He looked like an abandoned puppy, and a pang of guilt stabbed Oliver's heart. "No, man, it's cool. I'm just…. I don't know, edgy or something. I'm sick of starving myself and no one even noticing a difference. I'm sick of passing up cookies and cakes and burgers and pizzas, all the stuff I love to eat. For what? It's been a whole month, and look at me. No difference. No fucking noticeable change!"

"But I *did* notice. Ollie, you didn't put on the extra weight overnight, and you can't take it off that way. You said yourself, your clothes are starting to feel loose. You're losing, man. You've probably lost way more than you even expected you would."

"Do you really think so?"

"Why don't we go weigh you right now? I know you wanted to wait a month, but it's close enough, and you need the ego boost."

"But… but what if I haven't lost any? What if I've gained or lost only a little?"

"Trust me, you've lost weight." Benjy slid off the stool and stepped into the kitchen to grab hold of Oliver's wrist. "C'mon, let's go see."

Reluctantly, Oliver allowed his friend to drag him out of the kitchen and down the hall to the bathroom. He'd purchased a special scale that went up to four hundred pounds, and his first official weigh-in had registered three hundred thirty-two pounds. He honestly didn't know what to expect, what to even hope for at this point. It had been just four days shy of a month.

"Hop on!" Benjy ordered, pointing to the scale.

"I don't know."

"Ollie, please."

Oliver sighed, then smiled sheepishly. He held up both arms, fingers crossed on each hand. "Okay, let me kick my shoes off." One at a time, he toed them off and then took a step onto the scale. It felt like the world had shifted into slow motion as he balanced himself, then stepped on with the other foot.

"What did you start at?" Benjy asked.

"Three thirty-two."

"Oh my God!" Benjy started clapping, jumping up and down.

"What? What is it?"

"Three oh six! That's twenty-six pounds! You fucking lost twenty-six goddamn pounds already!"

"Really? That can't…. Wait, are you sure?"

"Look!" He pointed at the scale as Oliver stepped off and gazed down at the digital readout. The scale was programmed to continue displaying the weight for a few seconds.

"Benjy! Oh my God! Oh my effin' God! I lost twenty-six pounds!" He grabbed Benjy and pulled him into a tight embrace that lifted him right off the ground.

Benjy giggled excitedly, hugging back with a tight squeeze. "I told you! I told you you looked thinner."

CHAPTER THREE

OLLIE JOLTED awake, as though he'd stepped off the sidewalk and jarred himself back into reality. He woke like this regularly, fighting for breath, and his heart seemed to kick-start life back into gear. He fell in and out of sleep during the day too. Simple activities most people did with ease, like walking to the end of the block, standing for an extended period, or even mowing the grass, presented challenges for a young man Oliver's size. Walking any distance left him winded and achy all over. His knees and back hurt, the backs of his legs throbbed, and his feet felt like they'd been crushed in a vise.

Even sitting for long periods made him sore. And he didn't sleep well because he couldn't breathe normally. He'd awaken numerous times throughout the night, gasping or choking, and had contemplated scheduling a sleep study to determine if he needed a CPAP breathing machine.

For all these reasons and more, his determination to lose weight became about something far more important than vanity. Sure, he wanted to look better. Being only twenty-four, he especially wanted to someday go on a real date with someone special, not just a group outing or a meetup with a gang of friends. He dreamed of one day going to a beach and taking off his shirt without embarrassment, or—dare he admit it?—making love to another man.

But at this stage, those superficial issues of changing his physical appearance remained fantasies he couldn't fully conceptualize mentally. He tried looking in the mirror and imagining what he would look like as a slender man, and the mental picture wouldn't even form. He couldn't see himself that way in his mind's eye. So the idea of a date or of a shirtless stroll on the beach didn't even toy with his psyche. He had more important things to worry about.

Things like his heart health. Being this obese placed a terrific strain on his cardiovascular system. He knew by the way his chest ached after the slightest physical activity that he was killing himself by carrying around so much excess baggage. And the day he decided to start an exercise program, he also scheduled a long-overdue appointment with a general practitioner. He wanted guidance, not judgment, so he used the internet to choose a doctor who specialized in weight loss.

He rolled out of bed, heaving himself up from the mattress. He shouldn't be obsessing about what lay in store, but all he could think about was his doctor appointment. This first one terrified him, and a half hour later when he pulled his SUV into the parking space at the clinic, he almost backed out immediately. Hey, he'd lost twenty-six pounds already on his own. Maybe he didn't even need a doctor. But he sat in the vehicle for a few moments, taking deep breaths, trying to reason with himself. He should have brought Amanda or Benjy for moral support, but he'd been a bit self-conscious about the whole thing. Which, of course, made no sense whatsoever. They both knew he was dieting and trying very hard to lose weight, and Benjy especially had been incredibly supportive. He certainly would have accompanied Oliver had he asked. But no, he had to confront some of his demons alone. His fear of all things healthy—doctors included—was something he had to face head-on.

"Good morning!" The exaggerated cheerfulness of the receptionist at such an early hour of the morning both annoyed and bewildered Oliver, but he offered an obligatory half smile.

"Oliver Paxton, here for an eight-fifteen appointment with Dr. Evans."

"Nice to meet you, Mr. Paxton. May I call you Oliver?"

"Sure."

"So happy to serve you this morning. I'm Shirleen." She smiled sweetly. "If you'll just sign in on the clipboard, I'll get you some paperwork to fill out, and I'll need your insurance card and co-pay, if there is one."

"I believe it's twenty bucks." He removed his wallet from his back pocket and pulled out his insurance card along with one of his credit cards.

"Thank you." Shirleen thrust another clipboard into his hand. "Please fill out everything, front and back, and when you're done, the doctor will be right with you."

Oliver took a seat in the empty waiting room, squeezing his oversized body into the normal-size chair. His belly protruded to the point he was able to use it as a shelf for the clipboard. Thank God he'd scheduled the early appointment after all. Only crazy people and the terminally obese were up at this hour of the fucking morning.

When he finished the extensive medical history form, he pushed himself up from the chair and stepped back to the desk.

"All set?" Shirleen looked up, smiling broadly as ever.

"All set." He nodded and passed the clipboard over the countertop.

"Very well. The doctor will be with you shortly."

He sat back down, involuntarily huffing as he did so, and debated digging in his pocket for his phone. Before he could decide, the inner door to the examining rooms opened, and Oliver looked up to see who'd be escorting him back to see the doctor.

"Hi, Oliver? I'm Brad Evans, your doctor." He extended his hand.

Oliver gulped as he stared at the man's face and into the most gorgeous eyes he'd ever seen. Fuck, not just the eyes—the whole face was perfect. The doctor looked like he'd stepped off the runway of a fashion show. He couldn't be a day older than Oliver, and was physically perfect in every imaginable way, from the broad shoulders straight on down the V-shaped torso, to the narrow, thirtyish inch waist.

"Hi" was all Oliver could manage.

"We're pretty much on a first-name basis here. Hope you don't mind." The doctor—or, Brad, rather—smiled. "If you'll follow me, we'll just get your height and weight and get you situated in an exam room."

"You do that?" Oliver stared at him, surprised. His mouth had dropped open, and he probably needed a tissue to wipe the drool from his chin. He closed his trap and gulped nervously. "I mean, um, don't you have nurses?"

Brad laughed and nodded. "We do indeed have a nurse, but his shift starts a little later. For my early-bird patients, I take care of all the vitals myself. Hope you don't mind."

"Uh, no. That's fine." He followed the doctor down the hall until he stopped at a digital scale. It didn't look like any Oliver had seen before, a far cry from the old-fashioned type where they moved bars back and forth along the top until they balanced. This one consisted merely of a mat to stand on and a digital readout on the wall about eye level.

"If you'll just step right up. You may remove your shoes if you desire."

He did desire. He didn't want a single unnecessary ounce of weight registering for his official weigh-in. It had been over a week since he and Benjy had weighed him at home, and he was starting to feel anxious, concerned maybe something was wrong with his scale, or even worse, that he'd gained back some of what he'd lost.

"That's actually why I'm here... my weight." Oliver looked at the doctor as he toed off his shoes. He did not yet move toward the scale, though. "I'm trying to, um, ya know...."

"Take off a few pounds?"

"Take off a *lot* of pounds, actually."

"Well, good!" Brad patted him on the shoulder. "Then you've come to the right place." Keeping his hand against Oliver's back, he steered him forward, urging him onto the scale.

Frightened, Oliver closed his eyes and took a deep breath.

"You're okay," Brad said in the most soothing, sultry voice Oliver had ever heard. "You're in a judgment-free zone here."

In spite of how corny the doctor's words were, they placated Oliver just enough to boost his confidence. He opened his eyes and stepped onto the mat. Nervously he bit his bottom lip as he stared at the digital readout that flashed a couple of times and then suddenly displayed what he initially thought must be an erroneous weight.

"Two ninety-seven."

"What? Wait, that's not right."

"Sorry," Brad said, "but I'm pretty sure our scale is accurate. It's calibrated regularly."

"But that's nine pounds lighter than I was ten days ago. And my scale at home is brand-new."

Brad smiled. "Then I guess whatever you're doing must be working, right?"

"Wow! Doctor... or I mean, Brad, this means I've lost thirty-five pounds so far!"

"Congratulations!" He patted Oliver on the shoulder again. "Want to stand over here, back flat against the wall, and I'll record your height?"

Afterward Brad led Oliver into the exam room and motioned for him to have a seat in the chair, which came as a relief. He didn't like the idea of trying to wiggle his fat ass up onto the exam table in front of the sexy doctor. "Let's just have a little chat, shall we, while I take your vitals?" Brad slid smoothly onto the stool and scooted toward Oliver, blood-pressure cuff in hand. "Right or left arm? Do you have a preference?"

Oliver held out his left arm, it being closest to the doctor. "Either is fine."

As Brad slid the cuff over Oliver's hand and up his arm, goose bumps arose on Oliver's bare skin. The doctor's fingers pressing against his arm sent a shiver down his spine while at the same time igniting a warmth within his chest. He gazed into the blue eyes, momentarily losing track of all space and time.

"Have you had your blood pressure checked recently?"

"I haven't been to a doctor since high school. Well, wait. In college I went to urgent care once with an earache. That was probably the last time I had it checked, and I don't remember what it was. Normal range, probably."

"Good to hear." The doctor tightened the Velcro on the cuff and inserted the stethoscope's ear tips in his ears, then held the chest piece against Oliver's inner arm just below the cuff. He pumped the bulb of the blood-pressure cuff and listened as he watched the dial. "One twenty-seven over eighty-four. Pretty good pressure. Do you smoke?"

Oliver made a face. "No."

The doctor smiled. "That's also good to hear. Drinking?"

"Not much. I did some in college, but other than my best friend's wedding three weeks ago, I don't even remember the last time I drank."

"Any other issues, besides your weight? Have you had your blood sugar checked?"

He shook his head. "My employer announced they're going to start requiring an annual health screening. It's to comply with the Affordable Care law, I think."

"I'm familiar." Brad nodded. "We're probably going to want to schedule you for a complete physical anyway, and that should satisfy your insurance company's requirement. The good news is that it's usually covered at 100 percent under the new law."

"Oh, okay." That was going to mean he'd have to get naked in front of the drop-dead gorgeous doctor. Good thing he'd already taken the blood pressure, because Oliver could feel it spike just thinking about the physical.

"Oliver, let's talk about your obesity."

The word sliced like a knife into Oliver's heart. It sounded so insulting, especially coming from the young doctor's mouth.

"Does the word bother you?" Apparently Oliver had been obvious with his facial expressions.

He lied, shaking his head. "No."

"Well, it's a clinical word, not an insult. It simply means that according to our height and weight chart, you ideally should weigh within the range of a hundred forty to a hundred eighty. So you're roughly a hundred twenty pounds overweight right now, which is considered obese from a medical standpoint. When a patient is extremely obese to the point that their weight affects their overall health and could potentially contribute to their untimely death, we call that morbidly obese."

"Which is what I am?"

"Possibly. We'll find out a lot more when we do the physical, check your heart, test for diabetes. But I can tell you as a general rule that obesity is a major contributor to a lot of other health problems."

"I know. That's why I'm here."

"Can you tell me a little bit about yourself? Have you always had issues with your weight?"

Oliver didn't want to get too personal. He didn't want to offer his whole life story. "My parents are overweight, but not as much as me. I started getting chubby in middle school. Before that, I was more or less normal. Then by the time I started high school, I began getting heavier. I weighed about two eighty when I graduated."

"So right now you're about the same weight you were then."

"But I'd gained some. Like I said, I've lost thirty-five pounds in the last few weeks. I started dieting a couple months ago."

The doctor made notes on his clipboard, then placed it on the counter beside him. He turned to direct his full attention to Oliver. "What kind of diet?"

Oliver took a deep breath. Was he on trial here? The doctor had so many questions, but Oliver supposed it was good he was so thorough. "I did some research online, and I have some experience with this. I mean, I've been trying to diet on and off for the past ten years or so. Basically I keep track of calories and fat grams."

Brad nodded, a serious expression on his face. "Good. Low-calorie, low-fat. That's exactly what I'd have prescribed, along with exercise."

Oliver felt his cheeks warming as he looked down at the carpeting. "That's kind of the other reason I'm here. I want to maybe get a personal trainer or join a gym or something. I've been doing my own workouts in my garage, but…."

"You're not sure what is effective? You need some guidance."

"And I don't want to kill myself. When I first started, I'd get so out of breath and my chest would hurt—actually, my entire body, every part of me, seemed to hurt. I thought I was dying."

"What kind of exercises do you do?"

"It's kind of embarrassing."

Brad reached over to place his palm on Oliver's oversized thigh. "Don't be embarrassed. I want to tell you something. There's a reason I specialize in weight-loss therapy. I was obese once myself."

Oliver looked up into his face. "No way."

Brad smiled. "Bigger than you were when you started your diet. I understand everything you're going through."

"But…." Oliver couldn't believe it. "How did you do it?"

"Diet, exercise, lifestyle change." He ticked off the components on his fingers. "And eventual skin surgery. People say I look young, but I'm thirty-six."

He had to be lying. "No way," Oliver repeated.

The doctor smiled. "Swear to God. Anyway, if I had to guess, I'd say you started simply with walking, just moving your body around."

"Yeah. I cleared out my garage, which was a workout itself. Then I got out my boom box and turned on the music and just started walking in a big circle. I just walked and walked until I was so out of breath I couldn't continue. I took breaks, drank water, and started all over."

"And now, you probably have advanced at least to jogging?"

Oliver grinned. "If you can call it that. I wouldn't want to do it in front of anyone."

"Well, it won't be long before you get comfortable enough to work out in front of people. I'm going to give you a business card." He turned and opened one of the cabinet drawers, then removed an embossed card. "This is a friend of mine, Adam. He's a trainer down at the Fitness Warehouse. He'll be sensitive to your initial feelings of self-consciousness. He can probably work with you one-on-one privately. You might have to schedule your appointments early morning or late evening, but he's very accommodating."

Oliver took the card, wondering how expensive he was. It didn't matter. He'd max out his credit card if he had to. He'd even sell his extra computers and game systems on eBay if it meant actually succeeding this time.

"Adam was my trainer. He got into this kind of work because he's passionate about helping people."

Oliver looked at the card again, examining it more closely. He liked the rainbow colors and wondered if they bore any significance. In Dr. Evans's internet ad, he had listed, among other things, that he was LGBT-friendly. It would make sense he'd associate with like-minded professionals.

"I'm going to set you up with all the nutritional information, our complete diet plan. I'll have Shirleen schedule you with a nutritionist who can work with you on your long-term plan. People start diets, and when they're as heavy as you were—or as I was—they do lose a lot of weight quickly in the beginning. But at some point, probably soon, you're going to plateau. You'll start losing more slowly, and when that happens, it'll be easy to feel discouraged. You might be tempted to throw in the towel and just go back to eating whatever you want."

"I get that. In fact, it's happened already. Sometimes I ask myself, 'What's the point?' I doubt I can go on the rest of my life eating salads and clear soups."

"Exactly. You can't, and you won't. The dietician will teach you ways to incorporate many of the foods you like into your diet. Some of the best-tasting desserts and typical comfort foods can be prepared in ways that are lower fat and lower calorie."

"I completely gave up fast food."

"Good. Avoid those places like the plague."

"Pizza, fried chicken, donuts…." His mouth was practically watering as he visualized the taboo foods. "I've had nothing like that for over six weeks."

"Let's prioritize your appointment with the dietician. Her name is Jan, and I might be able to get you in to see her this afternoon."

Oliver was planning to go in to work after his appointment. He'd be late, but he'd already requested permission to use half a sick day. "Um, okay. I can call work…."

"Hold on." The doctor held up his hand as he picked up the handset of the wall phone. "Shirleen, can you call Jan and see if she has time to zip over here for a conference?"

"Sure, one sec."

Brad turned back to Oliver, holding his hand over the mouthpiece. "Her office is next door."

"She's on her way, Brad."

"Awesome! Thanks, hon."

Hon? Oliver resisted the urge to smile.

"Oops." Brad laughed. "Well, I tried to warn you, we're informal here. Shirleen and I have been friends since grade school."

"I have a friend like that. Her name's Amanda." Okay, that settled it. Brad had to be gay.

"Well, while we're waiting on Jan, let's get the rest of your vitals. I want to listen to your heart, check your eyes, ears, and throat… all that good stuff. And we'll run an EKG. Don't worry. It's quick and painless. So if you'll hop up on the table…." He patted the cushioned, paper-lined tabletop.

For some reason, Oliver no longer felt anxious. He rose and stepped onto the small stool, then pivoted his body before plopping down on the edge of the exam table. As the doctor leaned in close and held the stethoscope's chest piece against Oliver's back, the warm, fuzzy glow that had ignited in his chest a few minutes ago returned. He turned his head slightly and stared into the doctor's eyes. Brad smiled but didn't say a word, simply listened as Oliver's heart beat like a bongo.

Chapter Four

OLIVER HATED mirrors, avoided them at all cost. When he approached his car every morning and reached out to open the door, he averted his eyes so he wouldn't see his reflection in the window. When he walked up to a glass entrance door at the supermarket, he looked down at the ground rather than straight ahead, lest he accidentally catch a glimpse of his reflection. Even when he shaved and brushed his teeth, he looked at only his mirror image from the neck up.

But a few people had started to notice the subtle change in his appearance—people other than Benjy and Amanda. One of his coworkers, a middle-aged woman from the claims department, commented that he looked different. His boss asked if he'd gotten his hair cut.

He'd had to dig into the recesses of his closet and find some of his old clothes, items he hadn't worn in years. They were still huge. The forty-one pounds had made a difference, but he had a long way to go until he got to a point where he'd be considered a normal size. It felt good, though. It felt damn good.

He now used a chart Jan had provided, which he'd posted right on the refrigerator door. He used it as his meal plan and followed it religiously. Continuing with his exercise routine in the garage, he spent at least two hours every evening walking and performing improvised calisthenics. He still had the business card Brad had given him, the one for the fitness instructor. He just hadn't built up the courage yet to make the call.

At two hundred ninety-one pounds, he was nowhere near ready to expose himself to potential ridicule at a gym, regardless the assurances that it was a "judgment-free zone." He did, however, purchase a stationary bike that he set up in the garage.

"We should ride bikes together!" Benjy spotted the new exercise equipment as he followed Oliver into the house.

Oliver stopped in his tracks and turned to him. "I don't wanna ride bikes. If I did, I'd buy myself a real bike. I got this stationary one so I could use it in my garage where no one can see me."

"But riding a real bike is so much more fun, and we could do it together."

"No! Are you deaf or what? I said I don't want a real bike."

"Sorry."

Why did Benjy always have to be that way? He seemed to get under Oliver's skin unlike anyone else, even worse than Oliver's mother.

Once inside the house, Benjy removed an object from his pocket and held it out to Oliver. "I got you something."

"You what?" Oliver looked at him, scowling. Still irritated by Benjy's remarks in the garage, he wasn't yet ready to be congenial. "What is it?"

"It's an odometer you can wear on your wrist or ankle. It keeps track of how many miles you've walked or run. When I saw it, I thought you might be able to use it with your workouts."

"Really?" Benjy had a way of making him feel like a heel. Why'd he always have to go and be so goddamn nice when Oliver felt so grumpy? "That's cool. But why? I mean… um, why'd you buy it for me?"

"We're friends, aren't we? Isn't that what friends do? Think about each other and do nice things for each other. It's just a cheap little wristband."

It didn't look cheap to Oliver. He'd have to look up the price on Amazon and pay his friend back somehow. But it really was cool, and he'd definitely use it. This way he could set specific goals based on actual distance, not just pushing himself until he was drop-dead tired. "You wanna help me make a pizza? Then we can play Overwatch."

"Sure." Benjy smiled, beaming ear to ear. "But I didn't think you could have—"

"Well, it's a low-fat, low-calorie pizza. You might not like it, but we could order you your own pizza if you want."

Benjy laughed. "Don't be a moron. I'm not ordering my own pizza. I'm sure I'll like the one we make together much better. Homemade shit is always best."

Oliver grinned. There was something charming about Benjy's air. He seemed almost boyish at times, so naïve and innocent. Well, at least he projected that kind of vibe. It was too bad the guy was so fucked-up emotionally. With his anxiety disorder, his social development had stalled. At times he seemed more like a teenager. On the other hand, he was scary smart. He knew tons about science and literature and mathematics.

Benjy never talked about girls, though. He seemed to have zero interest in dating, and since the topic never came up, Oliver never mentioned anything about his own nonexistent dating life. It really didn't matter. There'd have been no point talking about that sort of thing with Benjy. Even if he were gay, he would have no interest in a fat guy like Oliver. And for Oliver to come out to him would be awkward and could jeopardize their friendship. Chances were that Benjy was asexual. He didn't seem to express interest in anything sexual. Period.

Since he'd started dieting, Oliver had substantially decreased the size of his meal portions. This had been particularly challenging in the beginning, because contrary to the rationalizations he'd made to himself about how he didn't eat any more than an average guy his age, he actually did. His prediet eating habits would have included consuming an entire large pizza by himself. He might eat two or three pieces at a sitting, but then a few minutes later, he'd go back and eat a couple more, then a couple more. He wouldn't stop until the pizza was gone.

But after three months of controlled eating, he now ate smaller portions and allowed himself to feel full. As long as he ate slowly, thoroughly chewing every bite, he found that one plate of food filled him up, as opposed to the second, third, and fourth helpings he'd consumed prior to his weight-loss effort.

He and Benjy created a vegetarian pizza masterpiece on focaccia bread, using fat-free mozzarella. They didn't skimp when it came to the toppings because all were extremely low-calorie and all fat-free. "We've probably burned off more calories making this pizza than we'll consume when we eat it." Benjy laughed as he slid the pizza tray into the oven.

"Just 'cause I'm on a diet doesn't mean you've got to be. I told you, we could order you a real pizza."

"And just 'cause I'm skinnier than you doesn't mean I don't need to eat healthy." He looked up at Oliver and winked, his trademark smile lighting up his face. How'd a person get to be so positive, and why did someone like Benjy waste so much time hanging around a sourpuss like Oliver? He didn't mean to be so cynical all the time. He didn't mean to be grouchy or irritable toward his best friend.

"You know what, Benjy?"

"Huh?"

"This is going to sound really corny…."

"What?" Benjy smiled even broader than before. "Just say it."

"I really don't deserve a friend like you."

Benjy laughed dismissively. "Don't be a dork. Of course you do. If not for you, I wouldn't even have my job. If not for you, I wouldn't even have any…." He trailed off, seemingly unable to complete his sentence.

"I saved your butt that one time, but you'd have probably figured it out on your own. And since then, you've covered my ass more times than I can count. And half the time I'm a jerk to you, snap at you, get irritated."

"Dude, stop it." Benjy placed his hand on Oliver's shoulder, having to reach up to do so. "Dieting is tough. It would make anyone grouchy. I don't take it personally, and besides, most of the time you get pissed at me, I deserve it. I know I can be annoying."

Oliver sighed. Benjy's self-effacing personality was only making him feel worse. "Well, please promise me something, okay?"

"Sure, anything."

"If I treat you bad, tell me. Call me out. Tell me to quit being an asshole."

After laughing a few seconds, Benjy grew serious. "I would never say something like that to you. Ollie, you're my best friend."

"Please… if I ever hurt you in any way, you have to tell me."

"Okay, okay. But you won't, so quit worrying. Shit, I forgot to set the timer on the pizza."

"It's only been in there a couple minutes."

"You know what I think we should do tonight?" Benjy's voice climbed a full octave. "We should go to the mall and shop for some new duds."

Making a face, Oliver shook his head fiercely. "No fucking way."

"Yes, way! I bet you've dropped at least three or four sizes, and you should reward yourself."

"But I have a long, long way to go."

Benjy rubbed his hands together. "Think of how many shopping trips we have to look forward to!"

OLIVER COULDN'T remember the last time he'd fit into a size forty-two pants. When he started his diet months earlier, he had a fifty-inch waist. He'd dropped fifty pounds and eight inches, now down to a size 2XL shirt. Still two hundred eighty-two pounds, a far cry from slender, he was at least starting to approach the range where others might see him as "chubby" or "a big guy" rather than just outright fat. He'd lost enough weight that it was obvious to his coworkers, his hair stylist, even the cashier at the supermarket. People complimented him openly, offering words of encouragement and lots of praise.

It had finally reached the point where Oliver had to pick up the phone and make the call he dreaded most. "Hey, Mom."

"Well, what do you know? The dead has arisen. Do you think it's too much for a mother to ask for her only son to call once in a blue moon to check on her? Once a week, maybe? Once a month? Once every six months even! After all, I only gave birth to you. Sixteen long, unbearable, excruciating hours of labor to bring you into this world."

"Mom, I just called you a couple weeks ago."

"A couple weeks ago? After all your father and I did, the sacrifices we made to put our only son through college."

"Mom, I paid most of my own college tuition. Well, I should say I'm paying it... still."

"Is it too much to ask? Is it too much for a mother to expect to see her baby more than once or twice a year?"

"Actually, that's why I'm calling. I was thinking maybe I'd visit this weekend. My friend Ben and I, we were talking about a road trip."

"Your *friend*?" He could see her in his mind's eye, jumping up from her chair excitedly.

"He's *just* a friend. He doesn't even know about me. He doesn't even know I'm gay."

"But you're going to tell him, right? It must be serious.... Wait, Ollie. You're not falling for a straight boy, are you? Honey, he'll break your soft heart, smash it to smithereens."

Sighing, he picked up a celery stick from the plate in front of him. "It's not like that. We're friends, that's all. I haven't fallen for him and never will."

"Okay, okay. It doesn't matter anyway. I better get busy. I've got shopping and cooking... and I've got to change all the bedding. I'll make up the guest room for your *friend*. Unless...."

"Make up the guest room, yes. We aren't sleeping together." Both of Oliver's parents had been 100 percent supportive since the day he came out in high school. In that sense, he'd been blessed. Unfortunately, they were blind to the other struggles he faced. As far as his mother was concerned, Oliver was the most attractive young gay man on the planet, and she couldn't understand why guys were not lining up to date him. When she looked at him, she didn't see his rolls of fat, and she couldn't comprehend why others didn't see her son through those same rose-colored glasses. "But, Mom, please... don't overdo it."

"Overdo it? What are you talking about? How could I possibly overdo anything? My son is coming for a visit for the first time in at least two years, and he's bringing a special friend!"

Oliver sighed, resigned to the futility of pointing out it had only been months, not years, since he'd visited, and that Ben was not the kind of special friend she was implying. She was going to believe what she wanted to believe, and facts would not deter her.

"Fine, but please just remember, I'm not out to Benjy."

"Benjy? You call him *Benjy*? Oh darling, that's so sweet. Does he call you Ollie?"

"I've got to go. We'll see you Friday evening. We're both taking a half day off work. Should be there...."

"By dinnertime!"

"By dinnertime, yes. And remember, I'm dieting."

"Oh dear. I've got to go too. So little to do, so much time to do it in." She laughed at her own joke, a standard misspeak she'd picked up years ago from *Willy Wonka and the Chocolate Factory*.

"Love you."

"Love you too, baby. Call on Friday when you're on your way."

OLIVER'S BELLY no longer rubbed against the steering wheel when he squeezed into the driver's seat of his SUV on his way to work. Actually, he no longer had to squeeze in at all. He still had a hefty, oversized torso, a protruding gut, and embarrassing man boobs, but overall he'd shrunk. When he sat upright in a chair, he could finally suck in his belly somewhat and was even aware that underneath the remaining roll of cellulite, he possessed real abdominals.

He made a mental note to bite the bullet and call Adam, the personal trainer Brad had recommended. He'd call when he returned from his weekend away. He'd procrastinated because he still couldn't envision himself exercising in front of anyone, even a trainer who did that sort of thing for a living. He wasn't even close to being able to bend at the waist to touch his toes. His attempts to complete a sit-up were a joke. And even the way he ran, more of a rapid waddle, was embarrassing. He just had too much fat on his body, and though a substantial amount had already burned off, it wasn't melting away nearly fast enough.

Maybe visiting his parents at this stage wasn't such a great idea. He made it to the office and slogged his way through the morning, dreading what lay in store that evening. His cubicle neighbor countered his lackluster attitude with an equivalent dose of enthusiasm. Benjy, who admittedly led a boring life, could barely contain his excitement over their imminent road trip.

"I packed snacks!" He held up a portable canvas cooler. "And an eclectic selection of CDs."

Oliver's obligatory smile probably came across as more of a smirk. "Dude, you know I don't snack anymore."

"Healthy snacks! Carrot sticks, celery, fat-free ranch dip. And I picked up some low-calorie crackers and SunChips."

"Trust me, once we get to my folks' house, you won't be hungry. You've got to promise me you'll eat a lot."

Benjy's face twisted into a look of bewilderment. "Huh? I pretty much make a point of *not* pigging out when we're together. I mean, I think it would be kind of rude with you being on a... or, I mean... with you trying to lose weight and stuff."

"Well, you don't know my mom. She will have made enough food to feed an army, and she's gonna try to force-feed me. But if she sees you scarfing down all her pies and cookies, she won't be as offended by me refusing them."

"Oh." He grinned in his typical ear-to-ear style. "Sure, I guess I can take one for the team."

Oliver laughed. "I doubt it'll be much of a sacrifice. My mom's a good cook. I didn't get this size by eating cafeteria food."

At 11:45 a.m., Benjy's head popped over the cubicle wall again. "You ready?"

"No." Oliver stared at his computer monitor. "I think I'm gonna puke."

"You do not. You're just nervous about seeing your parents." He stepped around the cubicle wall, walked up to the back of Oliver's chair, and placed a hand on his shoulder. Oddly, the softness of his touch stoked a warmth within Oliver's chest. Turning his head slightly, he looked up at Benjy. "Trust me, I know what you're going through. I don't even talk to my parents. Or, they don't talk to me."

"Really?" Oliver would have thought Benjy to be a mama's boy, particularly due to his hypersensitivity and emotionalism. Then again, maybe he wasn't being exactly fair. Technically there was a big difference between emotion and anxiety. "Where *are* your folks?"

"Missouri. That's where I'm from, but I left home when I was sixteen. Lived with a friend the last two years of high school, then left the state for college and never went back."

"What about your friend?"

"Oh, we still talk. Almost every day, in fact, either through Messenger or text."

Why a burst of unwarranted possessiveness suddenly gripped Oliver, he didn't know. Of course he wasn't jealous that Benjy had another close friend. It had been silly of him to assume he was the only important person in the guy's life. Well, actually, how could he even consider himself *important*? They didn't even know all that much about each other. Besides, Benjy was entitled to have whatever friends he wanted. Why, though, had he never mentioned this person?

"Sam's been my best friend since junior high, pretty much."

"Oh really."

"Her family took me in when my folks disowned me."

"*Her* family?" He should be appalled by what Benjy had said, but he couldn't keep from smiling.

"Yeah. She's still in Missouri, now engaged. She wants me to be there for the wedding, but...."

"You're afraid of seeing your parents?" Oliver sobered his expression, turning farther to face Benjy full-on.

"Nah. I don't even care about them, really. Plus, they'd never get an invite to the wedding. I just don't handle that sort of thing, being in a crowd, being the center of attention."

"Tell her you want to go, but you can't stand up for her. She knows you, Benjy. I'm sure she'll understand."

He nodded. "Probably. Hey, I see what you did. You got me talking about this bullshit to stall for time. C'mon, let's get going! We have a road trip to take."

Oliver wanted to ask more about Benjy's parents. Why on earth did they disown their own son? And when he was only sixteen? Had he done something horrible, something so egregious that they'd excommunicate him from the family? Or was it because of who he was?

He was projecting again, making assumptions that were outrageous. Gay men did that all the time, and it irritated Oliver. They always wanted to fantasize about straight guys being gay. They assumed every man on the planet was like them. Well, this definitely wasn't the case with Benjy. Oliver had never seen him so much as look twice at another guy. He didn't have anything stereotypically gay in his apartment, no homoerotic art or posters or anything. He didn't even like Britney Spears. Benjy definitely wasn't gay.

BENJY HAD reclined his seat and now lay back with his socked feet against the dashboard, tapping out dance moves to "...Baby One More Time."

"You fucking like Britney Spears!"

"Huh?" He sat upright, reaching for the stereo dial. "You don't like Britney?" He cranked down the volume as he turned and gave Oliver his full attention.

"No... or I mean yeah. She's fine. I just... well, it just surprised me. I didn't know you liked Britney Spears."

"I told you I brought an eclectic selection."

Oliver glanced at him, conscious of the fact he was driving. Benjy had changed into shorts and a tank top, exposing the entirety of his twig-like arms and toothpick legs. If he weighed more than one twenty, Oliver would be surprised. But in that getup, with his hair slightly mussed, wearing his Harry Potter glasses, he conveyed a sort of geeky, boyish charm. "Break out the snacks."

"Really?" Benjy's face lit up with a broad smile as he reached behind the seat and retrieved the small cooler. "Oh, and I have pretzel sticks. Fat-free, ya know."

"Yeah, now you're talking. I'll have a pretzel."

Benjy unzipped the cooler and removed the bag of Rold Golds, then peeled it open and handed one to Oliver. "Your parents live in the boondocks or something?"

He laughed. "Pretty much." He bit into his pretzel, savoring the saltiness. "Sometimes northern Michigan feels more like rural Kentucky. Lot of hunters and card-carrying Republicans."

"Long live the Second Amendment." Benjy giggled. "I know what you mean, though. I'm from a small town too. I think we had one black family and a couple Native Americans. My mom and dad are born-again fundamentalists. Baptists."

"What happened? Do you mind me asking? I mean, why'd they…?"

"Disown me?"

Oliver nodded, then paused. "You don't have to talk about it."

"No, it's fine." Benjy sucked on his pretzel, sliding it partway into his mouth, then pulling it out slowly. Oliver raised his eyebrows but kept his gaze on the road. In the most casual, insouciant manner, Benjy tossed his head back. "What the hell, right? Might as well be blunt. I'm gay."

Oliver stared straight ahead, feeling his eyes widen as he gripped the steering wheel with both hands. "Oh."

He drove a little farther in silence, neither of them speaking. "I can take a bus back. I'm pretty sure there's a bus line that runs all the way to—"

"Oh my God, Benjy. Don't be stupid." He turned and saw Benjy's eyes were flooded with tears. "I'm pulling over."

"No! Just drive."

Oliver sighed. "Look, it doesn't matter. It's totally cool you're gay, and I'm… I'm… I'm perfectly fine with it." Why couldn't he come out himself? "It doesn't change anything."

"Really?"

"You're my friend, man. My… um, *best* friend. Gay, straight, whatever—it doesn't matter."

"I guess I kind of thought you knew. I know we never talked about it."

"Well, maybe I suspected, but ya know, it's none of my business. And like I said, it doesn't matter. It wouldn't matter to my folks either. They aren't prejudiced."

"What do you mean, it *wouldn't* matter? Don't you mean, it *won't*?"

"Well, if you told them, and that's up to you, but… well, we're only there for two days." God, he hoped Benjy didn't say anything. If he did, his mom would be all over that shit like white on rice. And she'd be trying to hook them up.

"I don't usually bring it up, but I have to be honest, I've felt kind of guilty lately. You've shared so much about yourself, and you've been so open. I really admire how determined you've been with this diet, and I'm so proud of all you've already accomplished."

Oliver swallowed hard, forcing back the lump that formed. "Thanks, man."

"And I wanted to come out to you sooner, but I was afraid. After what had happened before…."

"When your folks kicked you out?"

"Yeah, and high school was awful. I got beat up every day."

It explained a lot of the social anxiety. Oliver's heart was cracking down the middle. He had to tell Benjy. He had to confess he too was gay. "I'm sorry, Benjy. I hate that happened to you."

"I was afraid of losing you as a friend."

"That'll never happen. I swear. Nothing is ever going to come between us, our friendship."

He looked over once more, and Benjy was smiling at him.

"I don't even know what to say." The tears flowed freely down Benjy's cheeks. "You're the best friend I've ever had. Besides Sam, I mean. You know, I probably wouldn't tell anyone but you this, but I'm kind of having a meltdown about Sam getting married."

"You don't like the guy?"

"No, it's not that. He's a great guy, and I'm really, really happy for her. But I just feel… well, I feel like I'm losing her. I know that sounds stupid."

Oliver glanced at him before refocusing his attention on the road. "No, it doesn't. That's how I felt with Amanda. Since I was so fat, I felt really cut off from most people. Isolated, I guess. She was my one true friend, and it was scary knowing things would never be the same for us."

"So you *do* get it."

"You'll get over it. You'll be fine, trust me. Your relationship with Sam will change, but you'll always be close. And you'll continue to make new friends."

Benjy laughed as he wiped his eyes with his fingertips. "I'm not so sure about the last part."

"I'm going to pull off at this rest area. It's the last one for, like, fifty miles." He pulled onto the exit and slowed the car as they approached the parking section. "Let's just have fun this weekend, okay?" He pulled in and turned off the ignition, then directed his full attention to Benjy. "No worries about gaming or work or weddings or being gay."

Benjy grinned. "Or being fat."

Oliver couldn't help himself; he smiled. "Or being fat. But that doesn't mean I'm going off my diet."

"Thanks, Ollie."

Oliver took a deep breath, wanting to lean in or possibly to reach out—to connect with his best friend physically. Instead he looked into Benjy's eyes for a few bated seconds. "Anytime, Benjy." He turned and grabbed the door handle before sliding out of his seat.

CHAPTER FIVE

"OH, MY God! Let me get a look at you. Ollie, you look so… so gaunt, so peaked. You're so thin!"

Oliver, standing in front of his mother as she held on to his shoulders, smiled as he looked into her eyes. "Mom, I'm not peaked. I lost fifty pounds, and that's a good thing."

"You must be starving."

Just then his dad cut in, patting Oliver on the shoulder. "Son, you look great."

They stood by the car, on the driver's side, and Benjy walked around, waiting and smiling as he stood at the front of the vehicle.

"Mom, Dad, this is my friend Benjy."

"Oh, isn't he adorable!" His mother held her hand over her heart.

"It's nice to meet you, Mr. and Mrs. Paxton."

"Ed and Betty," she corrected. "And you, Mister, could stand to put on a few pounds yourself."

"Mom, is it your goal to make the whole world fat?"

She stared at him, clearly crushed, but then smiled. "Yes, dear. That's exactly my goal. Keep them well-fed, and they won't have either the time or energy to fight… or to give me any shit." Oliver grinned, realizing he'd struck a nerve. "But for the record, you are *not* fat. Far from it, especially now."

Oliver gave Benjy a knowing glance. For some reason, his mother did not see him as overweight. She never had. And no matter how much he ate, it didn't seem enough to satisfy her.

"How'd you do it, Ollie?" His dad had stepped to the rear of the SUV and was retrieving their bags. "How'd you take off all that weight?"

"Well, I'm still working on it." Oliver walked over and took one of the two bags from his dad. "We can get these, Dad."

"Don't be silly. Well, you look like a brand-new b—young man. I'm proud of you, son."

"Thanks, Dad. Mostly it's been dieting, but I've started exercising, and I meet with a personal trainer this coming week." If he ever got up the nerve to make the call, that was. "I actually bought these clothes from a normal store at the mall. I didn't have to special order them like I used to."

His mother, oblivious to their conversation, had focused her attention on Benjy. "Do you have a girlfriend down there in the city?" Oliver wanted to intervene, save his friend, but Benjy seemed to be handling himself.

"I'm so busy with work, ya know. That's how I met Ollie. We work together."

"And you call him Ollie." She spoke almost to herself. "I knew you would." She placed her arm around Benjy's shoulders and led him toward the house. "You must be famished after that long drive."

"I really am, ma'am. I'm starving."

"Well, you came to the right place!"

Oliver had to stifle a laugh as his mom all but bolted for the door, ushered Benjy inside, and directed him to the kitchen.

Interestingly, Benjy seemed to instantly bond with Oliver's mother, and he helped her finish up with the meal preparation in the kitchen while Oliver toted the luggage to their respective rooms and settled in with his dad in the living room. His dad had a sporting event on TV, probably the Detroit Tigers. Since Oliver didn't really follow baseball, he picked up one of the magazines his mom had placed on the coffee table. "You guys subscribe to the *Advocate*?" Why were his parents subscribing to the national LGBT news magazine?

His dad looked up. "Your mother does. Has some interesting articles."

"You know, you can get an online subscription a lot cheaper."

His dad shrugged. "Your mother and me, we're not high tech like the younger generation. You, with your computers, just confuse old folks like us."

"You're not even fifty, Dad."

"I turned fifty last year. Don't you remember the big party?" Oliver did remember now that his father mentioned it, but he hadn't been able to attend. He had been in school, and to be honest, he didn't feel like subjecting himself to all the gawking and furtive comments about his weight.

"I'm sorry I missed it, Dad." Though he admired his father, barriers separated them on so many levels. He was gay, and his dad was straight. He'd always been obese, not exactly the athlete his dad had probably imagined he'd turn out to be. Oliver was a computer nerd, and his dad had been foreman at the same factory for the past thirty years. Oliver had been the first person from either side of the family to graduate with a college degree, and probably the first to be "openly" queer.

"Well, I'm glad you're here now. Finally." His father cleared his throat. "This young man you brought with you…."

"Benjy."

"Is he…?"

"He's just a friend. We're coworkers, and he's been really supportive of me these past few months. Without his help, I'm not sure I'd have succeeded in losing this much weight, not that I don't still have a long ways to go."

"Don't sell yourself short. You should be proud of your progress."

"I know." He sighed as he stared at the TV. How could it be, in the twenty-first century, his parents still had a console? The square picture seemed odd compared to the rectangular flat-screens Oliver was used to watching. "People still look at me, and all they see is my fat."

"That's not true." His father frowned. "Your mother and I—"

"You two see me differently than most people, especially Mom. She still thinks I'm her precious little baby, but I'm not. I'm all grown up now. I've grown up and *out*. Look at me—I'm as big as a house." He glanced down at his belly, which protruded in front of him. At close to three hundred pounds, his tummy still formed a shelf when he sat upright. He still couldn't cross his legs at the knees or bend over to touch his toes. Even putting on socks became a challenge.

"People are shallow." His dad seemed to be talking to the empty room, not looking directly at Oliver. "But as we get older, we change. Things like physical appearance matter a whole lot less."

Oliver shook his head. In so many ways, his dad defied the stereotype of a small-town factory worker. He didn't act or talk like a redneck, like so many of his coworkers. Maybe that's how he got the foreman position. Oliver often wondered if given a different set of circumstances, his father might have achieved far greater things in life.

"I'm not sure that's true, Dad. Some people are superficial their whole lives."

"True, but who gives a fuck about those people?"

Oliver raised his eyebrows and resisted the urge to grin. It wasn't like his dad to swear, let alone drop the f-bomb.

"You have your friend." He cocked his head toward the kitchen, indicating his reference to Benjy. "You have your job, and that other girl, the one who just got married."

"Amanda."

"And you have your family. Why do you care what some stranger says or thinks about how you look?"

"It's not just my looks, though. I can't *do* things normal people can do. Dad, I'm too fat to even go to an amusement park. I don't fit in the rides. I have to buy two seats when I book an airline flight. And you don't even want to see my fat ass on a bike."

His dad grinned. "I'm not exactly Mr. Universe myself."

"You're nowhere near my size. You never have been." His father was perhaps twenty to thirty pounds overweight, and it was hardly noticeable, especially compared to Ollie. His mom, on the other hand, was a bit heavier, but even she wasn't what he'd categorize as "obese."

"We're not going to care what your weight is, never." His dad looked directly into his eyes. "Don't let something like that keep you away from us. Ollie, being gone so long nearly broke your mother's heart."

The sting of tears threatened to flood Oliver's eyes, and he gulped to swallow the lump forming in his throat. "I'm sorry. It's just hard coming back here. I get that you're proud I got my degree and all, but...."

"You're embarrassed."

"When I see people from this town, and I notice how they look at me and stare, wondering exactly how fat I'm going to get before I... before I die, or before I end up on one of those shows, *My 600-lb Life* or *Biggest Loser*...."

"Ollie, you're nowhere near that size."

"But I'm on course—or I was—to become that huge. Dad, I'd gained over fifty pounds since I graduated high school. What you see now is the same me that left this town five years ago. After all this work, months of dieting, I'm down only to my original fat self that I was when I finished high school."

"But now you're on track, you're actually losing, and a few months from now you'll be even smaller."

"I just get so discouraged."

"But you said your friend is helping you."

Oliver nodded. "I came back here, not to show off my progress. Not even to get your approval. I came to let you and Mom know that I want a different life. I want a whole new me, a person not defined by my obesity."

"You didn't need to come back here to declare that, son. You know your mom and I have always wanted what's best for you. We only want you to be happy, and if losing weight will help you along the way, we support you."

"And it's better for my health. I feel so much more energized after just losing this much."

Benjy came through the archway and stopped by Oliver's chair. "Mom said to tell you dinner's ready."

"Mom? You call her 'Mom' now?" Oliver looked up, smiling.

"She told me to, said she would adopt me. I told her about my folks."

Oliver gulped. "Really? What did she say?"

"She hugged me, said I was welcome in your family."

"That totally sounds like something she'd say." Oliver and his dad pushed themselves up from their chairs and followed Benjy to the dining room. "Oh. My. God." Oliver stared at the massive spread of food that extended from one end of the rectangular table to the other. "This is like Thanksgiving."

His mother suddenly appeared in the doorway between the kitchen and dining area, holding a cream pie that had at least six inches of meringue on top. "Have a seat everyone. Dinner is served!"

WITH A Scrabble board between them, the foursome sat around the kitchen table, recovering from the massive feast. Oliver had managed to stick fairly close to his diet, splurging a little compared to his normal routine, yet still fastidiously counting his total calories. He passed on all the desserts, gravies, and anything he wasn't sure of the calorie count. His mother's sighs and disdainful glares were countered quickly by Benjy, who jumped right in and asked for extra-large helpings of each item Oliver had declined.

In spite of his effort to moderate his eating, Oliver felt stuffed. Over the previous three months, he'd effectively shrunk the size of his stomach. He felt bloated, in need of exercise, and more than once almost excused himself to go for a walk. He didn't want to walk the streets of his hometown, though. Not even late in the evening. If he were at home, he'd be in the garage, burning off every bit of fat he'd consumed.

But the Scrabble game had proven much more fun than he'd have expected. His dad broke open a six-pack of beer, and his mom and Benjy were sharing a bottle of cheap wine. Oliver drank bottled water in spite of his parents' assurances he'd be okay to imbibe just a little. Benjy sat in the kitchen chair, with one leg tucked under his butt, looking all serious as he sipped his wine and examined his rack of tiles. When he played the word *SHIT*, Oliver started to object, then saw that Benjy wasn't done. He had used the *S* to form a new word off of *HIT* but was also playing the word *COWARDS* vertically. He'd used every one of his tiles.

"Bingo!"

"You little shit!" His mother gasped.

"Well, that's one of the words he played," Oliver's father pointed out. "Is that even legal?"

"No. It's cheating!" Oliver tried to sound as indignant as possible.

"You're just jealous you didn't think of it." Benjy took a sip of his wine, grinning.

"Fine!" Oliver's mom spun the board in her direction. "If you can play naughty, then so can I." Oliver's mouth dropped open as his mom slapped the tiles onto the board one at a time. *BLOWJOBS* intersected with the *W* in *COWARDS* to form a brand-new bingo. "Bingo!" she shouted. "And don't forget my fifty bonus points."

Benjy instantly face-palmed, laughing his ass off, while Oliver felt his cheeks blaze like a campfire. "Mom! You didn't!"

"What? We're all adults here, aren't we?"

Benjy's laughter, bubbly and infectious, got the whole table cackling. "I can't wait to see what your husband plays!" Benjy turned to Oliver's father. "Do you two need a little private time?"

Oliver's dad sat up straight in his chair, his own face red as a beet. "I might just have to get out our toy box."

"Edward!" His mother guffawed. "You hush your mouth."

"Toy box?" Benjy threw a hand over his mouth, guffawing as he grabbed the edge of the table with his other hand. "Do you have toys in there that require batteries?"

"Mom, don't answer that!" Oliver couldn't believe his ears. His parents had never behaved like this. They were both cracking up, though, and his mother didn't seem the least bit embarrassed.

"Oliver, I'd have never expected you to be more of a prude than me, your mother." She pointed to the tablet next to Oliver. "Go on, record my score. Benjy's too. And then it's your turn."

"Fine!" He quickly calculated the scores and wrote them down, then played his word on the board.

Benjy stared in disbelief. "You can't play that. That's five points, just three letters." He slapped his hand on the table, laughing.

"Hey, I refuse to lower myself to your level and play smut words." He stared at his three-letter word, *CAT*, with pride, and spun the board to his father. "It's your turn, Dad."

"I just have one question," his dad said in all seriousness. "Did you play *CAT* because you don't have the letters to play *PUSSY?*"

With that, Benjy and Oliver's mom flew into a fit of hysterics, and Oliver, utterly humiliated, slumped over against the table, burying his face in his arms. "I give up." He moaned miserably, then finally looked up to make eye contact with a very giddy Benjy, smiling.

"WHAT DID my mom say when you told her about your folks?" Oliver and Benjy had decided on a late-night walk downtown. Of course, nothing was open in the small rural town. His parents didn't live far from the business district, which consisted of two intersecting streets, and they strolled through town and made their way down to the waterside in the solitude of a warm summer night. After walking about three miles, they at last made their way back to the house, and the moon shone brightly overhead. Benjy seemed to be glowing himself, perhaps from the three glasses of wine he'd consumed.

"Um… she cried, actually. And that made me feel like crap."

"She cried 'cause it's a sad story. I can't believe your parents disowned you."

Benjy nodded and took a few steps up the sidewalk toward the porch.

"I'm sorry I didn't come out to you," Oliver finally said. He stood a few feet back, still cloaked in the darkness. He didn't want to look Benjy in the eye. "I'm sure she mentioned I'm also gay."

Benjy looked down at the pavement, with Oliver still a couple steps away from him. Finally, Benjy looked up. "Can you hear that?" His voice was barely a whisper. "It's my heart beating. I'm sure you can hear it clear over there."

"Benjy…." Oliver took a step closer.

"For the past two months, I've fantasized about telling you about myself. I imagined that I'd come out to you, and you'd say you were the same way, you were gay too. And then…."

Oliver's eyes had adjusted to the dim light, and as he stared at Benjy's smooth, boyish face, he saw the tears streaking down his cheeks. He moved even closer, reaching out to frame Benjy's face with his palms. Leaning in, he kissed him softly, just a gentle peck against his soft lips. "I'm sorry I didn't tell you. I just couldn't. I couldn't tell… anyone."

"Oh, Ollie." Benjy stared into his eyes.

"I'm more than twice as big as you. You're cute. You're… sexy. And I'm a big blob."

"Ollie, you're not."

Oliver pulled away. "I shouldn't have asked you to come here." He turned away and raced up the steps, then quickly pulled open the front door and charged inside. He hurried up the staircase, into his bedroom, and closed the door behind him.

Slumping onto the bed in the darkness, Oliver buried his face in his hands, weeping. What had he just done? And why? Why'd he just kiss Benjy, and why did he then push him away? They weren't right for each other. A guy like himself, so big and fat, could never be with a cute, skinny little guy like Benjy. What was he thinking, and why'd he do something so stupid?

He walked over to the bathroom, located on the far side of the bedroom, and flipped on the overhead light. Stepping inside, he looked up at his reflection. He saw a wide, puffy face and a fat neck. He saw huge pillows of fat couching his pectorals, giving him embarrassing man boobs. He saw a round, flabby body that made him want to puke. Everything about him the exact opposite of Benjy, and he was reminded once more how wrong this whole trip had been.

He turned off the light and slogged back to his bed in the dark, then collapsed and rolled onto his side. He cried silently until he at last fell asleep and the darkness enveloped him.

CHAPTER SIX

OLIVER AWAKENED before five the next morning. He got dressed and sneaked downstairs, hoping to be the only person up and around. After grabbing a water from the fridge, he headed out the door and walked for two hours. Exhausted and sweating profusely when he returned, he checked the wristband Benjy had bought for him. Almost nine miles.

Of course, everyone was awake when he returned, but he headed up the stairs without a word, ignoring the gathering in the dining room. It sounded as if more than just the three of them had congregated for breakfast. His mom had mentioned inviting his aunt and uncle. Oh great, more people to gawk at his grotesque body.

He showered and changed, then stood before the mirror, carefully styling his hair. In spite of his physical shortcomings, he'd always remained fastidious about his hair. Perhaps he'd always been so particular because it was the one aspect of his appearance he could control.

The light rap on the bedroom door didn't really come as a surprise. He knew someone would be up to check on him, and he couldn't put off the inevitable forever. He walked over and opened the door to a freshly showered and rather demure Benjy, who offered a weak smile to Oliver, at first not speaking. Finally, Benjy asked to come in, and Oliver stepped aside.

"I'm sorry about last night." Oliver spoke first, not looking Benjy in the eye but staring down at the carpeting.

"Which part?" Benjy asked. "Not coming out to me right away or kissing me? Or are you sorry for turning tail and running from me?"

He shrugged. "All the above." He chanced a quick look at Benjy's face, his heart seizing as he saw Benjy's wide-eyed gaze. "I shouldn't have kissed you."

"Jesus, Ollie, that's the one thing you *shouldn't* be apologizing for."

"Benjy, I'm not ready for this now. Just look at me." He held out both arms.

Benjy sighed. "I don't even know what that means."

"It means I have to focus on taking care of me right now. I have to concentrate on getting healthy, getting this body in shape. Don't you see? I can't even stand the sight of myself naked. How could I ever expect someone else to—"

"Make love to you?"

He wasn't going to cry. Not again, not right now. Damn if he wouldn't drop to his knees at that very second and suck Benjy dry. He wanted to—God, how he wanted to. Everything about him was utterly adorable, and Oliver imagined running his fingertips over Benjy's smooth skin. He thought about worshiping every inch of him, making love to him. "How can you even say that, Benjy, without throwing up a little in your mouth?"

Benjy's face twisted, astonished as he stared at Oliver. He obviously couldn't believe what he'd just heard. "Ollie, if I were a little bit bigger, I'd fucking coldcock you right now. What a horrible thing to say about yourself!" His voice broke as it swelled with emotion. "Of course I don't want to throw up when I think about making love to you. I—"

"Just stop. Will you please stop pretending? I get that you're my best friend. I get you have anxiety and all that. We've been great for each other. But that's as far as it goes. That's as far as it ever can go, at least not with me—"

"What? At least not with you what?"

"Looking like the goddamn Goodyear Blimp! Jesus Christ, Benjy. You know what they called me when I graduated? You know what the teacher said over the loudspeaker instead of my name when he called me to pick up my diploma? He fucking called me Baby Huey! 'Baby Huey Paxton.' He held out my diploma and the whole fucking town busted into laughter, and I had to walk up there... in front of everyone!"

"Oh, Ollie...." Benjy took a step forward. "I'm sorry."

"I don't want to be a sympathy fuck. And I don't want to be your Baby fucking Huey!"

Tears streamed down Benjy's cheeks as he gazed at Oliver, hands at his sides. "What they did to you was wrong. It was so very wrong, but you know what? They did the same thing to me." He spoke in a hushed tone, barely a whisper. "I told you they beat me up every day, and it's true. But all that is behind us. Look ahead of you, Ollie! You're losing weight every fucking day, and I'm not going anywhere. I'm right here at your side. I'll help you every step of the way."

"But what about now?" Oliver slumped onto the bed, sitting on the edge of the mattress. He buried his face in his hands, not wanting Benjy to see his tears. "What about *right* now?"

He felt Benjy's weight on the mattress as he sat and wrapped his arm around Oliver's back. The gentleness of his soothing touch stirred a warmth in Oliver's chest.

"Right now we'll still be friends. We'll take things slowly if we need to, let them happen if they happen. No labels. No declarations. But please don't shut me out."

Oliver pulled his hands away and looked at Benjy. "What if I fail?"

Benjy smiled and shrugged. "Then you fail, and we keep trying. I don't... um... I don't *like* you only because of your looks. I like the person you are. If you're three hundred pounds or one hundred pounds, it doesn't matter."

"So you're saying we should just continue? We should just keep being friends and see what happens between us?"

Benjy nodded, sidling up a little closer and squeezing Oliver tightly. Oliver leaned back, raising one arm to wrap it around Benjy, then pulled him in against his chest. "And you'll help me? You'll help me reach my goal."

"Oh God, Ollie. You know I will."

Oliver held him for a few seconds before pulling back and kissing him sweetly on the forehead. "Did I ever tell you that you're really cute sometimes?"

Benjy laughed. "Only sometimes?"

"Well, um... no. All the time, but sometimes more than others."

"When I'm not in the middle of an anxiety attack?"

Oliver sighed. "Let's just enjoy the rest of the weekend together... as friends."

"And let what happens, happen." Benjy leaned in, pressing his lips softly against Oliver's. Though a bit startled, Oliver responded, parting his lips slightly as he kissed back.

As they pulled apart, he felt himself smiling a bit broader than he had in a very long time. "You taste better than a banana split with extra whip cream."

"See, I told you I'd help you reach your goal. When you're hungry and craving dessert, all you have to do is kiss me."

"Deal."

OLIVER'S MOM busied herself in the kitchen with her sister's help. They'd planned a huge barbecue for the afternoon. Everything always had to be centered around food. Oliver and Benjy lounged around the house for most of the morning, playing video games, and when his mom called for them, they assisted by carrying everything outside to the canopied dining area. Guests began arriving around one o'clock, and Oliver's dad volunteered to man the grill.

People his mom knew from church showed up along with relatives, neighbors, and friends Oliver hadn't seen since high school. In every case, he introduced Benjy as his friend and coworker, which was accurate but somehow felt deceptive. What was he supposed to say, though? *This is Benjy, my love interest, the man I've kissed twice and secretly want to make out with. Someday we might be boyfriends, but I can't honestly call him that now.* No, he couldn't say any of that because it wasn't anyone's business, and he had no idea how things would pan out for Benjy and him.

Benjy had his own set of baggage. He battled his own demons—awkward in social situations, prone to panic attacks. The guy sometimes was too skittish to pick up a phone and order a pizza.

When Benjy sidled up closely to Oliver, pretty much following him around like his shadow, Oliver didn't allow himself to feel annoyed like he often did. There were times when Benjy acted so reserved that he seemed frightened to speak up for himself, to complain when warranted, to ask for help or directions. He wasn't a mingler like Oliver, didn't demonstrate any degree of extroversion around strangers. In a crowd, he seemed to recede, pull into himself.

The way he'd taken so quickly to Oliver's parents had surprised Oliver. But now, amid this sea of new people, Benjy seemed different.

When Oliver got up to talk to one of his cousins, Benjy found a chair in the corner, sat with his legs crossed, and smiled nervously as people walked by.

After a few minutes, Oliver separated from the crowd and walked over to Benjy. "Hey, are you okay?"

Benjy looked up, smiling. "Yeah. Fine. See, you really do have a ton of people who like you. Look at all these relatives and friends."

Oliver took a seat beside him, rolling his eyes. "Trust me, you wouldn't want to hear what they say behind my back."

"And yet you're so friendly with them."

"Does that make me a hypocrite? See that lady over there, the one talking to my mom? She's my mother's cousin, and she called and asked my mother if I'd been tested for HIV when I came out in the tenth grade. She was worried about her children, both teenagers, associating with me."

"Oh my God."

"And that dude over there, that's her son, Walter. He teased me so bad when I was in middle school for being fat that I hated his guts. And that guy over there talking to my dad, he once called me Fat Albert as a joke. And that girl on the other side of my aunt, she and her friends used to sing 'Fatty, fatty, two-by-four' at the bus stop every morning."

"Ollie, please don't tell me any more." Benjy's eyes brimmed with tears.

"So yeah, I know I'm a hypocrite. I should tell them all to go fuck themselves, but I don't. I just smile and pretend none of it ever happened."

"Did you eat anything?" Benjy slid his hand onto Oliver's thigh, and the gentle touch felt good. Oliver smiled.

"A chicken breast, some watermelon, and a teeny-tiny serving of Mom's potato salad. I shouldn't have, but God was it good."

"Your mom's a good cook." He took a deep breath. "I shouldn't say this, Ollie, but I want to get out of here."

Oliver grinned, widening his eyes excitedly. "Let's go."

"We can't just leave. These people all came to see you."

"And they've seen me. They've all eaten the free food, and they'll have plenty to talk about afterward, how I'm just as huge as I've always been."

"But you're not." It looked for a second like Benjy was going to reach up and touch him. Instead, he twitched nervously. "You've lost a lot."

"I know a place we can go. It's secluded and quiet."

"Okay."

"I'm gonna tell Dad we're leaving for a while. He won't care, and he can tell Mom later when she figures out we've gone."

OLIVER HAD watched his share of sappy movies. He'd read books with romantic plots. He'd often thought he understood how two people were drawn together, the feelings of attraction they shared. Hell, he'd even crushed on other guys a number of times in high school and college. But nothing had prepared him for the warm feeling Benjy ignited in his chest. The odd mixture of excitement, anticipation, and uncertainty all but overwhelmed him. He wanted nothing more than to just *touch* him.

They held hands in the SUV.

"This isn't much of a beach." Oliver's tone apologetic, he turned to Benjy. "But the actual beach will be crowded right now. This is just a little lake where people come to launch their rowboats and fish."

"Deer Lake." Benjy read the sign posted just inside the small dirt parking area. "There's a picnic table."

"Yeah, and it looks like someone's here, but they're out on the lake. They left their pickup and trailer."

Benjy let go of his hand and reached for the door handle. "Let's walk down by the water."

"Sometimes there are swans or ducks."

"Oh." Benjy looked over to him. "We should have brought bread."

Oliver smiled. Benjy truly did not have a selfish bone in his body. He always thought of others, never said an unkind word, and he even had compassion for the wildlife. "They'll be okay. Trust me, they get enough free food from humans."

As they approached the water, a sandy shoreline extended only about five feet up until it met with grass. Benjy led the way, walking over to an embankment, where he slid to his butt and sat with his feet dangling over the edge.

"The water's probably warm. You can dip your feet in if you want, but it's not great for swimming. The sand on the floor of the lake is all mushy-like. Feels like quicksand."

"Really?" Benjy grinned. "I want to feel it." He pulled up his leg, pretzel-like, and removed his shoe, then did the same with the other and rolled up his pant legs. Oliver marveled at his agility. With his slender body and skinny legs, it was nothing for him to bend in any direction. Oliver still couldn't even cross his legs at the knees, let alone sit cross-legged.

Oliver lowered himself on the embankment, far less gracefully than Benjy, but he ended up in the same position, sitting beside his friend. Benjy slid down the embankment and stepped out on the sand, toward the water. "Are you joining me?"

Oliver shook his head. "I'll watch. Don't go far out, though."

Benjy placed both hands on his hips in protest. "I know how to swim, ya know."

"Well, suit yourself, but it's yucky in there. Plus, once you get out a ways, there's a lot of reeds. And this lake has lots of big fish too. Pike. They get three or four feet long."

Benjy's eyes grew wide and Oliver laughed. "Do they bite?"

"Go on!"

Benjy walked out a few feet, then stopped. He turned to look at Oliver, contorting his face. "Ew. It totally *does* feel weird. It's like I'm sinking into it."

"Oh, and I forgot to warn you about the leeches."

"Leeches!" He spun around completely, glaring at Oliver accusingly. "What the fuck are leeches?"

"Little slimy slugs that attach to your skin and suck your blood."

"Gross!" Benjy raced back up to the shore, staring down at his feet, examining himself furiously. "Are there any on me? Oh my God!"

Oliver cracked up laughing. "No, you're fine." He looked at Benjy's round little ass, the fabric of his pants smooth and tight across his behind. *Wow. Fucking wow!*

"You're a jerk, ya know."

Benjy jumped back up on the embankment to sit beside Oliver. With his legs dangling over the side, barefoot and pant legs cuffed, he brushed against Oliver.

"It's so pretty out here."

Oliver glanced out over the lake. Although a few hundred yards from where they sat, the lake expanded significantly. From their vantage point, they could see the other side. A thick patch of trees rose up, and Oliver wondered if the wooded area surrounding the water was what had given the lake its name. Perhaps the wildlife, including deer, frequently came and drank from the water.

"The sky is so beautiful, so clear." Benjy leaned back, staring up at the clouds. "It's like we forget about the world around us. Living in the city, I never take the time to even look up at the sky."

As Benjy leaned all the way back, flattening himself on the grass, Oliver dared to mimic his posture. Assuming an identical supine position, staring straight up at the billowy clouds, he couldn't bring himself to glance over at Benjy. He wondered, though, if Benjy could hear the beating of his heart. Benjy had asked him the same question the night before when they first kissed.

The graze of Benjy's fingertips against his arm sent goose pimples all the way up to Oliver's shoulder. He closed his eyes, trying not to think that he must look like a beached whale lying there on his back next to the water. He heard Benjy rustle, repositioning himself alongside Oliver's body, then felt his hand again, this time pressed flat against his chest.

"Benjy…." He opened his eyes, and Benjy was right there, his face in front of him, gazing into his eyes.

"You're wrong," Benjy whispered. "You're wrong about how you look. You're wrong about how I see you—how all the people who love you see you."

"How do you see me?"

Benjy smiled as he raked his fingers back and forth across Oliver's chest. "I see you as big and strong. You can wrap your arms around me and squeeze me into a tight, protective bear hug."

Oliver smiled. "I don't have to be fat to do that."

"You aren't that fat. Lying flat on your back like this, you barely have a belly."

"Benjy…." Oliver laughed. "You're so sweet, but stop lying."

Benjy reached down to the tail of Oliver's polo and slid his hand beneath, ghosting his fingers against Oliver's bare skin. He slid his arm upward and grazed his fingers across Oliver's pecs. "Mmm. Oliver, you make me rock-hard. I think you're amazing, the sexiest man I've ever known."

Oliver reached up and wrapped his arm around Benjy, then pulled him in. Leaning forward, he kissed him, strong and passionate, driving his tongue deep into Benjy's mouth. Benjy responded, squirming against him and running his fingers through Oliver's hair.

As they kissed, Oliver held Benjy, clung tightly to his slim body, and allowed his hands to move back and forth, up and down. He loved Benjy's tight, toned frame. He loved the smell of him, the taste. God, he was so adorable, so beautiful.

When at last Benjy pulled back, Oliver throbbed, aroused more than he'd ever been his entire life. "Benjy…." He nearly cried. Reaching up with both hands, he removed Benjy's glasses and carefully set them aside, then cupped Benjy's face with both hands, memorizing every square inch of its beauty.

Again he kissed Benjy deeply, savoring the moment, their closeness, and the taste and feel of this magnificent young man who seemed in every way too good to be true.

"Oliver, you're so beautiful." It wasn't like him to use Oliver's full name. "Thank you. Thank you for making me feel so… normal."

How could Benjy's declaration so artfully echo his own thoughts and feelings? He stared up into Benjy's face, smiling. "Ditto."

THEY WENT to a movie that night, a comedy, and Oliver sat beside Benjy, holding his hand in the dark. He hadn't gone to a theater in a long time. The seats were too small, and he usually needed to allow at least one empty seat on each side of him because his torso extended to the outer edge of his seat and his arms needed room on either side. But this time was different. He'd actually lost enough weight that he fit into one seat, with Benjy right beside him.

As much as he despised his hometown, he didn't want to go back to the city. After the afternoon at Deer Lake with Benjy, he couldn't stop smiling. He felt like a new man, revived and inexplicably happy. He didn't find himself annoyed at the concession stand, waiting for popcorn. He didn't feel like screaming at the driver in front of him who'd failed to move when the light turned green. And even when his mother lightly scolded him for leaving the barbecue so abruptly, Oliver merely smiled and apologized. He even kissed his mom on the cheek.

They held hands again on the porch once they got home, and Oliver pulled Benjy close and kissed him deeply. The passion inside him roiled, and he had to resist his urge to ravage Benjy, to demonstrate aggressively how strongly he desired intimacy. Instead he oh so carefully and tenderly kissed Benjy and caressed his back, amazed this lithe, spunky little man saw anything in him at all.

When the spring on the screen door squeaked and Oliver pulled back from Benjy to see his mother standing just outside the doorframe, arms crossed over her chest, he knew he'd been caught. He looked over at her, smiling.

She took a deep breath, shaking out her arms on either side of her before waving her hands in front of her face. "I knew it," she whispered.

"Mom...."

"I can't say I'm disappointed." Her voice, overwhelmed with emotion, cracked as she spoke. "Actually, I was praying."

"It just sort of happened... since we got here."

"I... um... I suppose I should leave you two alone."

Benjy shook his head, turning to her with outstretched arms. "C'mere." He pulled her into an embrace, and then she hugged Oliver, sort of at the same time. She pulled back, looking from one face to the other, tears streaming down her cheeks.

"I have two boys, both of them beautiful."

"In that case...." Benjy grinned impishly. "Mom, do you have any of that delicious potato salad left?"

AS MUCH as Oliver wanted further intimacy with Benjy, he wasn't ready, and certainly not at his parents' house. He kissed Benjy good night, then lay in his own bed, staring up at the ceiling. His cheeks hurt from smiling so much, and yet he couldn't stop grinning, even there in the dark.

He woke up early, ready once more for a long, solitary walk. But Benjy met him in the hallway, sporting sweatpants and a T-shirt. "Not sure I'm up for eight miles, but I'm not letting you out of my sight for that long."

Oliver kissed him on the forehead, and they descended the stairs together. When they returned a little over an hour later, they bolted into the kitchen, dying for water. Oliver's mom was frying bacon and sausage and making hash browns. "And I suppose you're just having your usual?" She looked at Oliver.

"Low-fat yogurt and oatmeal please. Dry toast."

"I'll have extra bacon, please." Benjy beamed.

Oliver's mom attended church with her sister and brother-in-law, graciously inviting the rest of the family to join them, though to Oliver the invitation felt more like a guilting. He didn't much care for church and hadn't been to one, other than Amanda's wedding, since the day he came out in high school. The Baptists weren't exactly welcoming and accepting of the LGBT community, and it took Betty Paxton about sixty seconds to decide she'd become Presbyterian. When the preacher at First Baptist tried telling her that her son was an abomination, she told him to take his King James Bible and shove it where the sun don't shine and called her sister to inform her she'd be attending church with her from then on.

The denomination didn't really matter, though. Oliver wasn't even sure he believed in God. He believed in science, believed in cause and effect. But that was different from karma. Karma was justice, and when he looked around, he didn't see justice. He didn't see equality and fairness. Some people had harder lives than others. Some started farther back from the finish line. And the good guy didn't always win. How could he, believing in science, think that a God existed somewhere out there and actually cared about what happened with people?

Maybe growing up fat and gay had naturally jaded him. Perhaps he saw life through a far more cynical lens than the average person. But he watched as Benjy scarfed massive quantities of food into his tiny little body and never gained an ounce. He knew plenty of slender people who sat around smoking pot all day long, people who weren't active, never exercised. Back in high school, he observed guys he'd been raised with suddenly develop into toned muscle studs, and they barely seemed to even put forth an effort. It was just something in their genes. How was any of this fair? How was it fair that he'd been born into a family with fatty genes? Why did he have a predilection to overeat? And why did other people who ate even more remain so slim?

He'd concluded he simply had to play with the hand he'd been dealt. If looking and feeling like a normal person meant exercising for hours every day and eating like a bird, he'd do it. And he still wasn't quite over the shock that a guy—*any* guy—would be interested in him, would find him attractive.

They'd been at his folks' for only two days, but it seemed an eternity had passed. So much had happened in the past forty-eight hours. When he and Benjy packed up Sunday afternoon, his mom and dad stood beside the car, his mother all weepy. She'd packed Benjy a buttload of leftovers, stuffing them into a specially purchased Styrofoam cooler.

"I'm going to learn some new recipes," she whispered into Oliver's ear as she hugged him. "Some nonfattening treats so I can cook for you again."

"Mom, you're fine. The food was amazing, as always."

"Did you check your oil?" His dad patted him on the shoulder.

"I get the oil changed every three thousand miles, Dad. It's on a maintenance schedule."

His dad frowned and nodded, then leaned in for a quick, manly hug. "Well, don't let the gas gauge drop below the half-full line."

"I know, but thanks."

"Benjy!" His mom pulled Benjy into her, hugging him fiercely. "You have to promise to come visit… a lot!"

"We will," he promised. He lingered in the hug for a few seconds, then finally pulled back and stepped over to hug Oliver's father.

An oddly surreal feeling swept over Oliver as he backed out onto the street and pulled away. "I can't believe I actually dreaded this trip." He spoke softly, not really directing his comment at Benjy, but Benjy responded, reaching over to take hold of Oliver's hand.

"These have been the best two days of my life." Benjy gulped, then stared out the passenger window. Maybe he was crying, but even if so, they weren't tears of sadness.

"Can we think of this as the start of a new life?"

"I like that." Benjy squeezed his hand. "You're going to be working on your weight, and maybe I should work on a few things too."

Oliver paused, wanting to respond but not quite sure what to say. Finally he whispered, "You're fine just the way you are."

"You know, I keep the ringer turned off on my phone because I'm too frightened to answer."

"Benjy, that doesn't mean anything. I do the same thing."

He looked over at Oliver, shaking his head. "It's not the same. I do it because I'm genuinely scared. I won't go to a store or restaurant if there seems to be a lot of cars in the lot, afraid it'll be too crowded. I get freaked out standing in lines, and every time I have any kind of deadline, I seize up, completely panic."

"We always have deadlines, Benjy. It's part of our job, how we function at work."

"I know." He sighed. "You have no idea what a fucked-up mess I am most of the time. But…."

"What?"

"But everything's different with you. You calm me. You make it all okay."

He turned on the blinker, slowing in preparation for his turn onto the expressway. "Well, you've helped me so much. Why don't you let me help you? We'll take it one day at a time."

Benjy smiled. "You're afraid of being naked in front of me, and I think it's silly. I've already fantasized a million times about you and me naked together."

Oliver felt his cheeks warming. Again, how did a person respond to a comment like that? He raised his eyebrows and stared straight ahead at the highway. "And it didn't gross you out?"

"Shut up!" Benjy pulled his hand away but only far enough to slap Oliver on the arm. "If I told you my fantasies, you'd probably really be embarrassed."

"Uh, yeah. I would." He couldn't hear them, not now. He couldn't let Benjy get any more detailed in his descriptions. That might just be enough to send Oliver completely over the edge, but oh how he wanted to know. Did Benjy dream about getting his dick sucked? Of sucking Oliver? Did he want to climb on top of Oliver, straddling him as Oliver lay on his back, and ride his cock like a cowboy riding a wild bull? "Don't say any more. *Please!*"

Benjy laughed. "Just wait till you take off a tiny bit more weight. I'll give you road head."

"Benjy! Stop!"

"I could do it now, maybe… if you pushed your seat all the way back."

"Benjy, for God's sake! No, my seat's already back as far as it goes, and that's just…."

"Too risky, I know. But maybe a hand job?" He slid his hand onto Oliver's thigh, rubbing back and forth.

"Why are you so horny?" Oliver grabbed Benjy's wrist and pulled it back.

"'Cause you kissed me a thousand times this weekend but nothing more."

"Well, you're the shy one, the one with anxiety disorder. You're not supposed to be so… um… assertive."

Benjy giggled. "That's what I mean. I'm an entirely different person around you. But think about it, Ollie. When you lose all this weight and turn into a supermodel, all these superficial guys who didn't give you the fucking time of day are gonna be all over you. Then you'll look at me and see me as I really am—a pathetic, neurotic little twerp."

Oliver's mouth dropped open, and he glanced over at Benjy, whose expression remained somber, dead serious. "You know that's not true."

Benjy took a deep breath. "I know," he conceded. "It's not fair, and I shouldn't say things like that. But that's my biggest fear."

"It's crazy, man. Baseless. I want to lose the weight so I can be more attractive *to you*."

"Ollie, I do want to help you continue losing your weight, but please believe me. It doesn't matter to me. I'm going to lo—feel the same way about you no matter what."

"And you've got to believe me too. We're both flawed. We both have our baggage, and so what? It's called being human. I like you as you are, right now at this very minute, and nothing's gonna change that. Ever."

CHAPTER SEVEN

TOO KEYED up to sleep, Oliver spent an hour or so online, playing Overwatch, then finally switched off the PlayStation to try watching TV. He couldn't stop thinking about all that had happened. Dropping Benjy off had been bittersweet, to say the least. He'd toyed with the idea of inviting Benjy to stay with him overnight, but Lord only knew where that might have led.

Yearning to take their intimacy to the next level, Oliver fantasized about so much more. He thought about Benjy shirtless, stark naked, even. His narrow waist and tight, solid core of abdominals depicted the polar opposite physicality to what Oliver's body exemplified. Oh, how he'd love to wrap his hands around that skinny little waist as he sucked on Benjy's rigid cock. It would be big, had to be. They always said skinny guys had huge cocks. With Benjy being short, it would definitely *look* disproportionately large against his diminutive frame.

As he pushed himself up from the chair, he thought of how lithe and agile Benjy was. He seemed to easily contort his body, sitting with his legs tucked beneath him, pulling his knees up to his chin, crouching and stretching so effortlessly. All of his antics contradicted Oliver's. Oliver heaved himself out of a chair, lumbered when he walked, and gasped for breath when he so much as tried to bend at the waist.

Sure, things were starting to improve. He wasn't winded anymore after a long walk. He could look down and see the lower half of his body much easier than before. He didn't struggle so much raising his leg enough to slip on his socks every morning. As he stepped into the bathroom, forcing himself to look straight ahead into the full-length mirror, he peeled off his polo shirt.

Was he smaller? Did he detect any difference at all? His face certainly looked thinner. He didn't display such an obvious double chin anymore. The man boobs disgusted him, the wretched pillows of fat that extended outward from his pecs to his underarms. But had they shrunk at all? Maybe a little. His tummy seemed smaller, and he was beginning to detect a waistline that had previously merely been enveloped with flab.

What exactly did Benjy see in him? He'd said Oliver was big and strong. In spite of himself, he smiled. Strong? He turned and flexed his bicep. Yeah, maybe. He certainly had more muscle than Benjy with his tiny twig-like arms. He repositioned himself, righting his posture to face the mirror head-on, and sucked in his belly. Puffing his chest a bit, he was able to imagine himself more defined. If he concentrated on the pecs and biceps, he could pack on some muscle for sure. If he lost some more of his gut, he wouldn't even be that disproportionate.

He closed his eyes for a few seconds and recalled the soft, tender touch of Benjy's fingertips traveling across his pectorals. Oh God, it had felt so wonderful. He opened his eyes and flicked off the light switch, then hurried to the bedroom where he peeled off his pants and underwear and flopped down on the mattress. Lying on his back with his eyes squeezed tightly closed, he envisioned Benjy. With one hand, he tweaked his nipple, and with the other, he found his hardness. Benjy's warm, wet mouth enveloped him, surrounded the entirety of his penis, and began to lave him. The heat of the suction surrounded Oliver's arousal, and as he stroked himself, it wasn't his hand that delivered such soothing ministrations, but Benjy's worshipful tongue and mouth.

Within minutes he lay panting on the mattress, a glob of semen splashed across his heaving torso. "Benjy…," he whispered. "Oh, Benjy, that was amazing."

HOPEFULLY BENJY didn't think Oliver had just brushed him off. He'd declined the invitation to Benjy's apartment after work, stating he had an appointment. He wasn't lying, and now as he parked his SUV in front of the Fitness Warehouse, he had a clear idea of what Benjy went through on a daily basis. His anxiety had kicked into overdrive, and it was all he could do to force himself out from behind the wheel. Somehow he managed, though, and made his way to the double glass doors at the building entrance.

As he approached the counter, he glanced around, peering for a few seconds into the exercise area of the gym. Thankfully, people of varying sizes were using the equipment. At least they all weren't buff muscle gods.

"Hi, can I help you?" a bubbly, blonde receptionist greeted him. He nodded and cleared his throat.

"I'm Oliver Paxton, and I have an appointment with Adam Wilcox."

"Sure, I'll page him." She picked up her handset and keyed a set of numbers into the phone. After a few seconds, she informed the trainer his five-thirty was waiting. She then hung up and turned to Oliver. "He'll be right out."

Oliver thanked her and stepped back from the desk. No chairs were positioned in the customer area, so he couldn't take a seat. Instead, he moved over toward the window and tried to appear inconspicuous. Thankfully his wait wasn't long, and when a thirtysomething, drop-dead gorgeous man strode toward him, smiling, Oliver gulped. The tight-fitting T-shirt bearing the Fitness Warehouse logo hugged the trainer's well-rounded pecs. He also wore silky, midlength shorts, perhaps Under Armour, and a pair of the most fashionable and undoubtedly super expensive sneakers.

"Oliver? I'm Adam! What a pleasure to meet you!"

Adam's pearly white smile immediately mesmerized Oliver along with the man's sparkling, crystal blue eyes. A lump quickly formed in Oliver's throat, and all at once, he felt like nothing more than a huge blob. God, why'd his trainer have to look like *that*?

"Hi," Oliver managed. "Dr. Evans referred me."

"Brad? Oh cool. Great guy. Well, I'm glad to meet you." He placed his hand on Oliver's shoulder, patting it as if they were longtime friends. "Why don't we head on back to my office and have a chat, okay?"

As he followed Adam down the hallway, the walls seemed to be padded, perhaps lined with carpeting like the cubicles at work. He trailed behind Adam, noting his broad shoulders, V-shaped torso, and most obviously, his well-rounded bubble butt. Everything about the man, from his impeccably styled hair all the way down to his sturdy, glistening calves embodied perfection. This was the man Oliver had dreamed about all his life, every time he looked in a mirror. Adam had been blessed with a perfect storm of physical amenities. He literally could become a model or perhaps even the next movie star.

He led Oliver into a small office, which was really more of a cubicle, and Oliver took a seat as instructed. Adam did not slide into his own comfortable desk chair but instead leaned back on the desk, sitting on the very edge. He bent forward as he spoke to Oliver, who might have otherwise felt awkward by the man's close proximity. Adam's charisma and striking good looks offset all of Oliver's misgivings, however, and Oliver looked longingly into Adam's gorgeous eyes, awaiting further commentary.

"Tell me, Oliver, what brings you here."

"Well...." He gulped and looked down, fidgeting nervously with his pant legs, smoothing out the material on his fat thighs. "I've been quite overweight for some time now, since back, um... clear back to when I was in school."

"And you're how old now?"

"Twenty-five."

"You've certainly come to the right place, Oliver. You said Brad Evans referred you?"

"Yeah, I've been dieting for the past few months. I know it's hard to tell by looking at me, but I've lost about sixty pounds so far."

"Holy Moses!" Adam slapped his hand on his thigh as he grinned from ear to ear. "Congrats, man! That's fantastic."

Oliver smiled, somewhat shyly. Adam's praise embarrassed him for some reason. "When I first started, I couldn't do much. I mean, in the way of exercise, I was sort of limited. It was hard for me to even walk long distances."

"And now?"

"Now I walk every day, sometimes as much as eight or nine miles. I have a wristband odometer I use. And I recently bought an exercise bike I use in my garage. I try to go a few miles every day."

"Sounds like you're doing amazing. Have you had a physical?"

Oliver nodded. "Everything checks out. No problems with my heart or anything, and I don't smoke."

"Good, good." Adam nodded, all the while still smiling. "So at this point, you're thinking you might be ready to kick things up to the next level? Get yourself a personal trainer and a workout routine?"

He didn't know whether to nod or shrug. "Well… I at least wanted to talk about it, get your opinion."

"How long have you been dieting, Oliver?"

"A little shy of six months."

"Wow, sixty pounds in six months. That's incredible. Hmm, I think you're probably due to start slowing down significantly. You're likely to plateau anytime now. But if we can get you on an exercise program and ramp up your metabolism a bit, I think we might be able to keep you on the right track, sort of counter your body's natural tendency to protect its fat."

"Huh?"

"Your body, it operates in self-defense mode most of the time. It stores fat, probably as a result of the way humans used to more or less hibernate. It's going to try to protect that fat, not likely to give it up without a fight."

"Wow, I never thought of it that way."

"What you and I see as a toned, fit body, Mother Nature views as merely sustenance of the status quo. But we don't go for long periods of time without eating anymore. We don't need to store so much fat. It's not healthy."

Oliver nodded. What Adam said made sense. That still didn't explain how some people ate so much without gaining weight and others packed on the pounds with no effort whatsoever. Adam seemed to almost read his mind, though, and indicated as much with his follow-up comment.

"That's not to say some of us aren't genetically more predisposed to gain weight. Tell me about your family. Are your parents and siblings heavy as well?"

"My mom is heavy, but not as bad as me. And Dad, well, a little bit. I'm an only child."

"Did you grow up eating a lot of fatty, unhealthy foods?"

"Pretty much, but I didn't think of it that way at the time. Those comfort foods my mom made all the time were my favorites. And then… well, you know college. Fast food, pizza, stuff like that."

"Exactly." Adam nodded along with everything Oliver was saying. "And I'm assuming most of those are things of the past at this point, after losing so much already?"

"I honestly haven't cheated even once. But damn... I've been tempted. This time was different, though."

"Hmm. Do you know why? Why have you succeeded this time? I'm assuming you mean you tried before and failed."

"Yeah, lots of times. This time, I was getting fitted for a tux. I stood up in my friend's wedding, and as I looked at myself in the mirror, I just lost it. Sort of had a meltdown, and I hated what I saw. I decided that no matter what, I was going to lose the weight."

"So you're doing this for *you*? It's not to please your parents or to impress a girl or anything?" He grinned and winked.

"I should be honest." Oliver gulped. "I'm not into girls."

"Again, you've come to the right place!" Adam reached out and slapped Oliver on the shoulder, squeezing it. "Most of the staff and a big portion of the clientele here are gay. And that's probably part of the reason Brad referred you."

"Really?"

"I doubt he'd be upset with me outing him. He's pretty open about his relationship with Todd."

"The nurse that works in his office?"

"Is Brad's husband, yes." Adam beamed.

"Wow." So his gaydar hadn't been all whacko. He hadn't been projecting after all. But that being said, he now felt even more awkward in front of this gorgeous man. Adam was not only hot but also gay!

"I don't know if Brad told you, but he used to be quite a bit heavier than you are now. How much are you? About two-sixty?"

"Two seventy-four. I was three thirty-two when I started."

"Yeah, I'd say Brad was at least four hundred, and look at him now."

"He's... um... gorgeous."

Adam smiled. "Don't you dare tell him that. He has a big enough ego as it is." Strange, Oliver hadn't gotten that impression. If anything, Brad seemed humble and self-effacing to him. Was it an act, perhaps, or was Adam just teasing?

"I probably wouldn't say this to most people." Oliver looked up into Adam's eyes. "But I'm interested in someone, and we've kind of, sort of... ya know...."

"You met someone you're hot for?" Adam raised his eyebrows, once again smiling his trademark grin.

"You make it sound so dirty. And delicious."

"I know, right? Isn't it, though? But hey, that's cool. Is this guy pretty supportive of your weight-loss efforts?"

"He's the best. Yeah, really supportive, but he's super skinny."

Adam shrugged. "You know what they say about skinny guys."

Oliver felt his face heating up. "Yeah. Um, I know."

"Well, that's cool, but just so you know, I'm going to try to keep you focused on your original goal. You have to remain determined to do this for *you*." He pointed his finger at Oliver's chest. "What's your honey's name?"

"My honey?" Oliver laughed. "His name's Benjy."

"Aww. Okay, just remember this is all about Oliver, not Benjy, not that Benjy won't reap some awesome rewards in the long run." He winked.

"But… but we haven't even talked about it yet."

Adam leaned back on the desk and pulled out a drawer from the other side. He retrieved a brochure and handed it to Oliver. "These are my rates. Let's start out privately. We can meet early mornings if you'd like, say eight o'clock. Most new clients aren't keen on having an audience."

"Yeah, that'll work great. I can come in before work."

"We'll make our first few appointments at eight, and when you get the routine down, you'll be able to arrive as early as you want. I get here around eight usually, but eventually you'll be able to start without me."

"How often should I come?"

"Why, every day. You should come every single day. We won't work the same muscle group every day, but you'll need to get in the habit of exercising daily."

"Oh. Okay."

"I'm not always here every day myself. I'm supposed to take a couple days off every week, which I sometimes do." He laughed. "I know, I'm married to my job. I love it that much. But even when I'm not here, there'll be a trainer available if you need assistance. And to start with, I won't leave you on your own."

"So, should I start tomorrow?"

"It's a date." He held out his hand to shake. "Oliver, I'm excited about this. Aren't you?"

Oliver nodded and smiled.

"I can't wait to get started." Adam patted him on the back.

CHAPTER EIGHT

AFTER RINGING for Benjy three times and getting no response, Oliver considered just dialing him on his cell phone. Perhaps he'd stepped out for a bit, possibly gone for a walk or something. His car remained in the lot, right next to Oliver's SUV. But as Oliver dug into his pocket for his cell, Benjy's voice finally crackled through the PA system. "Who is it?"

Oliver pressed the button and spoke into the mic. "Benjy, it's Ollie. Are you okay?" He didn't sound good at all.

"Yeah, sorry. I'll buzz you in."

The door clicked, and Oliver grabbed the knob and pushed it open. Benjy lived on the third floor, which usually meant using the elevator. Instead he took the stairs two at a time. Slightly winded, he huffed down the hallway and stopped in front of Benjy's door. Before he could knock, the door opened.

"Benjy, are you okay?" Oliver walked into the room as Benjy took a step back. His eyes were red, as if he'd been crying. What had happened?

"Sorry, I was taking a nap."

"Really? I didn't know you took naps after work."

"Oh." Benjy shrugged. "I guess I don't usually, but maybe I'm still tired after this weekend. You want a beer or something?"

Oliver shook his head. He tried avoiding all alcohol, especially beer. "Maybe just a water if you have one."

He followed Benjy to the kitchen, and as he might have expected, it was spotless. The whole apartment was neat and tidy, the opposite of Oliver's. But that was Benjy, fastidious about details, neurotic when it came to keeping everything organized. It wasn't the apartment itself that concerned Oliver, though. It was Benjy. He wasn't acting like Benjy.

"Are you mad at me?"

Benjy opened the fridge and removed a bottled water, then handed it to Oliver. "No. Why?"

"You just… um, I don't know. You seem pissed or something."

He shook his head. "You didn't have to come over. You already said you were busy, and that's fine."

"Wait, Benjy… no, I think you misunderstood what I said. I didn't say I was busy."

"I thought we had the most perfect weekend ever. In fact, I thought of it as life-changing."

"It *was!*"

"But then last night, you just dropped me off here. I was surprised. Disappointed, even. But I just thought you were tired or something. Then you hardly talked at work, and when I asked you over, you brushed me off. Ollie, I can take a hint. If you don't like being around me—"

Oliver set the bottle on the countertop, perhaps more forcefully than he intended, then immediately grabbed Benjy by the shoulders. "Are you fucking nuts or something? Benjy, I dropped you off last night because… well, because if I hadn't, I'd have fucking ravaged you! I wanted you so damn bad, and you're all I thought about all night."

"I was…?"

"And today, God, it was just a busy day. After the weekend, we had so much shit to do. And I told you, I had an appointment after work. I was worried about it. It was…." He took a deep breath. "It was with the dude down at the gym, my personal trainer. I joined the gym today, and I'm starting a workout routine with him. We had to talk about it."

"Wh-why didn't you tell me?"

"I don't know. I… um, well, I wanted to wait to see what he was like first. I hadn't decided if I was even going to be able to do it. But he seems really cool, and I think what he's offering is perfect for me. And you know what? He's gay! And I told him about you."

"You told him about me?" Benjy stared up at him, his eyes wide and magnificently brown. "What did you say?"

"I said you're a fucking pain in my ass."

Benjy continued to stare at him, neither frowning nor smiling.

"No, I didn't say that. I said you're amazing, and I'm interested in you. I said you motivate me."

Finally, Benjy smiled. "I think you had it right the first time. I think I *am* a pain in the ass."

"Benjy…."

"What?"

"Shut up." He grabbed Benjy and pulled him in for a passionate, tongue-on-tongue kiss. Benjy wrapped his arms around Oliver, standing on tiptoe, and pressed his body against Oliver's. Oliver slid his hands down Benjy's back, caressing him as they kissed.

On impulse, Oliver reached down and swept Benjy into his arms with an uncharacteristically smooth and chivalrous movement. Startled, Benjy clung to his neck, all the while continuing to plant sloppy kisses, deep and passionate against Oliver's lips. Oliver stumbled, then righted himself as he moved toward the archway. After twisting his body awkwardly, he carried his little man into the living room, where he gently laid him on the love seat.

Oliver slid down in front of him, first on one knee, then the other, and faced Benjy at eye level. Benjy held on to his shoulders as Oliver leaned in to kiss him, starting with his lips and working his way downward. He found the smooth, sensitive area on Benjy's neck, and as he kissed and sucked, Benjy squirmed. He spread his legs wide, wrapping them as best he could around Oliver's wider body, and Oliver pressed himself forward, his pelvic area now grazing against the sofa cushions.

Aroused and throbbing rock-hard, Oliver moaned. He reached toward Benjy's shirttail, grasping frantically. At last he lay hold of it and pulled it upward. He backed off momentarily in order to peel the shirt over Benjy's head. The smooth, lean torso now lay bare before him, a delicious playground. He stared down at it, amazed by Benjy's slender beauty and his tight, rock-hard abs. There wasn't an ounce of fat on the dude's body.

Oh so carefully, so worshipfully, Oliver ghosted his fingers along the unblemished flesh. He leaned in and kissed Benjy in the cleft of his pecs, though they weren't exactly what you'd call well-defined. They were perfect nonetheless, and his fingers soon found Benjy's nipples. Working his way down, he continued to kiss and lave. Benjy squirmed on the miniature sofa, thrusting his pelvis against Oliver's torso.

Oliver at last reached Benjy's waistband. He grasped it and began to tug downward.

"Oliver... oh God! Take your shirt off!"

He shook his head. "No. Please, Benjy." He looked up at him, stared him directly in the eye. "Please let me make this about you. Please. Just let me… let me pleasure you this once."

"Oh, Oliver." Benjy's eyes grew wide and moist, and he nodded.

With Benjy's cooperation, Oliver peeled the shorts and underwear off, tugging them down past his thighs and calves and eventually discarding them beside him on the floor. He looked down at the gorgeous body in front of him, now completely naked, and marveled that Benjy was every bit as enticing as he'd imagined. His cock indeed seemed oversized on a body that compact. It jutted upward, extending to his navel, throbbing in anticipation.

Smiling, Oliver wrapped his hand around the shaft and pressed his fingers against the underside of Benjy's cock. As he squeezed, a pearl of precum emerged in the slit and slowly oozed out. Benjy bit his bottom lip and moaned. He held his hands to the side, gripping the cushions of the loveseat.

"You're beautiful," Oliver rasped. "Only about ten times more awesome than I'd fantasized."

Benjy reached up and grabbed Oliver's shoulders, then tried to lean forward for another kiss, but Oliver used his free hand to press against Benjy's chest. "Lay back, baby. Just enjoy, okay?"

He scooted back a tiny bit and leaned forward, bending at the waist. Pressing his nose against Benjy's shaft, he inhaled deeply as he licked Benjy's swollen ball sac. He'd never smelled it before, other than from his own body. He had no idea how intoxicating the scent of another man's musk actually was. He licked furiously, darting his tongue back and forth, dancing across Benjy's sensitive nuts. Benjy moaned and laughed, squirming on the sofa, all the while spreading his legs wide and holding on to Oliver's shoulders. "Ollie! Oh fuck, Ollie!"

Finally, Oliver licked his way up the throbbing cock, then parted his lips and pressed them against the massive swollen cockhead. As he slid downward, he pressed his tongue against the shaft, careful to guard against any contact of his teeth. He formed a suction around the shaft and savored the smoothness of the flesh in his mouth. This act—sucking dick—had been a product of Oliver's masturbatory fantasies for so long, he didn't even remember exactly when it had started. He'd jacked off to the mental images. He'd viewed porn. He'd experienced nocturnal emissions. But he'd never actually done it. Benjy was his first—his *very* first.

"Ollie, oh my God, it feels… it feels so amazing."

Excited, Oliver began to bob, sliding up and down on the shaft. He continued his ministrations, wrapping his fist around the base of the cock in order to deliver a hand-mouth combo like he'd seen a million times in porn. Benjy's reaction was every bit as exciting as the porn stars—more so, in fact. And it didn't take nearly as long as he expected.

"Baby, oh God. You're gonna make me come!"

Oliver sucked madly, sliding down the shaft as far as he could. Taking it deep, over three-quarters of the way down, he held his position and sucked furiously. At last, he felt the cock twitch against his tongue. It pulsed as the cumload fired through the shaft and erupted voluminously into Oliver's hungry mouth. Gulping, he swallowed as Benjy cried out, squirming on the sofa and grasping Oliver's shoulders. He thrust his pelvis upward reflexively, moaning in ecstasy.

Oliver at first pulled back, staring directly into Benjy's contorted face. He leaned in to kiss him, pressing his lower body firmly against the sofa cushion. He too was throbbing, more excited than he'd ever been, and as he pressed his body inward, the friction against his groin sent a shiver throughout his body. He moaned and spontaneously erupted in his underwear, firing his load without even touching himself.

Shaking, he closed his eyes, and Benjy pressed both palms around his face, framing it as he kissed him passionately. Goddammit! Why'd he have to ruin everything by busting his nut like that? He kissed Benjy and pulled back. "Fuck," he whispered.

"Oh my God, Ollie, that was fucking amazing."

"I… uh… I made a mess."

Benjy smiled. "What do you mean?"

"I got so excited."

"You came? You came in your pants?"

Oliver felt about two inches tall. His face must have been fire-engine red. "Sorry."

"Oh my God, Ollie. That is so hot!" Benjy wrapped his arms around Oliver's neck and kissed him deeply. When he pulled back, his eyes glistened as he watched Oliver. "You want me to clean you up? I will…."

He shook his head and pushed himself up, staggering a bit as he got his bearings. After quickly turning away so Benjy didn't get a good look at his wet spot, he stumbled toward the bathroom. "I'll just take care of it best I can before it dries."

"Wait!" Benjy jumped up from the loveseat, still stark naked. "I have a bathrobe you can wear. I'll just throw your clothes in the wash real quick."

Oliver stopped and turned back to Benjy. That would mean sitting around practically naked for an hour or so. And if the bathrobe fit Benjy, surely it'd be too small for him. "You don't have, like, any oversized basketball shorts or anything?"

Benjy giggled. "You mean for all the hot athletes I so frequently entertain?"

Oliver sighed and rolled his eyes.

"Go take a shower," Benjy said authoritatively. "I'll run over to your house and get you some clothes. I'll be back before you're done."

"I have some shorts and a T-shirt in my car, in my gym bag."

"Cool, I'll run and grab them."

Oliver pulled out his keys, then tossed them to Benjy. "Benjy... I'm sorry."

"That's like the lottery apologizing 'cause you only won a million dollars." Benjy smiled. "You just gave me the most amazing experience of my life, and you're saying you're sorry?"

Oliver opened his mouth to explain, but Benjy gave him a warning look that said he'd be wise not to argue. He nodded and headed down the hall into the bathroom.

"I'm taking you out to dinner!" Benjy shouted. "Whether you like it or not!"

A couple times during dinner, Benjy had hinted he wanted to return the favor, so to speak. He even went so far as to suggest Oliver go back to his apartment after eating, but Oliver wasn't ready. As much as he'd loved giving Benjy head, he couldn't imagine taking his clothes off in front of his lover. He couldn't bring himself to even conceptualize the image of Benjy staring at his naked body.

When he dropped Benjy off, they kissed in the car, and Oliver begged off the invitation, stating he really was now tired. He had to get up earlier the next morning and begin his workout. Benjy offered to join him, and Oliver once more declined. "Eventually, yes. But just wait. I have to spend the first few days working with my trainer. Once I get onto a routine, we can go together."

"Cool." Benjy grinned wickedly, as if he'd hatched an evil plan. "Hey, what if I blew you right here, right here in the parking lot, in your car?"

Oliver laughed. "Very funny."

Benjy slid his hand onto Oliver's thigh. "I'm not joking."

Oliver reached down and grabbed Benjy's wrist. "I don't think so... not tonight."

"But I still owe you...."

Oliver sighed and shook his head slightly. "You don't owe me, Benjy. What happened between us was... well, it was the most amazing experience I've ever had. You saw how excited I got."

"But I want to please you like you pleased me."

"Honestly? You probably pleased me more. Benjy, you're the very first guy I've ever been with."

Benjy smiled, and Oliver could see the twinkle in his eye as the dashboard lights illuminated his face.

"You're gonna make me cry."

"I've been fat and disgusting my whole life. Nobody's ever wanted to be with me, and... well, I haven't really wanted to be with anyone either. I've never wanted other people to see me."

"Ollie, you told me tonight you're two seventy. For a guy your height, that's hardly even fat! Why can't you see yourself the way other people see you? Sure, you've got a bigger build, but I *love* guys who are bigger. If you only knew how much you turn me on...."

"Just give me a few weeks, okay? With this rigorous workout schedule, it hopefully won't be long till I start putting on some muscle and losing some flab."

This time Benjy sighed. He ghosted his fingertips up Oliver's arm. "Please don't tell me this means you expect me to wait weeks before I can blow you, or before you... ya know."

Oliver wasn't even about to let his mind go there. He took hold of Benjy's hand, mainly to stop him from tickling his arm, but also so he could capture his full attention. "Benjy, what if I tried to force you to be in situations you knew you couldn't handle?"

"What do you mean?"

"You have anxiety, right? What if I said 'Tough shit' and just tried to force you to face your fears and do things you were nowhere near ready to do?"

"I'd freak. I'd have a meltdown, an anxiety attack."

"So please don't ask me to do shit I'm not ready for."

Benjy stared at him, mouth agape. Slowly he nodded, then squeezed Oliver's hand. "Baby, I'm sorry. You're right. Please believe me, though. I didn't mean it that way. I didn't mean to pressure you into anything."

"I know. I totally get it." Oliver smiled at him and leaned in to kiss him softly on the lips. "You're so beautiful," he whispered. "I get you want to make love, and it's a lot for me to ask, making you wait."

"No. No, Oliver. It's not, and I promise I'll never pressure you again. But please understand, the offer is always open. Whenever you're ready, I'll be waiting."

A single teardrop from each eye streamed down his cheeks. "Thank you."

They kissed good night.

CHAPTER NINE

OLIVER DIDN'T normally roll out of bed till around seven, but he got up early that Tuesday, slapping the alarm clock when it buzzed at 6:00 a.m. After stumbling to the kitchen, he slid a mug into his Keurig and popped in a K-cup, not even bothering to check the flavor. He'd purchased a variety pack a few weeks ago—not a big coffee drinker himself—because Benjy liked it. He rubbed his eyes as he waited for the brew cycle to complete, then glanced around his kitchen.

Without question, his housekeeping skills sucked. How did a single person manage to accumulate so much clutter? Perhaps the biggest difference between Benjy and him when it came to tidiness was lifestyle. Benjy had a place for everything, and he painstakingly kept everything in its place. Oliver, on the other hand, left everything out in the open. Wasn't that also a metaphor of their lives?

All of Benjy's problems remained bottled up inside. You'd never know by looking at him that he battled his own demons on a daily basis. But in Oliver's case, everyone could see he was fat. He maintained no facade, had no false pretenses. Oliver was who he was… for the most part.

He'd done some online research and found it odd his trainer planned to work him every day. Most trainers suggested a day of rest between every workout. Maybe Adam was just a diehard, and if that was the case, it wouldn't surprise Oliver. The man seemed extremely dedicated, and he couldn't deny Adam knew his craft well. Just look at him. Not only did he possess the body of a god himself, but he'd also transformed Dr. Brad into a soap opera star.

He removed the fat-free nondairy creamer from the fridge and poured some into his coffee cup. As he pulled out the silverware drawer to find it void of clean spoons, he shrugged and grabbed a butter knife, which he then used to stir his coffee.

For some strange reason, his life seemed so foggy. At this time of the morning, he felt almost as if he was still asleep, dreaming. A few months ago, he'd have never imagined getting up at the crack of dawn to exercise. He sipped the coffee, savoring the taste. Vanilla something-or-other.

He'd already laid out his work clothes, had them folded neatly on the dresser. He'd take them with him, in his gym bag, and shower after his workout. From there he'd head to work. Though officially scheduled nine-to-five, his hours were somewhat flexible. Neither he nor Benjy punched a clock, and if they arrived a few minutes late, they could work over or shave their lunch to make up the time. The company was more concerned with overall productivity than time clocks.

After washing his face, shaving, and brushing his teeth, he slipped into his shorts and oversized tee. He took a moment to examine his reflection in the mirror, nearly laughing at the imposter who stood before him. "Ollie, you're not a jock." He shook his head. He didn't look the part, not even in his workout clothes. He'd never be like Brad or Adam, no matter how hard he worked at it. He styled his hair and tossed his toiletries into the duffel along with his change of clothes.

Surprisingly, the morning traffic seemed even heavier at this early hour. Did other people actually have jobs that started so much earlier than his? For all this time, he'd been proud of himself for managing to maintain such an early schedule. When he pulled into the lot of the gym to find it nearly empty, he heaved a sigh of relief. At least all the crazies were at work rather than working out. Only the real nutcases like him subjected themselves to such torture.

As he pushed through the front door, he immediately spotted Adam, who was already in the gym, using one of the machines. He took a few tentative steps closer, wondering if he should interrupt or just wait, but at that very moment, Adam finished his set and slid off the machine, panting and wiping his brow. He looked across the room, spotted Oliver, and smiled, heaving himself up from the bench. He bounded over to Oliver, as energetic as a three-year-old.

"Hey, big guy! You ready? Ready to get started?"

To Oliver's surprise, Adam slapped one hand on his shoulder and with the other patted his flabby belly. Astonished by the uninvited touch, Oliver gawked at him and tried to smile. "I was wondering... um, you did say we were working out every day, right?"

Still grinning, Adam nodded. "Absolutely! But we're just going to do cardio exercises on Tuesdays, Thursdays, and the weekends. We'll alternate upper and lower body workouts on Mondays, Wednesdays, and Fridays along with a shorter cardio workout."

"Oh, okay."

"That way you're exercising every single day yet giving your muscle time to rest."

"Should I put my stuff in a locker or something?"

"Yeah, man. Let me show you around. We'll get you set up with a locker and then do the rundown on your first day of cardio." With his hand on Oliver's shoulder, he led him down a hallway and toward a staircase that presumably led to the locker room. All the while, he kept talking. "For a guy your age, we need to get your heartrate up to about two hundred BPM."

"BPM?"

"Beats per minute. And you want to sustain that a minimum of twenty minutes."

He wondered how fast his heart beat when he walked in circles around his garage. He'd certainly managed to work up a sweat every time, and he definitely had maintained the routine longer than twenty minutes.

As Adam led him into the locker room, he noticed a group of four guys on the far side of the room. They all glanced over at him but didn't speak. Instead, they talked among themselves, laughing and smiling. Oliver looked away, directing his full attention to Adam.

"You'll get to know everyone eventually," Adam said dismissively. "Some of our diehard regulars."

They looked the part with their sculpted, nearly perfect bodies. In fact, from Oliver's perspective, they *were* perfect. As he opened his locker to store his personals, he overheard one of the others call his friend "bitch," and then froze in his tracks when he distinctly identified the phrase "power bottom." They were gay gym bunnies, the four of them. Of course he'd heard about them. He'd seen lots of evidence online and in magazines that they existed, but he'd never actually known one personally. They were the popular guys, the in-crowd, the young, hot-looking studs who got A-listed at all the cool clubs.

"Okay, are we ready?"

78

Oliver glanced back at Adam and nodded. "Sure." He followed Adam out of the locker room and back up the steps into the gym.

"Let the games begin."

"OLLIE, ARE you sure you're all right?" Benjy stood over him, waiting for him to rise from his chair. It was after five, time to leave work, and Oliver couldn't move.

"Oh, God. Every inch of my body... every fucking inch...."

"It hurts?" Benjy stared at him sympathetically, his face sad like a puppy dog.

"Ohh, you have no idea. No *fuck*ing idea. Some of the muscles in my body that hurt right now I previously didn't know existed. How can my abs hurt? I didn't know I even *had* abs."

"You have abs." Benjy smiled. "Trust me, I look at 'em all the time."

"Benjy, don't make jokes. It hurts too much to laugh."

"Who's joking? Let me come home with you. I'll draw you a bath and give you a massage."

Oliver thought about himself stripping naked in front of Benjy and immediately shook his head.

Benjy sighed dramatically. "I'm not taking no for an answer. You don't have to take off your clothes in front of me, and I can even massage you through your shirt, if you insist."

"Really?"

"And I'll even fix you dinner."

"You don't have to. Benjy, I'm just sore, and it's a good kind of sore. I'll get used to it."

"I just want to know how you're supposed to go back tomorrow already. After that kind of workout, your body needs rest. Does this trainer even know what he's doing?"

"Trust me, he knows." Oliver groaned as he pushed himself up from his seat. He held on to the desk as the pain ripped through his calves. Even his calves hurt? "You should see what he looks like. He's fucking sex on legs, absolutely perfect. I can't even believe he's *my* trainer."

"Well, I don't care what he looks like." Benjy sidled up to him, wrapping his arm around Oliver's back. "You can lean on me if it helps."

Oliver laughed, then grimaced. "If I fall on you, you'll be dead. Squashed flatter than a pancake."

"Don't flatter yourself." Benjy *tsk*ed. "I know you're tough, but I'm not some kind of wuss, ya know."

"I didn't mean it *that* way."

"And quit moaning and complaining all the time about how fat and unattractive you are. You're neither. To me, you're hotter than any fucking gym trainer. You know, when you go on about him being so hot, it's kind of insulting."

Seriously? Were they really having this conversation? "I didn't even say anything about you, Benjy. You're hot too. You're *way* hot, but in a totally different way."

"The nonsexy way?" He placed his hand on his hip, stepping away from Oliver for a moment.

"No, my trainer is nonsexy hot. *You* are sexy hot. Hotter than a fucking two-dollar pistol."

Benjy's mouth dropped open as he stared in astonishment, and then he smiled. "Ollie, that's one of the nicest things you've ever said to me." He slid back beside him and gave him a partial hug. As he did so, his fingers dug into Oliver's tender sides and Oliver groaned. "Oh… sorry."

As HE lay back in the sudsy water of the tub, Oliver marveled at the way Benjy had doted on him. He had stopped on the way home to pick up Chinese takeout and met Oliver back at his house. As soon as he entered the door, he'd headed straight for the bathroom, where he drew Oliver's bath.

"Go on, relax for a few minutes. I'll tidy up and keep this food warm. We can eat when you're done."

As Oliver closed his eyes, he allowed himself to sink down, and the steamy water soothed his aching muscles. Obviously, it would get better. Guys who worked out all the time weren't in constant pain. At least he didn't think they were. If so, they really had some incredibly high pain-tolerance levels.

He recalled how Adam's entire demeanor had changed once they got into the gym and began their workout. He almost instantaneously became a sadistic drill sergeant. He was good at it, though, pushing Oliver to his limit and beyond. Surprisingly they had used very little equipment. The cardio, Adam had said, was not about building muscle. They didn't need the resistance machines or free weights, although they'd incorporated dumbbells into one of the routines.

Tomorrow they'd start on the upper-body workout. Oliver cringed just thinking about it. His midsection already ached from his half-assed attempts at performing crunches. Adam hadn't mocked him, though. He'd assured Oliver that he'd done as well or better than most beginners. "Just wait. A month from now, you'll be doing a hundred crunches and will barely break a sweat." Oliver didn't quite believe the hyperbole, but offered an obligatory nod.

Other than obey orders, pretty much the only thing Oliver did that morning was nod. He didn't argue, rationalize, or complain. He simply obeyed. Adam seemed to like it, and when they finished their round of sets, he dismissed Oliver to the showers.

He'd initially felt good about the whole experience, and to begin with, he wasn't even sore. As he walked out, the gay gym bunnies walked past him in the hall, talking loudly to one another. Three of the four turned to him as he walked by, staring with their plastic smiles plastered on their faces. Slowly they morphed to looks of amusement, disgust possibly. Oliver redirected his gaze, staring straight ahead, and marched past them. Cruelly, they crowded over to the far side of the hallway, affording him an extra-wide berth. God forbid he might brush against them with his huge, unfit body.

It wasn't until later that morning that his body began to ache. He felt sore all over, and by the time five o'clock rolled around, he didn't think he could move. Thank God for sweet Benjy. He truly had become Oliver's motivator. In the tub, with his eyes closed, he allowed himself to relive the night before. It had been amazing, a dream come true. Sharing such intimacy with a guy as awesome as Benjy had always been something he'd imagined but in a very impersonal way. It was sort of like dreaming about winning the lottery or becoming famous. It was nice to pretend, but he never imagined he'd experience it, at least not without having to pay a prostitute.

And Benjy was anything but a hooker. He was sexy, though. And smart, compassionate, funny. He represented everything Oliver had always valued in a partner. After a few minutes of relaxation, he pushed himself up and dried off with the blanket towel Benjy had laid out for him. Crap, he hadn't brought his clothes in from the bedroom. He couldn't put back on the work clothes he'd just discarded. Maybe he should call for Benjy and ask him to bring him his robe.

He stood for a moment in front of the vanity, examining his reflection. After combing his hair, he lifted one arm and flexed. It was so silly of him. Why was he doing this? He nearly laughed at himself, but as he stared, his smile began to fade. Viewing himself like this, seeing only the upper part of his body, he didn't look so bad. He actually had kind of a sculpted chest already. His pectorals were certainly more defined than Benjy's. And he did have biceps already. He'd already begun losing some of the fat on his arms, and his skin felt a little looser. He reached up with one hand as he pumped his muscle into a knot. Oh yeah, it was solid.

The problem, though, was his odd pear-shaped torso. His entire midsection reminded him of Fred Flintstone. Strangely, the soreness he felt in his abs assured him that the roll of flab that hadn't yet disappeared merely covered something much more appealing beneath. What if the trainer and the doctor were right? What if, a few months from now, that fat was gone? What would he look like? He'd be a whole new person.

He smiled as he recalled Benjy's words. He'd said Oliver wasn't fat. He wanted to scoff, but he knew how sincerely Benjy had spoken. He truly didn't see Oliver as a big fat blob. Well, soon he wouldn't be. Soon he'd be that new man the doctor had promised. In a few months, he'd be a better, even more appealing lover for Benjy.

He took a deep breath and turned toward the door. He'd just do it. He'd just march right out there, wearing nothing but a towel. Chances were Benjy wouldn't see him anyway. He'd be busy in the kitchen, "tidying up." As he swung the door open, he stopped dead in his tracks.

Benjy stood on the other side of the doorframe, arm raised as if ready to knock. "Oh! Sorry." Benjy laughed, then slowly lowered his arm. He gulped and stared directly at the nearly naked body in front of him. "Oliver… um, how was your, um, bath?"

On impulse, he wanted to slam the door shut, but he froze. He looked down at the wide eyes in front of him, and unlike the foursome of gym bunnies that morning, he didn't see disgust. He saw… *desire*?

"I forgot my robe."

"Oh." Benjy's gaze did not stray from Oliver's chest. "Want me to go get it…." His voice trailed off, then he added in a whisper, "For you?"

"No, no. It's okay. I'll get dressed in my bedroom."

Benjy's head snapped upward as he looked quickly into Oliver's face. "Okay, cool. I'm keeping the food warm in the oven. I'll go get it ready."

Oliver nodded as Benjy slowly backed away, catching one last glance before he scurried to the kitchen. In the bedroom, he got dressed, slipping on a comfortable tee and shorts. Socked-footed, he padded back down the hallway and found Benjy in the kitchen, setting the table. "Wow, this looks like a new home."

Benjy tilted his head to the side, smiling sheepishly. "Hope you don't mind me cleaning up a bit."

"How'd you have time to get both the kitchen and living room so tidy?"

"I guess I just worked my magic."

Oliver stepped closer, reaching out to take hold of Benjy and pull him in close. "I don't deserve you," he whispered, then kissed him squarely on the lips.

Benjy, who was holding silverware at the time, wrapped his arms around Oliver and hugged with care. "You smell so yummy."

"It's called Irish Spring. It's just soap."

"Mmm. Well, I want to taste every inch of you." As he gazed into Oliver's eyes, he seemed sincere.

Oliver cleared his throat, not sure how to respond. "Um, I've already tasted *you*, and trust me, you're delicious."

Benjy sighed, dropping his arms at his side. "You're making this very difficult. I want to just skip dinner and go straight to dessert."

Oliver laughed as he took hold of the kitchen chair next to him and pulled it out. "Then I guess we better eat. I'm starving."

"I didn't even think about it. Maybe you'd rather eat in the living room. We could watch a movie or play Overwatch."

Oliver slid into the chair, glancing in Benjy's direction. "No, this is fine. This is better. You and me." He held out his hand to Benjy, who took hold of it as he slid into his own chair. "Thanks for drawing my bath, for cleaning my house, for...."

"I hardly even cleaned. I just tidied up a bit." He handed Oliver his silverware. "You hardly ate any lunch. I think you can afford to indulge a little tonight. Take as much rice as you want."

Oliver chuckled. "I've gotten used to smaller portions. You know what they say? Nothing tastes even half as good as being slim feels."

With raised eyebrows, Benjy nodded. "I get it, but I've been slim all my life, and it's overrated. Ollie, you know I support you 100 percent, but if you never lost another ounce, I'd be fine with that. I like you exactly as you are."

Oliver scooped a small portion of white rice onto his plate, then added a generous serving of vegetable stir-fry. "You want me to be happy, right?"

"Of course, which is why I said I support you 100 percent. And I also understand your desire to be healthy. I just wonder, though, if a daily workout schedule where you're pushing yourself to this degree is actually healthy in the long run. I read online that all those people who exercised their asses off for that show *Biggest Loser* just turned around and gained back all their weight after the show."

"Because they didn't maintain it. They went back to their unhealthy eating habits. Benjy, I've changed my whole lifestyle. I haven't eaten any crap in the last six months."

He nodded as he loaded up his own plate, taking a considerably larger portion of rice than Oliver. "But they had those poor people exercising for eight hours a day, sometimes more. And they fed them hardly anything. As a result, their metabolisms crashed. That article said in order to maintain their new weight, they'd have to stick strictly to an eight-hundred-calorie daily diet. It just wasn't possible, which was why they all gained back their weight. I just think you should check around. Find out if this means you're going to have to work out every single day into infinity to stay skinny."

Oliver scowled, somewhat annoyed. Was Benjy raining on his parade, pissing in his Cheerios? Why couldn't he just be supportive?

"Well, this trainer's the same dude who worked with my doctor. I think he knows what he's doing."

"Please don't think I'm questioning *you*. Like I said, I support you all the way."

"*Do* you?" He set his fork on the side of his plate and picked up his water glass.

"Ollie, you know I do."

They ate in silence for a few moments until Oliver had at last allowed the surge of adrenaline and defensiveness to wash through him. "You're right. You really have been totally supportive."

"I promise, I won't say another word about it." Benjy looked up at him. "I'm sorry. Will you forgive me?"

"Don't be a butthead. There's nothing to forgive." Oliver smiled and reached over to playfully ruffle Benjy's mop of hair.

Benjy grinned affectionately. "Cool. I still get to give you a massage, ya know. You promised."

Under the table, Oliver's shorts began to tent. The thought of Benjy's hands all over him sent a ripple of excitement through his body that traveled straight to his groin. He shoveled a forkful of rice into his mouth without comment. Gulping, he picked up his water glass again and nodded.

How was it that Benjy made him feel like he was in ninth grade again? The thought of touching him and being touched by him excited Oliver, and that anticipation made him both aroused and nervous. His heartbeat quickened and his palms began to sweat. He could hardly concentrate on anything but what he hoped was going to happen, and his ravaging appetite suddenly disappeared. He pushed his plate away before picking up his glass once more and at last drained it completely of its content.

"You okay? Want more water?"

He shook his head. "I'm... uh, full."

Benjy stared in disbelief at his plate, then looked into Oliver's eyes. "Ollie, no way. You hardly ate anything, and you were starving."

"I might eat more later."

"Do you need to lie down?" His look of genuine concern was almost enough to make Oliver feel guilty, but then again, Benjy was the one who was doing this to him. He reached over the table and took hold of Benjy's hand.

"Let's go lie down."

"But I'm not—" He stopped midsentence, and Oliver noticed the glint in his eyes. "I can finish up later." He smiled and slid to his feet.

Oliver rose from his chair, still clinging to Benjy's hand, and together they walked down the hallway to his bedroom. Once inside, Oliver pulled Benjy into a hug and fiercely kissed him. Benjy's leg brushed against him, pressing into the silky basketball shorts. The smooth fabric rubbed against Oliver's inner thigh as Benjy's leg pressed into his throbbing erection.

Oliver slowly backed out of the kiss but continued to look at Benjy, who now stood on tiptoe, arms draped around Oliver's neck.

"Please take your shirt off for me so I can give you your massage."

"You said I didn't have to."

"I've already seen you, though. And I liked it." Benjy grinned.

"Really?"

Benjy nodded. He let go of Oliver's neck and reached down to grasp the tail of his T-shirt. Oliver stood there, his heart racing like a locomotive, and allowed Benjy to peel the shirt upward—slowly, oh so slowly, pushing it up to Oliver's chin. Oliver raised his arms and took a step back, then bent forward, allowing Benjy the chance to pull it the rest of the way over his head. As Oliver straightened his posture to stand before his lover, Benjy's palms were already pressed flat across his chest, his fingers trailing back and forth.

"Oh, Oliver." His breathy voice nearly caused Oliver's knees to buckle. He took a step back, toward the bed. Benjy moved closer. Another step. Closer again. Finally, Oliver lowered himself onto the mattress as Benjy moved between his outstretched legs, and for once Benjy towered over him. "This time," he whispered, "it's my turn. I get to pleasure *you*."

Benjy took hold of Oliver's head and held it with both hands as he kissed him deep and passionate. He pulled away only long enough to slide his lips down to Oliver's neck. Oliver tossed his head back as he slid his hands around Benjy's slender frame and caressed his back through the fabric of Benjy's work shirt. Benjy kissed and sucked Oliver's neck, which felt more amazing than Oliver had ever imagined it possibly could. He moaned, resisting the urge to squeeze Benjy tight. The sensation both tickled and aroused him, and his hard-on now throbbed mercilessly.

Benjy pushed him backward, not forcefully, but with grace and patience, a gentle urging. As Oliver pressed his back against the comforter, he realized the bed had been made, and he never took the time in the morning to make it. Benjy had even gone so far as to plan that. He'd made up the bed while Oliver was in the bathroom.

Benjy stepped back, allowing Oliver the chance to lift his legs and situate himself against the pillow. Oliver twisted his body on the bed, changing the angle in which he was lying, and Benjy lowered himself to sit beside him. With his hands now on Oliver's chest, he gently massaged, working his fingers into the tender flesh, and oh did it ever feel wonderful.

Oliver moaned and closed his eyes. "Benjy, will you please…?"

"Anything."

Oliver opened his eyes and looked at him. "Take off your clothes?"

"I thought we agreed. I get to—"

"I want to feel your body next to my skin."

Benjy's radiant smile warmed Oliver's heart. He nodded and began unbuttoning his dress shirt. He pulled it off and tossed it carelessly onto the floor. His smooth, tight abdominals didn't even press into the waistband of his dress pants, not even in his seated position. God, that tight body was so fucking sexy. He slid to a kneeling position and unbuttoned his pants, then peeled them back before stepping off the bed and sliding the pants down his thighs. He backed up just a bit, allowing Oliver to take in the sight of his entire body. The smooth, formfitting briefs fit him like a Speedo, accentuating the impressive bulge he was packing. Oliver reached for him, trying to graze his package with his fingertips but couldn't quite reach. Benjy giggled and grabbed the waistband. Slowly and in strip-tease fashion, he eased them downward, at first revealing only a portion of his swollen cock. When Oliver moaned in frustration, Benjy tugged them the rest of the way off, exposing his raging hard-on. It sprang up, ready for action.

"Benjy, I have to…. Please let me—"

Benjy shook his head, laughing. "Nope. No touchy for you. We have a deal."

"I don't remember agreeing to this."

Benjy slid back onto the bed and tucked one leg beneath his butt. He used one hand to gently caress Oliver's midsection. "Mmm, mmm." He leaned forward and kissed Oliver's pectoral, the one closest to him. After kissing, he pressed his lips against the nipple and sucked, then darted his tongue against it.

"Jesus!" Oliver bucked on the mattress, squirming frantically as he reached for Benjy out of pure reflex.

Benjy resisted, pushing back Oliver's arms as he continued to tantalize the sensitive nipple.

"You call that a fucking *massage*?"

Finally, Benjy pulled away and sat upright. He turned to direct his attention to the area below Oliver's waist. "I think I see something that needs massaging."

"Benjy, oh my God. You know I won't last long."

He shrugged. "Who says we can only do it once? If you come too soon, I'll just have to go a second round." He pressed his fingers against the silk shorts, instantly locating Oliver's bulge. "Oh wow." He smiled as he turned to look into Oliver's eyes. His own sparkled with excitement as he raised his eyebrows and licked his lips. "It ain't little."

People always assumed fat dudes had tiny penises, and probably in most cases it was true. At least it appeared that way because they had so many rolls of flab, and the length of their manhood seemed to be eclipsed by their huge bellies. He'd seen some photos of guys like that while looking at porn in the chubby chaser section. He hated it. He despised the stereotype, and those guys grossed him out. But wasn't that who he was himself? Wasn't he just another one of those big flat blobs?

"Ollie, look at me!" Benjy snapped his fingers in front of Oliver's face. "You weren't with me for a few seconds. You were spacing, and I don't think I want to know what you were fantasizing about."

He'd lost his arousal, and as he looked once more at Benjy, all the insecurity he'd managed to suppress suddenly returned in full force. "This was a mistake," he whispered. "I can't—"

Before he could move to push himself up from the mattress, Benjy leaned forward and placed both palms against his chest. "No, Oliver! You're not moving. Not till you tell me what just happened."

"I know what I look like. I know I'm… hideous."

"Ollie, I know what you look like too. I'm fucking looking at you! And you are *not* hideous. Far from it. Let me decide what I like and what I don't. Okay?" His fingers trailed softly down the center of Oliver's torso, all the way to his navel. "So far, everything I've seen and touched has been amazing, far better than I'd even imagined it would be."

Oliver pushed himself up on the mattress, propping his upper body with his elbows so he could see the entirety of his body, including his rounded tummy. No, it wasn't ripped. It wasn't completely flat with an identifiable six-pack. But as Benjy had earlier stated, it wasn't nearly as noticeable in this reclined position. And it sure as fuck was smaller than it had been in a very long time.

To his amazement, from this vantage point, he could actually see below his waist. He hadn't even tried lately to look. He'd gotten so used to avoidance. Even when he used the restroom, he didn't look down at himself. There'd been no point in trying because his fat stomach had always been in the way.

But not now. For the first time since middle school, he could actually see the area of his body that Benjy now touched ever so delicately. A surge of excitement jolted through him and his cock again sprang to life, beginning to swell right before his eyes. Benjy rubbed the growing bulge through the fabric, his eyes wide with anticipation.

Without further warning, Benjy slid his hand smoothly beneath the waistband of Oliver's shorts. Oliver moaned as Benjy grabbed hold of his erection. The soft caress of Benjy's palm and fingers felt so very different than Oliver's own hand—the only one to previously have touched him so intimately. Oliver gasped, closing his eyes for a couple seconds while tossing back his head.

"Benjy." He didn't even recognize the sultry whisper of his own voice. "Oh God, Benjy, that feels… amazing."

Benjy slid down on the mattress, agilely repositioning himself on his knees, between Oliver's thighs. Oliver spread his legs a bit, and couldn't help but feel awkward in the exposed position. He still didn't have his pants off yet, and as Benjy started to tug down against the waistband, he nearly panicked again. Keeping his eyes locked on Benjy's face, he thrust his pelvis upward enough to allow Benjy space to peel down his shorts.

Before he could even get the shorts all the way down Oliver's thighs, Benjy froze. His eyes grew wide and his mouth gaped open. "Oliver, holy fucking shit! Why on *earth* were you ever ashamed of showing me your—"

His cock sprang upward, the bulbous head swollen, and as Oliver stared down, he could hardly believe he'd at last exposed himself to another man. Benjy knelt between Oliver's legs, just inches from his junk. As Benjy slid back on the bed and tugged the shorts down farther, Oliver obliged, temporarily squeezing his legs together. Benjy tore off the shorts, tossed them aside, and dove onto the mattress. Now on his belly, he darted out his tongue to lick Oliver's ball sac, all the while grasping his shaft firmly with one hand.

Oliver didn't know what to do with his own hands. He clutched frantically at the comforter beneath him. He wasn't anticipating how ticklish his balls would be. Washing and touching himself over the years hadn't prepared him for the distinct feeling of a warm tongue against the most sensitive region of his body. He squirmed and bit his bottom lip. Keeping his legs spread wide apart proved far more challenging than he'd ever have imagined—such sweet torture.

Benjy licked him, lapping furiously at his testicles for a few minutes until at last he backed away and reached up to remove his eyeglasses. Placing them on the king-sized mattress beside him, he looked up into Oliver's eyes as he held his cock firmly by the base. He smiled, then opened his mouth and pressed his tongue against the sensitive underside, and it seemed to Oliver that Benjy was enjoying an ice cream cone. When his lips wrapped around the bulbous head and he felt the silky warm suction of Benjy's mouth around his shaft, Oliver cried out.

Words would never be able to describe the warm, slippery sensation of Benjy's mouth. "Oh fuck, Benjy. Fuck-fuck-fuck-fuck-*fuck*!" He first grabbed the bedsheets, then released them to grab Benjy's shoulders. Squirming on the mattress, he looked down to see Benjy sliding down his rock-hard shaft.

He'd seen the images hundreds of times in online porn scenes but had no idea exactly how wonderful it actually felt. As Benjy bobbed on his cock, the slickness of his tongue against the underside and the warm silkiness of Benjy's mouth surrounded him. Benjy's lips formed a tight suction around the shaft, and Oliver marveled as he watched his cock sliding in and out of the welcoming hole.

"Benjy! Oh Benjy, that feels so fucking good. Oh God!"

He couldn't help himself. He had to touch Benjy. He raked his fingers through Benjy's thick, unruly hair. Caressing, almost petting, he conveyed the pleasure of what he was feeling through the gentleness of his touch. "Oh, baby, you're gonna make me shoot. You're gonna make me come. Oh God! Benjy! Benjy!"

He couldn't hold out much longer. Though the experience hadn't taken that long, it didn't seem to matter. He cried out one more warning to his lover. "Here it comes! Benjy!" Pressing his palms against Benjy's shoulders, he tried to guide him back. He didn't want Benjy to assume he expected him to swallow the load.

But Benjy didn't even hesitate. He dove farther onto the cock, taking its entirety into his mouth and pressing his lips against the ball sac. Forming a seal around the shaft, he sucked all the more furiously, and as Oliver at last felt himself cross his glorious point of no return, he grasped Benjy's shoulders and released his load. Like a geyser erupting, he blasted deep into Benjy's mouth, firing straight down his throat. Benjy gulped and moaned simultaneously, swallowing every drop as jet after jet pumped out of Oliver's cock.

Shivers rippled through Oliver's body and he moaned again, tossing his head back and squeezing his eyes tightly closed. He shook on the mattress, draining himself, then opened his eyes and looked down at Benjy, who now stared up at him, smiling as best he could with his mouth full of Oliver's manhood.

"Son of a bitch…. Benjy!" He reached for him, and Benjy slowly slid off the shaft, licking his lips, then climbed up on top of Oliver and slid into the crook of his arm as they kissed with passion. Oliver could taste himself on Benjy's lips, but more importantly, he felt the smooth warmth of Benjy's skin against his own. He wrapped both arms around him, holding him against his body. "Benjy, you're amazing. I… I can never repay something like that."

Benjy smiled and kissed him once more. "You already have, Ollie. You already have."

CHAPTER TEN

TWO FULL weeks of nonstop workouts had begun to yield some noticeable results. Although Oliver didn't see a remarkable change in his appearance, he certainly felt a lot different. Particularly, as he worked his upper and lower body with the resistance training and free weights, he felt the burn induced by his torturous routines, but the effects did not debilitate him, as had been the case in the beginning. And his cardio routines were beginning to energize him more than exhaust him. Funny how it worked that way. Instead of feeling tired, he felt revitalized.

As promised, the exercises he'd originally found challenging became easy. Adam had said he'd be doing a hundred crunches at a time by month's end, and he was already up to fifty. Discouraged that the scale wasn't immediately reflecting his progress, he talked to his trainer, who assured him the fat would continue to diminish, but he might not see drastic results in terms of his weight. While losing fat, he was also gaining muscle. And he couldn't really deny that. His clothes were looser, and so was his skin. He was starting to feel more defined.

Perhaps it was the boost in confidence he suddenly felt that led him to speak to one of the gym bunny foursome early one morning. The most gregarious of the group, Devon, entered the locker room alone. Though he generally arrived first, the others were always soon to follow. Oliver had learned their names simply by inadvertently eavesdropping. Devon possessed a boyish face and seemed to always be smiling. He wore a short, conservatively styled haircut that suited his naturally wavy hair, and had big brown eyes like Benjy. Of course, he also had a body to die for, not a noticeable ounce of fat on his godlike frame.

Oliver could only aspire to one day be as fit as a guy like Devon. It seemed too distant a goal to seriously envision himself with that kind of body, and the very idea of a dude like that talking to him or even giving him the time of day made butterflies flutter in Oliver's stomach. Like back in high school, he admired the jocks from afar, secretly. He watched them in movies, on TV, and online. And occasionally he'd even interact with one in person, usually about something work related. But he didn't have jock buddies. He'd never be a part of their group, a member of their "in-crowd."

"Morning." Oliver managed to muster the courage to actually speak as Devon strutted past him. Devon stopped briefly, turned, and looked down at Oliver, who was sitting on one of the locker-room benches, lacing his sneakers.

"Oh, hi." He smiled, and in that split second, the eye contact they shared sent a thrill through Oliver's extremities. The vibe resonated sincerity and honest cordiality. Granted, the guy had only spoken two words, but it was more the way he said them and the look he gave Oliver that felt so right.

"Have you guys been coming…?" He started to ask if they'd been coming to the gym long, then realized how cliché the remark sounded.

"Have we been coming here long? Sure. Nearly every day for the past three years. Well, my friends Roger and AJ started coming about a year ago. They're a couple."

As if on cue, the other two walked through the door. AJ, the shorter one, probably younger, stopped and looked from Devon to Oliver, a puzzled expression on his face. He wore his blond hair swept back stylishly, high on the top and shaved on the sides and back.

"Our other friend, Ethan, is the veteran. He's been a member since this place opened eight years ago."

None of them looked that old. Oliver knew who Ethan was. He'd have guessed him to be in his mid- to late-twenties, and like the others, possessed a solid, sculpted physique. He seemed quieter, though. But Oliver had observed all four of them. He'd had plenty of opportunity out in the gym. They did a lot of the same exercises and used many of the same machines Oliver used. Of course they all were way more advanced than Oliver.

"New duds?" AJ said to Oliver. He hadn't bothered to even officially greet him, but he was referring to the new sleeveless workout shirt and shorts Oliver had just purchased. He smiled as he looked up at AJ, pleased the guy had been observant enough to notice.

"Yeah, actually."

"That's what I thought. You've been wearing those same ol' clothes every single day the past two weeks. Glad you scrounged up the cash to get yourself something new."

"Oh." Oliver laughed. He looked at the three of them, all smiling. "Yeah. Well, I've never had a gym membership before."

With the same plastic smile on his face, AJ nodded. "Trust me, it shows. Where'd you get your cool new knockoffs? No, don't tell me, let me guess. Hm. Salvation Army Thrift Store?"

"AJ…." Devon moved closer to AJ and placed a hand on his shoulder while AJ's boyfriend, Roger, laughed.

"No, no, no! Of course not!" AJ continued. "You got them at Walmart."

Actually, Oliver *had* purchased the new clothes at Walmart. For so many years, he'd been too fat to shop in the same stores most people patronized to buy their clothes. Most of his wardrobe had been mail ordered. With him losing so much weight within the past five months, he wasn't sure where to even shop. He and Benjy had gone to the mall once and gotten a few basics—shirts and pants—but they were mainly for work. And it didn't make sense to spend a fortune on gym clothes, especially when he just wore them to work out. Plus, he hoped to continue losing weight, which meant he'd have to buy newer items in a few weeks.

He stared up at AJ, who was grinning smugly. His boyfriend, all smiles, laughed beside him. "Oh my God." He slapped AJ on the back. "I can't believe you just said that." The guy seriously found the comments amusing, though. He couldn't seem to stop laughing, which only encouraged AJ.

"No offense, man. It's got to be challenging, a guy in your condition." AJ continued his stand-up routine.

"My condition?"

"You know what they say about heavy people? They're like relationships. A lot of times they don't work out."

At this point, Roger literally doubled over, laughing so hard. Devon stood beside them, smiling, but didn't offer commentary. Finally Devon grabbed AJ's shoulder and spun him around. "C'mon," he said. "You're a doofus. Go get changed." AJ's boyfriend grabbed his other arm and pulled him away as the two continued laughing hysterically.

"Uh, sorry about that," Devon said to Oliver, then turned away and headed across the locker room to join his friends. The fourth member of the group, Ethan, then walked in and strutted straight past Oliver without a word, to meet with his group. Oliver heard the four of them laughing as AJ recounted the story of his humorous antics moments earlier.

Red-faced, Oliver stored his personals in the locker and headed up the stairs to the gym. He felt nauseous and on the verge of tears. More than that, he felt two inches tall. He'd never been more humiliated in all his life. Even at three hundred thirty pounds, he hadn't felt so inferior.

His face burned as he pushed his way through his routine, not even caring if he did the exercises properly. He just needed to get out of there. When Adam arrived a few minutes later, Oliver apologized, explained he wasn't feeling well that day, and stated he needed to leave early. He didn't even finish all his cardio.

When he got to his car, he tossed his duffel carelessly in the back seat, slid behind the wheel, and slammed the door angrily. At last the tears erupted, an agonizing sob bursting from his core. All this for nothing. It was never going to matter. He'd never be good enough. He'd never look like those guys or even know how to act like them if by some miracle he *did* lose all his weight.

For so long, he'd laughed at all the jokes. Fuck, he'd often been the one to tell them. A fat joke was so much easier to endure if you were the one saying it. People didn't see the pain. They didn't understand the struggle.

Wiping his eyes with the back of his hand, he dug out his cell phone from the console beside him and speed-dialed his employer. Requesting a sick day, he explained he thought he had the flu or something. As he peeled out of the parking lot, he could hardly see the road because his eyes had again flooded with tears, but his car knew his destination so well it could practically drive on autopilot.

The one thing he'd always loved about the McDonald's not far from his house was that you could order from the main menu twenty-four hours a day. They didn't exclusively serve breakfast until ten thirty like many of the restaurants in their chain. He pulled up to the drive-through board, not bothering to even glance at the menu. He knew it all by heart. It was all too familiar.

The rush of excitement that surged through him perhaps resembled the feeling a crack addict experienced when they knew they were about to get their fix. "I'd like a number nine with a large Coke and a large fry, a twenty-piece McNugget with sweet and sour, an extra order of large fries… oh, and two apple pies… and wait, can you add a Big Mac?"

OLIVER'S PHONE log had recorded the missed calls from Benjy. Obviously, Benjy was worried about him, and Oliver kind of felt like shit shutting him out. He should call Benjy back and at least try to explain his absence at work. Forcing himself upright, he sat up and swung his legs over the edge of the bed, holding the cell out in front of him.

He didn't press Benjy's number, though. Instead he stared at the phone, chastising himself mentally for allowing those assholes to get to him. He'd nearly sabotaged himself because of them and their cruelty. At this point, he no longer felt sad, and his feelings of self-loathing had completely vanished, replaced by ferocious anger and justifiable indignation.

When he heard the pounding on his side door, he set the phone down on the bedside stand and rose to his feet. He marched out the bedroom and plodded down the hall toward the kitchen, through the utility room, and opened the door to the garage. There Benjy stood, hands completely full.

"Benjy…."

"Ollie, I've been so worried. I brought you some soup."

Oliver smiled and ushered him inside. "Thank you. That's so sweet." He'd apparently left the garage open, so Benjy had parked in the drive and simply walked in through the open garage door. Usually they arrived together, so the side door was the entrance Benjy was used to taking.

"That soup smells good."

"Are you even hungry, though?"

Oliver nodded. "Starving, to be honest."

Benjy walked through the utility room and set the package on the kitchen counter. He turned to Oliver. "Even after all that Mickey D's?" He raised his eyebrows as he looked into Oliver's face.

"Oh that." Oliver shrugged. "You must've seen the fast-food bags in the garbage out in the garage?"

Benjy nodded. A disappointed expression, not so much judgment but more sadness, eclipsed his face.

"Don't worry, I didn't eat any of it. Well, not true. I had two french fries. I threw the rest away."

"Ollie, what happened?" He stepped closer, placing his hand on Oliver's arm. On tiptoe, he leaned toward his boyfriend and kissed him on the lips. *Boyfriend?* Was that what Oliver considered him? He smiled as he thought about it. Benjy smelled and tasted as delicious as the soup. "Was it just a moment of weakness? A temptation?"

"Something like that, and I'm sorry I worried you. I should have called or texted you or something. I should have called you back, but when I got home from the gym, I honestly didn't feel well and ended up taking a nap."

"Well, let's sit down. I'll get you some soup."

"Why don't we save the soup? Let me take *you* out for a change? We can go to that restaurant over by the mall that has the enormous chef's salads, and you can order anything you want. You can even get a hot-fudge sundae."

A broad, excited grin spread across Benjy's adorable face. "I guess you really are feeling better, huh? I'm dying to hear what happened, but I'm telling you right now, I don't need ice cream for dessert. I'd rather have *you* instead."

Oliver swept him into a hug as they kissed once more. He'd love to just carry Benjy into the bedroom right then and make passionate love to him, but he really was famished. "Okay." He lowered Benjy to the floor. Oliver had hugged him so fiercely, he'd literally swept him off his feet. "I'll tell you all the details. Let me get my keys."

On the way to the restaurant, Benjy told Oliver all about work that day, what he'd been working on and reiterated every word their boss had said. No, she hadn't seemed upset at all that Oliver had called in. It was the very first time he'd ever missed work, so she was certain he was truly ill.

Oliver didn't talk about his experience at the gym, not while in the car. Instead, he waited until they were seated in the restaurant and had already placed their order. He then looked across the table in their booth and directly into Benjy's eyes. He took hold of his hand and began to explain. "I had a bit of an embarrassing situation this morning."

"What was it?"

Oliver could read the genuine concern in Benjy's eyes. "These four guys who are always there, other members who work out in the mornings, same time as me—they kind of gave me some shit."

Benjy scowled. "What do you mean? What kind of shit?"

"Teasing me… well, no, not really teasing. They were mocking me, my size."

"Oh my God!" Tears of rage instantly flooded Benjy's eyes. "I hope you filed a fucking complaint!"

Oliver shook his head. "No, not yet. To be honest, I was sort of pathetic. I didn't even defend myself or tell them all to go fuck themselves or anything. I just took the abuse and ended up leaving there a mess, bawling like a schoolgirl."

"Oh, Ollie." He actually did then begin to cry, tears streaming down both cheeks. "I'm so sorry."

"Baby, don't cry." Oliver reached across the table and wiped Benjy's face with his finger. "So I stormed out to my car, feeling sorry for myself. I was kind of having a pity party, whining about how nobody understood me or what it was like to be so fat, blah, blah, blah. That's when I called in to work and headed over to McDonald's, where I bought out practically the whole fucking restaurant."

Benjy shook his head. "I saw all those bags."

"But when I got home and rushed inside with all my fat food—or I mean, *fast* food…." He smiled and winked. "I peeled open the straw and shoved it in my drink, then took a sip. I was jonesing for it, Benjy. My mouth was literally watering, but when that sugar hit my palate, it just… I don't know, it tasted weird. I could feel the coating of sugar in the inside of my mouth and on my lips. Then I tried a couple french fries. You remember how much I loved McDonald's fries, right? Well, they tasted like tallow or something. I could feel their greasiness, and it grossed me out."

"You're not used to it anymore. The sugar, the fat—they're foreign to you."

"Yeah, I guess so. But that's when I looked down at the counter, at all that food in front of me, and even though it smelled so good… even though it *sounded* so good, I realized it wasn't. I just kept looking at it, and it was like for the first time ever this switch went on inside my head. That shit's poison!"

Benjy smiled. "It really is."

"And then I started thinking about what had just happened back at the gym. Benjy, I don't even know those fuck faces. They don't know me either. They have no clue what I've been through in my life, my genetics, my history, if I'm smart or funny or… or anything! They know nothing about me, but they were judging me simply based on what I look like."

The tears were now flowing again as Benjy nodded. Oliver ignored them and continued. "Benjy, I've worked too fucking hard these past few months to let some shit stains like those airheaded gym bunnies ruin everything for me. I almost threw it all away. I almost went back to my former three-hundred-pound self. If I'd have backslid in that moment, that's probably exactly what would have happened. I'd have just kept gorging myself, eating more and more until I was enormous again, probably bigger than ever before."

"But you didn't."

"No! No, I didn't. You know why? Because I want to be better than that. I *am* better than that, and I don't want to do that to my body anymore. And I want to be your… your… your…."

"What? Ollie, say it."

"Your *boyfriend*! Benjy, I love you, and I want to be your boyfriend!"

"I love you too!" He grabbed hold of Oliver's hand and squeezed it as the waitress arrived with their salads.

"Aww." She smiled sweetly as she slid the plates onto the booth table. "You two are such a sweet couple. Don't let me interrupt." She took a step back as Ollie leaned forward, across the table, and planted a passionate kiss on Benjy's welcoming lips. The waitress clapped her hands gleefully.

When they left the restaurant a half hour later, Oliver dropped a twenty-dollar bill on the table.

Chapter Eleven

WHEN OLIVER returned to the gym the morning after his epiphany, he entered with a newfound resolve. Wearing his brand-new Walmart workout gear, he marched confidently down the stairs to the locker room, brushing past AJ.

"Oh, excuse me." Oliver bodychecked the smaller though seemingly more muscular man, who stumbled backward, flailing his arms a bit before righting himself and regaining his footing. He leaned against one of the lockers and glared at Oliver.

"Dude, watch where you're walking. You're like a fucking ox plodding through here."

"AJ, is it?" Oliver stared at him. "You're right. I'm a big guy, always have been. I'm not nearly as toned and tweaked as you, and I probably never will be. But nothing's ever going to change the fact I'm bigger. Even if I lose all my excess weight and develop a perfectly sculpted, Herculean body, I'll probably still have a good fifty or sixty pounds on you. Right now, at this very minute, if I so desired, I could pick you up and snap you like a fucking twig." He stepped closer. "You have a big mouth, but that's about the *only* part of you that's big."

AJ's eyes grew wide, and his mouth gaped as he stared at Oliver. "Are you… uh… threatening me?"

"Damn right I am. Leave me the fuck alone. You made it clear yesterday I'm not one of you. I don't have the right body type, and I don't buy the right clothes. Newsflash, bitch. I wouldn't want to be a part of your inner circle if you paid me."

"Whatever." AJ took a step backward, away from Oliver. He didn't turn around but kept his eyes on Oliver's face as he inched his way down the corridor. "I don't think the management's going to appreciate you threatening the other members."

"And I doubt they'll appreciate you ridiculing my weight in their 'judgment-free zone' either. I'm like this close to filing a formal complaint against you." He held up his fingers to indicate an inch of space. "Don't push me."

AJ twitched his head, flicking his pomade-sculpted hairdo effeminately, and squared his shoulders. "You're nothing but a wannabe, and that's all you'll ever be."

"Exactly. I want to be happy with who I am, and I don't give a rat's ass if you like it or not. So fuck off, little man." He turned and opened his locker, then tossed his duffel inside before closing the door and spinning the combination lock. Without another word, he pivoted in the opposite direction and headed back out of the locker room and upstairs to his workout.

He pressed himself harder than ever before, pounding through the workout, a broad smile plastered across his face.

OLIVER'S PROGRESS, measured daily, seemed barely noticeable, at least from his perspective. Of course, he did notice how much easier it became to complete his workout routine, and as he relentlessly pushed himself to continue upping his game, he found himself performing exercises he previously wouldn't have ever dreamed possible. But he yearned to see drastic change in the mirror. And even though his clothes continued to feel looser on his body, he couldn't help but see himself as the fat boy he'd always been.

But Benjy noticed.

Saturday morning, three weeks after his confrontation with AJ, Oliver stumbled into the breakroom at work. He and Benjy normally didn't work weekends but had been asked to pick up overtime to complete a deadline. They pretty much had the office to themselves, the building empty but for the two of them and another computer geek working on the second floor. Oliver had already finished his daily workout at the gym and had showered and changed as usual before heading to the office. He hadn't seen Benjy yet but knew he was already busy at work. His car had been parked in the lot when Oliver pulled in. He smiled at the pot of fresh-brewed coffee. Benjy had even set out a cup of Oliver's favorite french vanilla creamers.

As he poured the hot coffee into his mug and stirred in his cream, he noticed a gift-wrapped package on the counter. He'd been so focused on his caffeine fix, he hadn't even noticed the gold metallic paper and bright, shiny oversized red bow. He took a sip of his java and looked closer. The small tag attached to the bundle stuck out from beneath the bow, and to Oliver's surprise it bore his nickname: OLLIE.

"What the hell?" He grinned and set down his coffee. Examining the tag first, he removed it and turned it over.

YOU'RE LOOKING MORE AND MORE AMAZING
EVERY DAY! CONGRATS ON YOUR PROGRESS. B.

Astonished, he nearly gasped. What was up with this? People didn't just give him gifts like this, not for no reason. Christ, he was lucky to even get so much as a birthday card or Secret-Santa present. For most of his life, he'd been the forgotten one, the guy nobody remembered unless they were teasing or fat shaming him. He picked up the wrapped box from the counter and held it in his hands, blinking rapidly.

"Open it."

Oliver looked up, glancing across the room to see Benjy standing just inside the door. "Benjy… why?"

"What do you mean, why? I thought we'd already had this conversation. It's okay for friends to remember each other, buy gifts for one another. Right?" Benjy repeated the line he'd used when he'd given Oliver the wrist odometer.

"But… but…."

"Open it." Benjy pointed to the gift.

"Benjy, I don't know what to say. What's the occasion?"

Benjy sighed, tilting his head slightly as he smiled. God, if he didn't have the most adorable face. And those eyes, usually dark brown but now cast with an amber hue, bore a hole directly through Oliver's heart.

The anger he'd felt toward AJ and the guys from the gym had dissipated, replaced at first with determination, a resolve to succeed and prove them wrong. But Oliver knew that AJ's brash and childish remarks, all his scorn and ridicule, merely echoed what most everyone else thought, though didn't have the balls to say out loud.

But for some reason, everything felt different when he was around Benjy. Oliver didn't feel like a circus freak. He sometimes didn't even remember how different he was from average-sized people. The way Benjy looked at him—like he was right now in this frozen moment of time—made Oliver feel… attractive?

"Open it. *Please.*"

Oliver gulped, then laughed nervously. Finally he shrugged and stepped over a couple feet and placed the gift on the breakroom table. Gingerly he peeled off the bow, then flipped the box to find the taped edge of the wrapping paper.

"Please tell me you're not one of *those* people. You don't save every little piece of wrapping paper and open your presents extra carefully so you don't damage them."

Oliver laughed, then turned to Benjy, smiling. "You know me. I'm nothing like that. As a kid, I used to just tear into my Christmas gifts. Wrapping paper wadded up everywhere, thrown across the room. You, on the other hand, seem like you'd be a careful present opener."

"Then why're you being such a pussy about opening it?"

Oliver bit his bottom lip and closed his eyes for about a second. "Good question." He chuckled, then quickly ripped through the wrapping paper, tearing it away carelessly. The plain white box beneath gave nothing away, and once the gift wrap was gone, Oliver removed the lid.

"Benjy!" He stared down at the contents of the box. Workout gear, but not just some el cheapo knockoffs from Walmart. "Under Armour?"

He reached into the box and removed the silky shirt, noting immediately it was way too small. "These are expensive."

Benjy moved closer, sidling beside him. Oliver's heart raced a bit as he felt the gentle touch of Benjy's palm against his back. "No, I got a good deal. It's to celebrate your progress."

"Benjy, they're awesome." He pulled the pants out of the box to reveal a pair of shorts beneath. "You got me shorts and pants both?"

"And a hoodie. I didn't wrap that one, though. It's in my cubicle."

"Benjy… I…. Uh. What am I supposed to say? You're too good to me."

"Those guys made fun of you 'cause of your clothes. Now you'll be the best-dressed gym bunny."

"Ha! Yeah right. Me, a gym bunny."

"Will you put them on for me? I wanna see you in them. I wanna see your muscle." Benjy gently squeezed Oliver's bicep, and Oliver turned to him, staring into Benjy's eyes.

"I love the clothes. I really do, Benjy. But I know I can't wear these yet. I'm not ready. I'm not small enough."

The smile never faded from Benjy's angelic face. "Yes, you are," he whispered. "You *so* are. Trust me."

Oliver held up the shirt, taking a step back to show Benjy. He pulled it against his torso. "I've never worn this size in my life."

"It's supposed to fit you tight."

"No… I can't wear tight-fitting stuff, not with all my rolls."

"That's just it!" Benjy giggled. "Oliver, your rolls are gone. You're now building muscle. That shirt's gonna show off your ripped body."

Oliver placed the shirt back in the box and grabbed Benjy by the shoulders. "Baby, how can you look at me and see that?"

"How can you *not* see it? Ollie, try on the shirt… and the pants. And then let me suck you off in your new gym gear." He'd lowered his voice to a whisper, sultry and sensual.

Oliver's heart skipped a beat as his cock pulsated in his khakis. "I can't believe you just said that." He felt his cheeks grow warmer.

"Please," Benjy pleaded. "I want to make love to every inch of your gorgeous body… with my lips and tongue. I want to deep-throat your big fat cock."

Oliver leaned in, pulling Benjy toward him, and planted a searing kiss on his dirty-talking little mouth. Benjy's arms snaked around Oliver's torso, his hands caressing Oliver's shoulder blades as they kissed. Oliver held Benjy close, driving his tongue into Benjy's eager mouth, and Benjy's fingertips ghosted down the back of Oliver's polo shirt until at last they slipped beneath the tail and pressed against Oliver's bare skin.

"Right here?" Oliver blurted a raspy stutter as he pulled back.

Benjy gripped the polo shirt and tugged upward. "Hell yes. Right here. Right now."

He managed only to pull it partially up Oliver's torso when suddenly Oliver realized if he removed the shirt, he'd be standing in the middle of the employee breakroom, naked from the waist up. What if, God forbid, someone were to walk in? The irony of his thoughts, the fact he was more concerned about being caught shirtless than being in the midst of sexual congress with another man, struck him as amusing, and he laughed spontaneously. Benjy grinned and laughed along with him, continuing to tug on the shirt, now pushing it upward in an attempt to raise it above Oliver's pectorals.

"Lift your arms, big guy." Benjy leaned in to kiss an exposed nipple. With their height difference, his head was positioned perfectly so Benjy's lips could easily press against Oliver's chest.

"I've never had public sex," Oliver whispered, as if saying the words quietly somehow made them secret. He took a step backward, bending slightly at the waist, which allowed Benjy to peel the shirt over his head. Before Ollie could reach for his new, silky Under Armour shirt, Benjy had cast the polo aside, and his hands were all over Oliver's chest, roaming freely.

"Baby, do you want me to try on my new clothes?"

"Mmm." He sucked Oliver's left nipple between his lips and nibbled ever so slightly.

"Aaahh!" Oliver cried out. "Jesus Christ!" He pulled back as the most erotic sensation traveled down his body, like a jolt of electricity from his nipples directly to his now-throbbing cock. He snatched the shirt from the box on the table and quickly pulled it over his head.

Benjy held back, smiling in the most teasing, seductive manner, and reached down to rub his own bulge as he watched Oliver pull the shirt down over his pecs. As Oliver felt the soft, stretchy fabric against his skin, he hesitated. This wasn't going to be good. He couldn't squeeze himself into this kind of shirt. He'd look like a big, bulging blob and would feel like a bloated beached whale. But as he pulled it down his torso, the shirt slid smoothly against his frame and amazingly fit him like a glove.

"Mmm-hmm. Now that's what I'm talking about." Benjy stared directly at Oliver's rather pronounced clefted pectorals. Could it actually be true? Did he now have normal pecs?

He still didn't look perfect. His skin was loose and saggy. He still had some excess weight around his midsection, and his loose, flabby skin, stretched by all the fat he'd carried around for so long, had begun to form an "apron." But damn, the tight-fitting shirt all but concealed these remaining flaws. Benjy moved closer once more, sliding his fingertips against the smooth fabric of the shirt. His touch felt amazing, a tantalizing tickle as his fingers danced across Oliver's chest.

"Sexy as hell," Benjy whispered as he trailed his hands down Oliver's torso, across his much-flatter and tighter abs, and found the button of his khakis. Benjy stood on tiptoe to kiss Oliver once more as he deftly unfastened the pants, peeling back the fly. His hand found Oliver's raging hard-on the exact same moment Benjy's tongue plunged into Oliver's mouth.

Stumbling backward, Oliver steadied himself against the countertop, gripping the cabinet ledge with both hands. Benjy danced the dance, keeping his body pressed against Oliver, gripping his rigid cock firmly as they continued to kiss. Now pinned against the counter, Oliver widened his stance, partially to afford Benjy easier access, and partly to keep his now wide-open pants from slipping down his thighs. As Benjy slid smoothly to his knees, though, he dragged Oliver's pants and underwear down past his thighs.

"D-don't you want me to try on the shorts too?"

Benjy cocked his head back in order to stare up at Oliver. Grinning, he grabbed hold of Oliver's shaft by the base. "Wouldn't want to get a cum stain on 'em or anything." He immediately directed his attention to Oliver's bulbous cockhead, which was now oozing a pearly white drop. Benjy's tongue darted outward, licking it up, and then he inhaled him.

Oliver moaned as the silky warmth of Benjy's mouth surrounded his throbbing cock. Without deliberation, he reflexively thrust his pelvis upward and out. Benjy swallowed the entirety of the shaft deftly, laving the sensitive underside with his moist tongue. Oliver stared down in awe as he watched Benjy's cheeks cave in while he sucked.

Slowly, perhaps worshipfully, Benjy serviced Oliver with the expertise of a porn star. And as he continued to bob, stroke, and suck, Oliver tossed his head back, soaring to the pinnacle of ecstasy when at last he moaned and released volleys of cum into Benjy's hungry mouth.

Benjy remained on his knees, sucking out every last drop as Oliver trembled. Chills and goose bumps traveled down his extremities.

"Oh. My. God. Oh my fucking God, Benjy."

"How'd you become so domestic?" Oliver stood behind Benjy in his apartment kitchen, wanting to wrap his arms around him, but conscious of the fact he'd just be interfering with Benjy's meal preparation. He really got into cooking, and he was damn good at it. Oliver marveled at his skill and appreciated how meticulously Benjy prepared each meal, using low-fat ingredients, ever aware of Oliver's diet restrictions.

Benjy cleared his throat as he tossed his head back, still stirring the pasta sauce. "Well, if you're not going to at least grope me, you might as well make yourself useful and set the table."

Oliver *harrumph*ed and reached down spontaneously to goose the perfectly rounded globe that presented itself. He slid his other arm around Benjy's waist and cupped his package, pressing his palm gently into his bulge. Leaning into Benjy's neck, he inhaled, savoring both the aroma of his cologne and the sweet-smelling marinara.

"Mmm, that's more like it." Benjy giggled.

"I'm a multitasker," Oliver whispered. "I can grope, goose, and suck neck simultaneously... *and* manage to set the table as well."

"If you make me burn this sauce, you're buying us takeout."

Oliver laughed, debating for a second if it would be worth it. He stepped back, pulling his arms away, and walked over to the cupboard, where he found plates and glasses. "If paying for takeout is all that's required for me to get into your pants, I'd say I got the better end of the bargain."

"As if you need to bargain for it." Benjy turned, tilting his head to the side, and offered the sweetest, most innocent smile.

"Well, no offense, but I'm almost as excited about the pasta as I am about the prospects of getting laid. I don't think I've had spaghetti since I started the...."

"I know. Diet's a four-letter word. But a serving of pasta's not going to hurt you. You don't have to completely sacrifice all carbs, especially with the way you've been working out."

Benjy was right, as usual. Oliver couldn't believe the rapid transformation his body continued to undergo, and at this stage, he found himself needing to eat a little more. It wasn't like before, though. He didn't binge or eat compulsively. He ate to satisfy his hunger and to fuel his ever-increasingly intense workout routine.

"Maybe after dinner we can go for a bike ride, just in case." Oliver chuckled.

"And stop again for frozen yogurt?" Benjy grinned. "With waffle cones."

Oliver sighed. "Are you making fun of me? You know that was the closest thing I've had to ice cream in the last year. *And* I only ate two bites of the cone."

Benjy tapped the wooden spoon against the side of the sauté pan, then turned to point it in Oliver's direction. "You might be bigger than me, but don't think I won't use this to warm your now tight, little, perfectly rounded asscheeks. I've never made fun of you, and never will. I just wish you'd accept that I love you exactly as you are, whether or not you lose another ounce."

Oliver gulped. "Sorry. I… um…."

"You need to set the table." Benjy placed a hand on his hip. Oliver bit his bottom lip, wanting to respond to Benjy's candid expression, but wouldn't it just seem disingenuous? He nodded and smiled meekly, then carried the plates over to the table.

"Remember when you said you wanted to join the gym with me?" Oliver lay on the floor in Benjy's living room, on his stomach with his knees bent, kicking his bare feet against the cushions of the sofa. Benjy sat beside him, cross-legged, eating a bowl of popcorn as they watched *Teen Wolf* together.

"Yeah, but that was a long time ago. You've been going there for months now, and you never said anything else about it."

Oliver shrugged. "Well, I'm saying it now. You wanna start going, at least on the weekends?"

"Do you think I need to?"

"No." Oliver laughed. "I love you just the way you are, but…."

"But you wouldn't mind me beefing up a bit, packing on some muscle?" He tossed a popcorn kernel into his mouth. Oliver reached over and playfully squeezed his slender arm.

"That's not what I said… or meant. I just think it'd be the healthy thing to do, and besides…."

"What?"

Oliver looked at him and smiled. "I wouldn't mind if those assholes saw with their own eyes what a hot boyfriend I have."

Benjy's mouth dropped open in astonishment. He gave Oliver the most puzzled look. "You mean like a trophy or something?" He set the bowl down on the floor, then leaned back, bracing himself with both hands on the floor behind him and laughed hysterically. "*Me*, a trophy?"

Oliver pushed himself up, pulling his legs underneath him. He now could do it quite easily. He reached out and grabbed hold of Benjy's sides, digging his fingers in playfully. "Are you laughing at me?"

Benjy erupted with another gale of fitful laughter, squirming in Oliver's grip. "Stop it! Stop it, that tickles."

Oliver leaned forward, no longer tickling, and kissed him on the lips. Benjy reached up, wrapping his arms around Oliver's much leaner, more toned torso, and moaned as he drove his tongue into Oliver's mouth. They clung to each other, tilting their heads side to side as Oliver continued to taste the salt from Benjy's popcorn. He at last pulled back to gaze into Benjy's eyes. Benjy raised his hand to Oliver's face and cupped his cheek affectionately, caressing it. "I'm not gonna get muscular like you," he whispered.

"I don't want you to." Oliver kissed his forehead. "I just want us to start doing things together, other than work, I mean. I want us to start going out places."

"We go to restaurants, movies sometimes. We ride bikes together."

"Places with other people. We've never gone to a bar together. We haven't made any friends."

"But…."

"I know it's hard for you, but let's at least do the gym together, okay? And I'm still going to the wedding with you." He'd agreed to be Benjy's date to his friend Sam's wedding.

So much had changed over the previous months. Oliver had changed, and not just physically. He'd taken off another fifty pounds and was now down to two hundred twenty, over a hundred pounds less than when he'd started his diet. But he'd not only gotten thinner. He'd also added muscle. He still had a paunch on him, but it was way smaller. He could feel the tight abdominals beneath the loose skin and remaining flab. He'd packed on muscle in his biceps, legs, and pectorals as well.

He still had a way to go before he'd be comfortable peeling off his shirt at the beach. And eventually he'd have to do something about his loose skin. But the remaining flaws he possessed, he'd learned to conceal. He wore tighter shirts like the Under Armour gear Benjy had bought him that held in the loose skin. He had a whole new wardrobe, picked out almost entirely by Benjy. And literally everyone now noticed how slender he was.

When Oliver looked at himself in the mirror, he now no longer saw a double chin and a bloated gut. He no longer possessed man boobs or pillows of fat beneath his arms. He could now even bend over at the waist and touch his toes, and he could sit in positions he'd only previously dreamed of.

And he could make love.

His first time with Benjy had been special. They both were virgins, and other than watching porn videos, had no idea what they were doing. But Benjy had volunteered to bottom, and as it turned out, he liked it. He just might possibly have liked it as much as Oliver had liked topping. They didn't use condoms. Didn't need to since they were each other's first.

Now holding Benjy in his arms, as they sat together on the living room floor, Oliver wanted to make love to him again. He slowly peeled Benjy's T-shirt over his head and grazed his fingertips across the smooth skin of Benjy's bare torso. Benjy responded with kisses, burying his face in Oliver's neck as he wrapped his arms around him and caressed his back. Oliver wore a tight-fitting ribbed tank top. It felt good, holding the loose skin in place, and Benjy seemed to understand. He never pressured Oliver to take it off. But at night, when they slept together, Oliver liked to strip down and feel Benjy's bare skin against his own.

Soon they were unbuttoning each other's pants. Benjy slipped his off, then pushed Oliver onto his back so he lay flat on the carpet. He tugged Oliver's pants down his legs, then his underwear, and pulled out a tube of lotion from the drawer in the living room stand. He slicked up his palm and began to stroke Oliver's throbbing cock.

Oliver moaned and closed his eyes, enjoying the feel of Benjy's ministrations. After jacking him at least a dozen strokes, Benjy reached behind himself and lubed his hole. He then straddled Oliver and held Oliver's cock by the base. He pointed it straight up, aligning it with his hole, then sat down, impaling himself.

Oliver moaned and bucked his hips, savoring the heat of the silky-smooth sensation that surrounded his cock. Benjy placed his fingertips against Oliver's chest and began to bounce up and down, riding him cowboy style. Oliver hardly had to do any work and received the benefit of an awesome show. He stared up at Benjy, taking in the entirety of his naked body as he bottomed from the top.

Oliver took hold of Benjy's cock and jacked it as the two edged closer to climax. "Oh fuck, Oliver! Fuck me! Fuck me hard!"

Oliver thrust his pelvis upward in time with Benjy's bobbing. Kneeling with his legs on either side of Oliver's body, he took the entirety of Oliver's cock deep inside him. At last Oliver reached his point of no return. He cried out, "Baby, here it comes," and released his load. "Oh God! I love you! I love you, Benjy Erickson!"

At that very moment, Benjy moaned and fired multiple jets of cum all over Oliver's tank top.

Trembling and gasping, Benjy finally dismounted. He slid onto the ground beside Oliver, who pulled him into a loving embrace. They kissed and hugged each other tight.

"I'm sorry. I shot all over your shirt." Tears flooded Benjy's big brown eyes.

"It was hot. You were amazing. Baby, please don't cry." Oliver ran his fingers through Benjy's hair.

"I love you too," he whispered. "And yeah, I'll do it."

"You'll do it? What do you mean?"

"The gym. I'll join the gym with you. I'll be your trophy boyfriend." Oliver grinned. "They're gonna be so fucking jealous."

CHAPTER TWELVE

"HOLY MOSES! Mister, you look *fabulous*!" Amanda gawked at Oliver as he walked out of the dressing room cubicle. Wearing all black, with a black tie, Oliver looked and felt like a new man. He and Amanda had spent the entire afternoon running up Oliver's credit card at the mall. He stood in front of the full-length mirror, gazing at himself and slowly turning, checking out his ass as best he could. "Do these pants make my butt look fat?"

She giggled. "I don't know. I need a good feel to really be able to tell." She reached down quickly and goosed him.

Feigning indignation, he pulled away. "Watch it, girl."

"Are you wearing a girdle?" She laughed again as she stared at him. It seemed so odd, the way their roles had somehow reversed. After her marriage nine months ago, she'd gained more than a few pounds while he'd lost an enormous amount of weight. Now down to a thirty-four-inch waist, which was probably about an inch too big, and a large shirt size, Oliver looked proportionally normal.

"Kind of," he admitted. "It's a one-piece compression undergarment, to be precise."

Puzzled, she stared at him. "Really? How come? You're not even chubby anymore. Why do you need that?"

"Trust me, you wouldn't want to see me naked."

Scoffing, she placed two fingers against her chin. "I wouldn't be so sure about that. You're looking mighty fine."

"You've seen the *Fantastic Four* movies, right? You know who Mr. Fantastic is, Reed Richards?"

"The stretchy guy?"

"Exactly. That's me now. Amanda, I have so much loose skin, it's disgusting. I mean, you can't tell so much on my arms. When I flex my bicep, it's not really noticeable, but I can literally pull the skin down below my arm for probably six inches or so. And on my legs, it's much worse. Remember how fat my legs used to be? I couldn't even cross them at the knees."

She looked down at his midsection. "Well, I'd be lucky if I could cross my legs at the knees right now. But you're right, you've lost a huge amount. I'm so proud of you. What're you going to do about that leftover skin, though? This sounds weird, but will it tighten up on its own?"

He shook his head. "I still have at least thirty more pounds to lose, and then I can have skin surgery."

"Thirty more pounds? Oh my God, you'll be a stick."

He cackled. "Well, maybe twenty. I'm a hundred ninety-eight, as of this morning. This is the first time since junior high I've been below two hundred pounds. I'm so psyched."

"And you wanna get down to one seventy?"

"Maybe one eighty. I have to be within a certain range for my height to qualify for the surgery. We have good insurance, but they're not likely to cover the surgery. They consider it cosmetic, so I'm going to have to lay out some cash."

"Ouch." She looked him over once more. "I like it." She nodded. "But are you sure you want to keep racking up your credit card? Sounds like you're going to need to save every penny."

He nodded. "I have some saved, and my folks are giving me twenty grand for the surgery."

"No way!"

"I know. I was shocked. At first I refused, but Benjy talked me into it. He said it would devastate my parents if I refused. I swear to God, he's closer to my mom now than I am."

Apparently tired of standing, she plopped down in the chair outside the dressing room cubicles. With a sigh, she yawned. "He seems nice. Quiet, though."

"Oh, wait till he gets to know you. He's a magpie who never shuts up."

"That's just it. After all this time, I still hardly know him. Ollie, I wonder if your Benjy even likes me." It seemed an odd thing for her to say. Amanda certainly wasn't the insecure type, and he'd always expected her to be 100 percent supportive if he ever did find a boyfriend. Now he had, and she was being pissy about the whole thing.

"No, he's just shy. He likes you a lot. Plus, he kind of has an anxiety disorder or something."

She scowled. "I just want to make sure you're happy, that's all."

"Of course I'm happy. We're buying these clothes more for him than me. I want to look good for him when we go to the wedding together."

"You should want to look good for you, Ollie. Not for Benjy."

He rolled his eyes. "What if I said something like that about you and Tyler? Don't you want to look good for your husband? We're happy," he said, a little too defensively. "Benjy makes me very happy, so happy I was thinking of…."

"What?" She crossed her legs at the ankles as she batted her eyelashes, looking up at him expectantly.

"I'm thinking of asking him to move in with me."

"Oh, that. Well, to be honest, I'm surprised that didn't happen a while ago. I thought you meant something more permanent."

More permanent than moving in with each other—was she talking about…. "*Marriage*, you mean?"

"You say he makes you happy. You both say you're in love."

"Wow." He turned and again stared at his reflection in the mirror. "I hadn't gotten that far, I guess. I hadn't even thought about that."

She sighed dramatically. "Well, I suppose this is as good a time as any to spring the news on you."

"The news?" He turned back to face her. "What news?"

"There's a reason I've put on so much weight recently." As she rubbed her tummy, her sheepish smile was what really gave her away.

"Amanda, no way! You're…?"

"Pregnant! You're gonna be Uncle Ollie in a few months."

"Oh my God! Oh my God! Oh my God!" He stepped over to her as she pushed herself up from the chair, a bit wobbly on her feet. He swept her into a hug, then backed off quickly, careful not to squeeze too tightly.

She laughed. "I knew you'd be happy for me. For *us*."

"I am! I'm just so… *surprised*."

OLIVER AGAIN found himself standing outside Benjy's apartment, waiting to be buzzed in. He'd arrived as planned, at seven in the morning. Benjy was supposed to meet him in the parking lot to go to the gym. They'd planned out the entire Saturday, beginning with their first workout together. They planned to get a healthy breakfast afterward, then hit the video game store. The county fair, one of the biggest in the state, was running that week, and they were going together.

But when Oliver pulled into the parking lot, Benjy was nowhere to be found. Of course, Oliver tried calling from his cell phone, and the call went straight to Benjy's voicemail. He must have overslept. That seemed strange, though. In all the time Oliver had known him, he'd never once been late for work. Benjy was never late for anything.

He pressed the button again, holding it for a few seconds. His concern had begun to morph into frustration. He didn't want to be pissed at Benjy, especially not today. He planned to pop the big question, to ask Benjy about possibly moving in together. But when the speaker crackled and Benjy's hoarse voice croaked out a tepid greeting, it felt exactly like déjà vu to Oliver. This is what Benjy did when he freaked out. He holed himself away, shutting out all the world, including Oliver.

He sighed in disappointment. "Benjy, buzz me in." After a few seconds, when nothing happened, he pressed the button again. "Benjy! Will you buzz me in, please?"

Finally the buzzer sounded, and Oliver pushed the door open. He bounded the three flights of steps and stopped abruptly outside Benjy's door. He didn't want to barge in there angry. Benjy's anxiety had kicked in again, and he couldn't help it. Still, the situation was no less maddening. How were they ever going to be able to plan anything? How would they ever make friends, experience anything together, when Benjy got all crazy every time Oliver so much as suggested they leave their comfort zone?

That right there had always been the problem. Benjy lived within a bubble, a zone of comfort. The more settled in he became with a particular setting or situation, the more difficult it was to step outside of his box. There were days he could hardly bring himself to go into a store. When he did finally muster the courage, he avoided people and went through self-service checkouts if possible. His position at the office mainly involved working alone. Seldom did he need to interact with others.

Conversely, Benjy was so wonderful with people, the ones he actually allowed into his life. He was the best boyfriend in the world—loving, attentive, devoted, and sexy as hell. He was great with Oliver's parents, especially his mom. And he was even well-liked at work, although most coworkers didn't really know him that well.

Oliver took a deep breath and knocked on the apartment door. He heard movement from the inside and waited. Finally the door opened and Benjy stood before him, clad in the most adorable workout suit Oliver had ever seen. Of course, anything Benjy wore looked adorable, but the navy-colored workout pants and matching hoodie, both bearing a strip of parallel white stripes, looked really classy.

"Are you ready to go?"

"Oliver, I don't feel well. I was planning... I mean, I had every intention. I got up early, got dressed and everything, but... my stomach—I think I'm going to throw up."

"You'll feel better after we get there, after you get used to the situation."

Benjy shook his head, taking a step back. "No, I don't think so. I... uh... I'm not very comfortable with the idea of working out in front of people."

"Benjy, you're the one who suggested it. Remember? When I first started at the gym, you asked if you could go with me."

With eyes as wide as saucers, he stared at Oliver, shaking his head. "Well, I changed my mind. And look at you. You look great. You don't need my help."

Oliver resisted the urge to sigh. He wanted to do worse than that even. He wanted to grab Benjy by the shoulders and shake him. He wanted to ask what the hell was wrong with him. Why did he always have to be so damn difficult? Instead he just glared.

"Please don't be mad."

"What about the fair? What about breakfast and the game stores? Benjy, we had the whole day planned!"

Benjy turned away from him and walked toward the kitchen. "I can't help it."

"You *can* help it! Benjy, this is nuts. You're acting like... like a crazy person!"

When Benjy spun back around to face him, Oliver knew instantly he'd said the wrong thing. The contorted, tortured expression on Benjy's face spoke a thousand words. Oliver reached out, taking a step toward him. "Benjy, I'm sorry—"

"Get out! Get out of my house!" Benjy screamed. "Go!" Tears streamed down his cheeks.

"No, please…. Benjy, I'm sorry. I didn't mean—"

"Just go. Oliver, I told you I can't go, and I mean it." He stormed past Oliver and rushed down the hallway to his bedroom and slammed the door behind him.

Oliver stood there, dumbfounded. He should go after Benjy, make sure he was all right. He should apologize again, beg forgiveness for what he'd said. At the very least, he should wait for Benjy to calm down. Instead, he shook his head, angry. Things didn't have to be this way. Benjy didn't have to turn every situation into an ordeal, a big, melodramatic scene. They were going to the fucking gym, not door-to-door preaching the gospel. What cause was there for anxiety in the first place? What exactly did Benjy fear? That someone was going to look at him the wrong way, say something mean, attack him? It just made no fucking sense.

It didn't matter what Oliver did at this point. Their day had already been ruined, and staying in that apartment, waiting for Benjy to suddenly become sensible, wouldn't help. They'd just have another argument when and if he ever did come out of his bedroom. Oliver sighed as he turned and headed back out of the apartment.

As he sped out of the parking lot, fury bubbled up inside him. Benjy wasn't a little kid anymore. He was a grown man, and it was high time he started acting like one. Yes, he'd faced hardship in life, but so had a lot of other people. He couldn't go on forever living within a cocoon. What his parents and family had done to him—the way they'd rejected and disowned him—was sad and tragic, but it wasn't the end of the fucking world. That was no reason for him to hole himself away in the confines of a tiny apartment. He'd created a self-imposed prison.

By the time he arrived at the gym, his frustration hadn't abated. He felt angrier than ever, in fact, and at this point he almost would welcome a confrontation with one of the gym bunnies. He'd probably deck them, and it would feel fucking fantastic. He allowed the testosterone to surge through him as he started his cardio workout, pushing himself harder than usual.

He now possessed muscle, and as he lay on the mat and rapidly counted out his crunches, he savored the burn in his abdomen, knowing every single time he stretched and tightened those core muscles, the firmer they became. In spite of the loose skin that sagged over his midsection, beneath it lay a solid, rippling washboard. As he performed the dumbbell presses, his biceps bulged, now at least twice their original size. His sturdy legs no longer twitched and ached miserably while on the StairMaster or during his calisthenics routine. The muscle burned on the days he did his lower body workouts, but even then, it was a pleasurable sort of pain, not exhausting as it had been in the beginning.

He rarely interacted with Adam anymore. Of course the trainer still checked on Oliver occasionally, monitored his overall progress. But Oliver had advanced in his training to a stage where he'd become self-sufficient. He didn't even need Adam to spot for him, because he generally used the resistance machines rather than free weights. He'd decided some time ago that his goal wasn't to pack on muscle like a bodybuilder. He wanted to ultimately achieve his weight-loss goal and subsequently stay in shape with a lean, toned body.

At his current weight, most people wouldn't even categorize him as overweight, not by looking at him. At first glance he now possessed a body not too different than most of the gay guys who regularly hit the gym. The only negative he still faced was the loose, saggy skin. It didn't embarrass him, though. In a way, it served as a reminder of his progress. Like the huge pair of pants he'd saved from when he was a hundred thirty pounds heavier, that sagging skin showed his original size compared to where he was now.

But he did look forward to the day he'd be able to have it removed. He allowed himself to occasionally fantasize about peeling his shirt off on a dance floor or at the beach. Currently he wouldn't dream of it. Even after his workouts, when he had to shower before leaving for work, he used a private stall where he dried off and got partially dressed before heading back to his locker. He always wore the one-piece compression suit, and the tight-fitting Lycra held everything in place, even accentuated the noticeable muscle beneath his skin. The legs of the suit extended down almost to his knees and thus held in the loose skin on his thighs as well.

He'd just finished pulling the ribbed tank over his head and smoothing it out over his skin-tight undergarment when Ethan, the quiet gym bunny, walked through the locker-room door. His wet hair dripped with sweat as did his brow and glistening, bare torso. Now, that was the kind of body Oliver hoped to have one day, when and if he ultimately hit his weight goal and had the loose skin removed. Ethan glanced at him, then stopped in his tracks.

"Hey." He stepped closer to Oliver, using the T-shirt he held in his hand to mop his brow. "How're you doing?"

Oliver hesitated before responding, unsure if their interaction would simply devolve into a confrontation like all his previous experiences with the four gym stooges. "Fine," he answered tersely.

"You've been coming here awhile now, but we've never officially met."

"I met your friends." He slipped onto the bench and bent over to pick his sneakers up from the floor. "Talked to AJ a couple times."

"Ah, right. I heard about that."

"But that was a long time ago, months back. He hasn't bothered me since."

Ethan laughed. "AJ has a big mouth, and he thinks everyone finds him hilarious. If only he were as funny as he thinks he is."

Oliver raised his head and looked at Ethan seriously. Their gazes locked. "He's not funny. He's mean, narcissistic, and shallow."

Ethan nodded. "I can't argue with that, but AJ is AJ."

"And so you guys just go along with it? It doesn't bother you when he mocks and ridicules others? You just laugh?"

The sweaty jock squared his shoulders, assuming what Oliver perceived as a defensive posture. With his shoulders pulled back, his pectorals looked even more appealing. Why was Oliver imagining his lips pressed against them, his tongue lapping the rivulets of perspiration?

"I think we're all guilty of shit like that. I can't say I'm proud of it, but haven't we all at one point or another laughed at an off-colored joke? Sometimes when the offender is a friend, it's easier to go along with them because… well, because it seems polite or something. You're afraid of offending the offender." He sighed and stared at Oliver with what seemed a look of genuine contrition. "I know it's not right, and I'm sorry."

Oliver looked down, stepping into his shoe. He pulled the laces tight and tied them. When he looked back up, Ethan was still standing there. "It's cool, man," Oliver said. "I get what you're saying. I've laughed at jokes and gone along with stuff myself."

"I wish I always appealed to the better angels of my nature."

"Me too."

"But, dude, you know how they always say success is the best revenge? In your case, that's totally true. Look at you. Look at your progress, your body. You're fucking ripped. I can't ever remember witnessing such a drastic transformation so quickly."

"Well, it's been almost a year. It was over nine months ago I joined the gym."

"Nine months ain't shit. I've been coming here almost nine *years*."

Oliver laughed. "It shows, man."

"Thanks." Ethan smiled and it warmed Oliver's heart. "But listen, I really am sorry, and I hope we can be friends. You should be proud of yourself." He held his hand out and Oliver stood to shake it.

"Apology accepted. I hope we can be friends too."

"You should come over to the café sometime."

"The café?"

"You know, the Rainbow Café, down the block, right on the corner. We usually hang there during the day, a group of us."

"Oh, really? Maybe I will sometime." Oliver smiled.

"You should come by tonight. They have poetry readings, acoustic performances, shit like that. There's an act tonight, sort of a one-man show." He winked.

"Hm. Is he good?"

Ethan shrugged. "Some people think so. You should come and judge for yourself. Afterward, there's still plenty of time to hit the clubs."

"Oh, I don't know about that."

"Well, at least come for the show."

"I'll think about it." He smiled again as Ethan patted his shoulder.

"Cool, man. Hope to see you there." Oliver watched the broad, muscular shoulders and delectable bubble butt as Ethan strutted away, over to the far side of the locker room.

Maybe he'd do it. Maybe he'd just go ahead and check out the café. What could it hurt?

Chapter Thirteen

AFTER PARKING his vehicle in the alley lot behind the Rainbow Café, Oliver sat in his car and pulled out his phone. He'd tried calling Benjy twice, but his unanswered calls had been sent to voicemail. He decided to call one more time. He wanted to smooth things over, make sure Benjy was okay. More importantly, he planned to invite Benjy to go with him to the café. It would be a way to salvage the day, and they could put the whole misunderstanding behind them. A small gathering in a coffee shop might actually be the sort of social event Benjy could handle.

But once again, the call went to voicemail. After leaving two messages already, Oliver didn't see the point in wasting his breath a third time. He ended the call and set the phone down on the seat beside him. As he checked out his reflection in the rearview mirror, he had to admit that another reason he wished Benjy were with him was because he was nervous. It wasn't as if he'd been a social butterfly at any time in his life. Back in high school and college, he'd maintained his standing within his circle of friends. They all proved superficial, and everyone eventually went their own way. He now had contact with none of them.

Since starting his new job and relocating to the city, he hadn't made any real friends other than Benjy. He attended some work functions— the Christmas party, a summer picnic, and even one of the company-sponsored conferences. In those settings, he mostly just made an appearance, chatted briefly with the few people he recognized, and got out as soon as possible.

It seemed food and drink became the focal point of every social event. For all these months, he'd strictly adhered to his nutrition plan, almost never straying from his diet. Alcohol wasn't any better. He could just as easily blow the whole thing by consuming high-calorie beverages.

That wasn't about to happen at the Rainbow Café, though. He'd checked out their website and was pleased by what he saw. Their menu featured the typical offering of cappuccinos and lattes, but also included pressed juices, flavored bottled waters, and a lot of healthy, nonfattening choices. They also boasted a novelty section where they sold LGBTQ souvenirs and knickknacks, CDs, videos, and books. The pictures and description made it sound like a quaint, cozy, little boutique coffee shop.

He pushed through the door of the rear entrance and had to walk down a hallway before emerging at the rear of the main seating area. A couple sofas had been positioned together to create a living room ambiance, and a few feet away, the coffee bar offered barstool seating. Small round tables were scattered throughout the dining area, and a smattering of eclectic, cushioned chairs gave the room a very informal feel.

There couldn't be more than twenty-five people in the café, and Oliver glanced around, hoping to spot a familiar face. He didn't see any of the guys from the gym. At the far side of the room, a staging area with a raised platform contained a single stool upon which a guitar rested. The guitar case sat on the stage floor beside the stool, but the performer must either have taken a break or perhaps hadn't yet started his show.

On the other side of the room, an archway led into an annex to the building. It must be the gift shop described on the website. Oliver walked across the café and entered the small room, then sauntered around the corner and down the aisle. He stopped in front of a display of picture frames. As he looked down, one in particular caught his attention. Rainbow stripes extended from a small lavender heart in the upper left corner of the frame, and in cursive script, the message "Love is Love" was scrawled across the top border of the frame. The stock photo in the picture slot displayed a happy, model-perfect gay male couple, embracing.

Immediately, Oliver's heart seized a bit. He thought of Benjy and reached down to pick up the frame, then inspected it more closely. He held on to the frame a while longer as he walked up and down the three narrow aisles of the small shop, then finally headed to the cash register. The employee, a college-aged male with a very slim build, turned to Oliver, smiling. He was shorter, like Benjy, and as he looked up at Oliver, his smile broadened even further.

Oddly, Oliver had noticed since losing all his weight how much friendlier people were to him in general. At the grocery store, the bank, even the mall, they engaged him more enthusiastically. It felt easier to maintain eye contact and to make small talk. He'd always believed in the harsh reality that people liked physical attractiveness. Scientific studies proved repeatedly that people trusted good-looking people more than they trusted average-looking or even homely strangers.

But he wasn't quite used to it. He didn't exactly know how to react when salespeople fawned over him, poured layers of syrupy sweet kindness into their interactions. In a way, it struck him as phoniness, and at the risk of being judgmental, he found it rather pretentious and hypocritical. If you're going to be nice, do it for the right reason. Treat people respectfully because they're people, not because they're *good-looking* people. Had he still weighed three hundred thirty-two pounds, would this salesclerk be so gracious toward him?

Nonetheless, Oliver smiled and returned the clerk's courtesy with an equal dose of politeness, and after the transaction was complete, while the salesclerk wrapped the frame, Oliver felt a hand in the center of his back. An arm extended into the air to the right of him, and a voice whispered in his ear. "Selfie time. Smile for the camera." Oliver looked up toward the phone and saw Ethan's reflection. He stood beside Oliver, his face pressed against Oliver's cheeks, and smiled. Oliver grinned as Ethan snapped the photo.

Oliver pulled back a bit, still smiling. "Hey, I looked for you when I came in. Did you just get here?"

"I've been here awhile. I might've been in the restroom or something. I'm so glad you made it." He glanced at the photo on his phone, clearly pleased. "Oh, I'm so relieved. Earlier I looked kind of blotchy. I tanned this afternoon, and it sort of distorted my complexion or something. I don't know. It was weird."

Oliver shrugged. "Looks fine to me, both in the picture and in person."

"Oh, you're so sweet." He leaned in to offer a hug, and Oliver obliged, allowing Ethan to brush his cheek against his own once more. "Mmm. What is that you're wearing? Smells so good."

"Really?" Oliver didn't know whether Ethan was being serious or teasing him. "It's just soap. Irish Spring."

"No kidding?" Ethan giggled. "I thought it was a new fragrance."

Maybe he should have doused himself with cologne. He hadn't thought about it. Obviously, Ethan was wearing something. "You smell pretty good yourself."

"Why, thank you." Ethan smiled proudly. "*Acqua Di Gio* by Giorgio Armani." His authentic-sounding Italian accent amused Oliver. How long had he had to practice saying it before he got it just right?

"Well, it's very nice."

The salesclerk cleared his throat and handed Oliver his bag. "Oh, thank you." Oliver nodded to the clerk as Ethan gripped his bicep. Oliver turned to him, unsure what to think about how touchy-feely his new friend had suddenly become.

"Should we go back inside and get a beverage?"

"Sure, sounds good." He followed Ethan out of the gift shop and back into the café, where they stopped at the counter. Ethan ordered a mineral water, and Oliver decided on a simple glass of unsweetened iced tea.

"You're kind of a no-frills guy, aren't you, Oliver?"

Self-consciously, he laughed. "Yeah, I guess so. It's just an iced tea sounds so refreshing. So, do you know a lot of these people here?" He looked around the room, which had filled up a bit more in the previous minutes.

"Yeah, a few of 'em. We're all kind of like family here." As if on cue, someone walked by, and Ethan waved, using just his fingers in a sort of toodle-oo gesture. An extrawide grin eclipsed his face for just a brief moment, then immediately faded. He turned back to Oliver. "In fact, I was talking about you earlier to a couple of my friends. I told them your story, how you'd transformed yourself. They agreed it's all very inspiring."

"Really?"

"Come on, let's go get a seat." He took hold of Oliver's wrist and dragged him into the seating area. They chose—or actually *Ethan* chose—a table close to the stage. "It's almost time for the next set."

"The next set?"

"The next set of my show."

Oliver's mouth dropped open. He stared at Ethan, astonished. "*You're* the one-man show."

"*Moi.*" He used both hands to point to his chest.

When he took the stage, a smattering of applause behind Oliver spurred him to clap as well. Ethan tilted his head to the side, briefly holding one hand over his heart. "Thank you. Thank you so much. And thank you for coming." He picked up the guitar from the stool and took a seat.

He then proceeded to strum the guitar for a few beats, and when he transitioned into a melody, Oliver had to admit he was impressed. The guy was good. He definitely had talent, and as he began to sing, Oliver liked his voice. He chose sort of folksy types of songs, and after the third one, Oliver pulled out his phone and snapped a couple pictures. Ethan looked awesome up on the stage, sitting on the stool with the top three buttons of his shirt open. He wore tight jeans that fit his long, muscular legs like a glove.

He performed a couple more songs before closing out his set. By that time, the café had filled up considerably. As he descended from his perch on the stage, several of the guys from the audience approached him, offering hugs and congratulations and more than a few bro handshakes. When at last Ethan pulled out his chair and sat down at the table opposite Oliver, another familiar face entered the picture.

Devon pulled up a chair and requested permission to join them. "Sure, man." Ethan motioned his approval. As Devon sat down, he looked at Oliver and nodded. "Oliver, is it? I remember you from the gym."

Not wanting to rehash any of the previous drama, he nodded his agreement. "Good to see you again, Devon."

"Dude, I gotta tell ya, you look amazing. You don't even resemble the person you were a few months ago when you started coming to Fitness Warehouse."

And you haven't changed a bit. Oliver forced a smile. "Thank you."

"Ethan said he'd invited you tonight, and I was pretty stoked about it. I'm really glad you decided to join us. You *are* going to Paradise with us?"

"Paradise?"

"The club. The gay bar...."

"Oh, right. Well, probably not this time. I have... um...."

"You already have a date?" Ethan sounded crushed, and Oliver immediately turned his attention back to his friend.

"No, no… nothing like that. I just can't go tonight."

"Oh, well, that kind of sucks. Party pooper."

Oliver laughed obligingly. "Remember, I'm the fat guy. Gay bars haven't exactly been friendly in my experience so far. I've got to build up the nerve, ya know."

"Oh, don't be silly," Devon chirped. "You are definitely not a fat boy anymore. You'll be just fine in any club."

Ethan shot him daggers, and Oliver wondered for a second what was going on between them. Ethan then looked at Oliver, placing his hand on top of Oliver's. "You just have to be quick-witted. If any of those bitches tries dishing you any smack, you just hit 'em with a snappy comeback. Once they know you're not a pushover, you're fine."

"That's my problem. I've never been great at the snappy comeback."

"That's not what AJ says." Devon laughed. "You scared the shit out of him."

"I meant every word of what I said to him. I never meant to dish him anything."

"Baby, you're overthinking this." Ethan squeezed his hand. "You really don't even need to worry about it. Looking the way you do, you can just stand there and be beautiful. You'll have the bottom boys eating out of your hand."

He thought of Benjy, his own "bottom boy," and he couldn't imagine ever referring to him so tritely. A hollowness manifested within his chest, and he suddenly wondered if maybe coming to the café alone had been a mistake.

"I kind of have someone already. I'm not really looking…."

"You have a boyfriend?" Ethan blurted out.

"Yeah, I think so. I mean, I did, but…."

"But there's trouble in paradise? You had a fight?"

"Yeah. And now he won't answer my calls."

"Dude," Devon said, "you're definitely coming with us tonight. You can't let a guy do that to you. Look, you've tried to call him, and he's blowing you off, so fuck him. Go out and have fun. If he doesn't like it, that's his problem."

"Exactly," Ethan seconded. "Who is this guy anyway? Someone you met at the gym?"

Oliver shook his head. "We met at work, before I started working out."

"Back when you were…?"

"Fat. Yeah. Back when I weighed over three hundred pounds. We've been good friends, and it became more than that these past few months."

"Dude! You can do way better than that. Look, you have to put all that behind you." Devon leaned in as he spoke. "If this guy was your friend back when you were a porker, he's probably…."

"Benjy's *not* even fat. He never has been." He glared angrily at Devon.

"No, I didn't mean it like that. I mean, think about it, man. You're in a different league now. You're not the same person you used to be."

He looked into Devon's eyes, then looked over at Ethan. "Maybe I'm not, but I'm not ready. I really should get going." He pushed his chair back and stood up. "Ethan, I loved your show. And it was good seeing you again, Devon. I've got to go."

CHAPTER FOURTEEN

WHEN OLIVER woke up Sunday morning, he debated skipping the gym for the very first time. Sure, there'd been plenty of times previously when he hadn't felt like dragging his ass in at such an ungodly hour to work out, but this time, it wasn't laziness or procrastination that gave him pause. He wasn't sure he wanted to face the likes of Ethan and Devon. At least it was Sunday, and the gym bunnies often didn't show up early in the morning, so maybe he could get in and out without a confrontation.

Speaking of confrontation, he had to go see Benjy. After plodding his way first to the bathroom and then the kitchen for a cup of coffee, he found his phone and immediately checked for messages. Still nothing from Benjy. He couldn't help but feel a bit miffed. He understood that Benjy had suffered an anxiety attack the day before. He realized he was very upset, but he should have long since been over it. He could have answered Oliver's calls and texts, if for no other reason than to say he was okay.

What if he wasn't okay? What if he'd suffered some sort of psychotic break, had a complete meltdown that rendered him catatonic? Oliver was no psychologist. He didn't know the risks, and it troubled him. After his workout, he'd definitely go to Benjy's apartment and check on him, whether Benjy liked it or not.

He looked over at the counter—a bar separating the kitchen from the dining room area. Benjy had left one of his books. Most of the computer geeks Oliver had known were not pleasure readers. They prided themselves in being analytical, mathematical thinkers and read only nonfiction. Statistics, scientific journals, internet articles. If they did read any fiction at all, it was usually science fiction or comics. But Benjy was different.

Benjy read voraciously, consuming on average two or three novels a week. He used his tablet, a Kindle Fire, for most of his reading, but certain books he refused to read in digital format. He admitted to the quirkiness of his eccentric distinction, but he insisted some books—the classics—were meant to be held in your hand. One such book, *Frankenstein* by Mary Shelley, sat on the counter in front of Oliver. Benjy had read it already, two or three times, he said—he couldn't remember. But he often reread books he liked.

A lump returned to Oliver's throat as his heart clenched. Why'd he feel so hollow? With his mind's eye, he saw Benjy curled on the sofa, one foot tucked beneath his butt and with his other knee raised. He often chewed his finger or thumb as he read, a peculiar habit. But he was always so adorable.

Well, at least that would give Oliver an excuse to go to his apartment. He'd say he came to return the book. Maybe he could talk Benjy into a walk or a trip to the video game store. They'd been through too much together to let something like this silly disagreement come between them. It would be okay. Oliver would apologize, smooth everything over, and they'd be back to normal.

Fortunately the gym was mostly vacant when Oliver arrived. He plowed through his workout, focused more on just getting it over with than accomplishing any particular goal. By nine o'clock, he was showered and changed and heading up the stairs to the facility's exit. As he pushed through the front door and stepped out into the parking lot, a red sports car whipped in. When it honked, he raised his hand to wave, assuming it had to be someone from the gym who recognized him. When Ethan climbed out of the car a few seconds later, Oliver wanted to make a mad dash in the opposite direction. Instead, he stood his ground and smiled.

"Hey, man. Are you done already?"

"Yeah." Oliver nodded. "I'm so used to the early schedule."

"That sucks. I was gonna work out with you. We can still do brunch, though, if you want to meet me back here in a couple hours."

"I'm on my way now to Benjy's, but thanks for the offer."

"Benjy? Is he the guy you were talking about last night? The one who blew you off yesterday? Oliver, you deserve better than that." He raised his eyebrows as if to scold. Ethan looked like he'd just stepped off the page of a fashion magazine, his hair perfectly coiffed, wearing his designer workout duds.

"Well, maybe he's feeling better today. I'll ask if he wants to go to brunch together."

"Great idea! If you patch things up, bring him along." He smiled sweetly. "And if not, give me a call."

"Oh, okay. Guess I'll need your number."

"Oh, right." Ethan pulled out his iPhone, and Oliver retrieved his Android from the pocket of his duffel. As they exchanged phones, Ethan stared at Oliver's quizzically. "We need to get you a better phone. C'mon, man, this thing's from the Stone Age."

"I've had it a couple years. I like the bigger screen."

"Christ, it's like a television set. I've seen tablets smaller than this." He laughed at his own joke, an obvious exaggeration. Oliver, who knew a lot about technology, hated being bullied into buying "the latest thing." And he'd encountered more than a few Apple users who were downright snobby about their preferences.

"To each his own, I guess." He punched his phone number and name, first and last, into Ethan's phone and handed it back.

"Dude! Now we're officially linked, connected digitally. I'll add you to Twitter and Facebook."

"Don't use Twitter, but Facebook's fine."

"You don't use Twitter?" Ethan made a face.

Oliver and Benjy had agreed months ago that Twitter was just too asinine to mess with—mostly just gossipy bullshit. He actually had a Twitter account but only checked it on his laptop occasionally. He wasn't interested in any celebrity opinions or chitchat about strangers' doctor's appointments and baby showers. That was the problem with social media. People shared everything, and they were all so quick to voice their opinions about anything and everything. Others got offended because their friends were constantly spouting off shit they'd never have the balls to say in person, face-to-face.

He and Benjy used Facebook to share cool stuff about Marvel or DC Comics, awesome new movies, and gaming info. He also shared photos with his mom and Amanda, and Benjy kept in touch with his friend, Sam, back in Missouri. His newsfeed would probably be boring as hell to a guy like Ethan, but what the hell?

"All right, have a good workout, and I'll try to catch up with you later."

"It's a date!" Ethan patted him on the shoulder. "Call me." He held his thumb and pinky finger up to the side of his face, the unofficial sign language.

"Later."

"Later, man."

By the time Oliver pulled into the parking lot of Benjy's apartment complex, his phone had chimed. He parked, then picked up the phone, hoping it was a text from Benjy. It wasn't. He stared at the text message from Ethan, who had sent him a copy of their selfie from the night before. He'd also sent Oliver a Facebook friend request. Sighing, Oliver reluctantly clicked the Confirm Friend Request button before shoving his phone into his pocket.

He got out of the vehicle and walked over to the door. Maybe he should try calling Benjy again. No, Benjy would just ignore it and let the call go to voicemail. Oliver pressed the button on the intercom that corresponded with Benjy's apartment number. Then he waited. Not even five seconds later, the buzzer sounded, and Oliver pulled open the entrance door. It seemed odd Benjy hadn't spoken through the PA system as usual, but Oliver wasn't complaining. He quickly bounded up the steps and soon stood outside Benjy's apartment door. He rapped lightly and waited again.

Benjy opened the door and stepped back, allowing Oliver space to enter. But Oliver didn't want space. He moved closer to Benjy, reaching out to him. Benjy took another step back. "Oliver, we need to talk."

"That's why I'm here. You haven't answered any of my calls."

"I know. I'm sorry." He closed the door and motioned for Oliver to step into the living room area. "Have a seat if you want."

"I don't want a seat, but I'd love a hug… or a kiss, maybe."

Benjy offered a weak smile, only curling the very corners of his mouth. Oliver could read the sadness in his eyes. He looked exhausted.

"Baby, are you okay?"

"Oliver, please have a seat." Benjy took his own seat in the only single occupancy chair, leaving the loveseat or sofa for Oliver to choose from. He slipped onto the loveseat, sitting on the very edge of the cushion in order to lean forward in Benjy's direction.

"I'm so sorry about yesterday. I never should have said you were—"

"No, it's okay. I overreacted, and you were right. Actually, I do have a mental illness. We should have talked about this a long time ago. I have severe anxiety disorder. I even take medication for it."

"Benjy…."

"Sometimes when I start to freak out, the stress and anxiety consume me. The symptoms become physical manifestations where I get intense headaches and severe nausea. Sometimes it feels like I'm having a heart attack, like that day you helped me at work back when we first met."

"I remember."

"And yesterday, I wasn't lying to you when I said I was sick. I'd been puking. I had a headache. I completely and totally went into a full-blown meltdown, and I'm sorry."

Oliver shook his head as he blinked, fending off the threat of tears. God, he'd been such a fucking ass to Benjy. If only he could turn back time and take back the words that had slipped out of his mouth….

"It's too much baggage to expect anyone to accept. Most of the time I can hardly accept it about myself. I have periods where I start to get better. Like when we went up to your folks, Oliver, that was the best weekend of my life. I only had one little episode, and that was at the picnic."

"It's not too much. Benjy…." He reached out, attempting to take Benjy's hand, but Benjy pulled away. "I was so wrong. I don't think you're crazy. I'm the crazy one for being such an asshole, for not trying harder to understand."

"No." Benjy shook his head. "You've been more than patient. I've been thinking about this a lot. Nonstop, actually." He tried to smile again. "I wasn't fair to you. In fact, none of this whole situation was fair. All this time there's been a part of me that secretly hoped you wouldn't be so successful with your weight loss."

"I don't believe that."

"It's true. Oliver, your weight was your baggage, just like my anxiety is to me. You needed me, and I needed you, and I was terrified you'd lose all the weight and not need me anymore."

"That will never happen."

"It's happened, Oliver. It's *already* happened."

"No! Benjy, that is *not* true. I love you, and for God's sake, I don't consider anything about you to be 'baggage.'" Again, he reached out, urging Benjy to take his hand.

Instead, Benjy picked up his phone from the end table. "Right before you rang the buzzer, I was on my phone, on Facebook." He tapped some buttons on his phone, pulling up the app. "Oliver, you apparently weren't too devastated by our *disagreement* yesterday." He held out his phone, handing it to Oliver.

He looked down at the image of Ethan and him, standing cheek to cheek. It had been posted to Oliver's wall and apparently had appeared in Benjy's newsfeed. Oliver had been tagged along with the date, time stamp, and location. His mouth dropped open when he read the caption. "My prospective love interest and soon-to-be boyfriend, Oliver Paxton."

"What the fuck!"

"I'm not mad." Benjy spoke in a calm, even voice, which sent a chill down Oliver's spine. "I understand. Look at you two, what an adorable"—his voice cracked as he spoke the final word—"*couple.*"

"No, Benjy! It's not like that. I have *no* interest in this guy whatsoever. You've got to believe me."

Benjy sighed, tears now streaming down both cheeks. "Then you're a fool. He's obviously interested in you."

"Ethan had no business posting this picture on my timeline. And this caption, it's pure bullshit. He knows about you. I told him—more than once—I'm in a fucking relationship."

Benjy rose from his chair and held out his hand to take back his phone. "Oliver, it's over. It shouldn't have continued as long as it did. I don't want us to part ways angry at each other. I care about you, and I want you to be happy."

"Then don't do this!" Oliver's voice rose three octaves as the hot tears flooded his eyes. "Please!"

Benjy stepped closer and reached out to brush his fingertips against Oliver's hair. He leaned forward and kissed Oliver's forehead, then removed the phone from his hand and stepped back. "I'll always be grateful for everything you did for me. You saved my ass that day right after I'd started at work. You befriended me when I was friendless. You've been so patient, so understanding. And I love your mom and dad."

"I don't accept this!" Oliver rose from his seat and grabbed Benjy by the shoulders. "I haven't stopped loving you. Benjy, you can't do this. You can't decide something like this for both of us. You're not fucking baggage!"

Benjy reached up to place his palm gently against Oliver's cheek. "I love you too, Oliver, which is why I'm letting you go." He pulled away and walked across the room briskly, toward the hallway. "Let yourself out. I'll see you at work tomorrow."

"Benjy!"

Benjy turned one last time before entering the bedroom. "Call Ethan. He's waiting." He walked over the threshold of the bedroom and closed the door behind him.

Oliver crumpled to his knees, devastated.

CHAPTER FIFTEEN

OLIVER DIDN'T call Ethan, not right away. He remained on his knees in Benjy's living room, crushed to the core, and cried for ten minutes. He debated marching down the hallway and camping out at Benjy's bedroom door. He wanted to beat the door down, beg and plead for another chance.

It didn't matter. Nothing he could do now would change what had happened. Benjy wasn't going to relent. Oliver already knew how stubborn he was. It felt as if his shoes were filled with lead as he plodded back down the staircase and out to his car. When he got there and opened the door, the first thing he saw was Benjy's book. He'd forgotten to take it with him, but he wasn't about to go back and wait for Benjy to answer the buzzer.

He drove home, barely able to see the road ahead of him. None of this seemed real. It had to be a dream—a horrible nightmare. Maybe somehow he'd find a way to win Benjy back. Maybe Benjy would think about it and reconsider. Clinging to this thin shred of hope was the only thing that mitigated the dull ache in his chest that otherwise would surely have crippled him.

As he drove past Burger King, Wendy's, Arby's, and McDonald's, he mustered every bit of willpower to avoid pulling in and commencing with a feeding frenzy. Oh, the comfort such delicious food would have provided, had he succumbed to the temptation. His mouth watered as he savored the imaginary taste of greasy fries, loaded burgers, and thick, creamy milk shakes.

What if he went home and waited a couple hours? Maybe he could write Benjy a letter, send it via email, explaining in detail what had transpired between Ethan and him. He hadn't even asked the dude to take his picture. He'd just done it. And Oliver had certainly given him no indication whatsoever that he was interested in anything with him beyond friendship.

When he got home, he looked around his house. As usual, he needed to clean. He had laundry to do, a dishwasher to load. He should scrub his bathroom and vacuum his floors. Beyond that, he hadn't even made his fucking bed. He never made the bed. What was the point? He was just going to mess it up again a few hours later. Why did he have so much energy and drive to work out, but couldn't force himself to clean? Why was he able to play video games for hours on end but couldn't take five minutes to make his bed?

Why were people so strange, so quirky? Benjy, so affable, to know him was to love him, yet he constantly feared the world hated him. The opportunity to be happy lay right there, right in his path. He need only claim it, but he wouldn't. He spent all his energy fretting about everything, constantly worrying someone might do or say something to him that would crush him. In the process, he behaved as if he'd already been crushed.

Well, he had. Oliver couldn't imagine the devastation Benjy must have experienced when his parents disowned him and kicked him out. He'd already faced hardship, a victim of abuse and repeated bullying at school. And in every way, he'd risen above the tragedy. He'd succeeded by finishing high school, acquiring a degree and a decent job. Why couldn't he allow himself to enjoy the life he'd created for himself?

Oliver tried cleaning the kitchen, thinking that in some weird way it would be appropriate. Benjy would approve of his effort. But every time he bent over to place another dish in the dishwasher, he thought of Benjy, how spotless his apartment always was. Every time he tossed an item in the trash, wiped the counter, or cleaned the stovetop, he envisioned Benjy flitting around the kitchen, so comfortable within his element.

He didn't get far in his cleaning efforts. After a half-assed attempt in the kitchen, he slogged back into the living room and collapsed on the sofa. He should fix himself a salad or warm up some soup. He wasn't hungry, though. A few minutes ago, he'd fantasized about consuming the entire menu at McDonald's, but now he didn't think he could even force himself to eat.

He grabbed his laptop off the stand beside him and opened his email. He began typing a letter to Benjy, but after two sentences, he stopped. What more could he say than what he'd already said? What creative words could he craft in order to show Benjy this had all been a misunderstanding? How could he convince him, win him back?

He shook his head and slid the laptop onto the sofa cushion beside him. He loved Benjy, but he couldn't force him to do something he didn't want to do. He couldn't magically change Benjy's mind, no matter what arguments he used. Benjy had decided it was over. He'd dumped Oliver without so much as giving him a chance to defend himself. Benjy was the uncooperative, uncompromising, unforgiving one.

Oliver could go on blaming himself for accusing Benjy of acting crazy, but what purpose would that serve? It wouldn't change anything. He'd already apologized, explained it was a poor choice of words. He'd already taken back what he said. Hadn't he?

No, an email wouldn't change anything. Getting on his hands and knees and begging wouldn't. Nothing would change the situation. He picked up his phone, debating whether or not to call Amanda. His mom, maybe? He certainly didn't want to talk to Ethan. In fact, he just might punch him in the face the next time he saw him.

He sat on the couch by himself—no food, no TV, no computer. He just sat there as if paralyzed, completely numb, and listened to the silence. He wasn't sure when he dozed off, but he awakened after dark, curled up on the sofa with his laptop on the floor beside him. He got up and stumbled to the bathroom, then grabbed a yogurt and bottled water from the refrigerator. He stood in the kitchen, staring at the digital clock on the stove. He couldn't believe he'd slept all those hours, the entire day. It was now after eleven. He'd really fucked up his sleep pattern. How would he ever get back to sleep? He had to work in the morning, after all.

But after he finished his snack, he stumbled to the bedroom and collapsed on the bed. He had no problem falling back asleep, and he awoke seven hours later to the sound of his alarm.

OLIVER FACED Monday morning the same way he did any other Monday. He suppressed his anger and sadness, deciding not to think about the situation. He'd go about his routine as if everything were normal. He arrived at the gym a little after seven and pounded out a brutal, upper-body workout. As he finished up with a set of leverage chest presses, he felt the burn not only in his pectorals, but also in his triceps and shoulders. He released the air from his lungs, then took another deep breath at the exact moment Devon appeared beside him.

"Nice!" He placed his hand against Oliver's shoulder. With his other hand, he reached around and patted Oliver's chest. "You're pumped, man."

Oliver looked up into Devon's face, unsure if he should be annoyed or flattered. Devon smiled, staring into his eyes. With their faces inches apart, Oliver immediately noticed the spicy scent of Devon's sandalwood cologne. He certainly didn't smell of man sweat like Oliver probably did himself. "You haven't worked out yet?"

Devon removed his hand from Oliver's chest, but lingered close, running the fingers of his other hand along Oliver's shoulders. "Just starting."

"That's what I thought." Oliver smiled. For the first time in several days, he felt a warmth within his chest, and not from the burn of his workout. Benjy had always ignited a warm, glowing feeling of contentment within him, especially when they were alone, intimate with each other. Why was he feeling this sensation with Devon? Maybe it resulted from his gentle touch, the cadence of his smooth voice, or even from that intoxicating, sexy smell of his cologne.

"I can't believe Ethan posted that pic of you two yesterday."

Surprised, Oliver widened his gaze. "How'd you know?"

"I saw it. I'm his friend on Facebook, and I saw what he posted. I sent you a friend invite, but you haven't accepted."

"Oh, sorry. I haven't been back on Facebook, not since my boyfriend—my *ex*-boyfriend—found the picture."

"What? No way. You're not saying he dumped you or something? Not because of *that*?"

Oliver heaved a sigh. "Sort of. Well, not *only* that, but that didn't help."

"Man, I'm sorry to hear that. But you know what? You're probably better off without a guy like that. He sounds like he was very controlling."

Was he? Was Benjy just being overly possessive? No, Oliver knew better than that. This wasn't about jealousy. Benjy's decision to end their relationship hadn't been rooted in selfishness. Insecurity, maybe, but nothing to do with his ego. In a weird sort of way, it might have been easier to accept had it been pure jealousy. "I haven't seen or talked to Ethan."

Devon leaned against the machine, tilting his head slightly as he spoke. "He never should have posted that comment with the picture, suggesting you two are a couple."

"No shit."

"That was very presumptive of him."

"Or flattering, depending how you look at it." Oliver turned to see Ethan on the other side of him. "I didn't mean to assume anything. I guess it was just wishful thinking."

"Ethan...." Oliver stared at him, unsure what to say. He should be angry. He should stand up and knock the guy's block off. "How did you expect me to explain that comment to Benjy?"

Ethan moved closer, unconcerned by Devon's presence, and placed his hand on Oliver's other shoulder. "I overheard what you just said, that your boyfriend broke up with you. That's pretty sad, man. But if he loved you, he wouldn't freak out over an innocent picture."

No, he freaked out because Oliver had been an asshole, had called him crazy. "I think he just wants me to be happy."

"Exactly!" Devon and Ethan said in unison. They glared at each other, then Ethan continued. "And you didn't seem too happy Saturday night. Dude, you're torturing yourself over this guy."

Oliver pushed himself up from his seat on the machine, stepping away from both of them. "Well, I gotta go get showered. I have work today."

"Come down to the café tonight," Devon suggested. "We'll hang together."

"I'll be there," Ethan added.

"I'll think about it." Without another word, he walked away, heading toward the staircase leading to the locker room. As he showered and got changed for work, he thought about what had just transpired. Had two hot guys just simultaneously hit on him? Were they...? No, no that was insane. Of course they weren't vying for his attention. Of course they couldn't be competing against each other for him. Could they?

He smiled as he buttoned his dress shirt.

WHEN HE arrived at the office, Oliver looked over his cubicle wall to find Benjy's workstation empty. He looked at his phone, checking the time.

Benjy was never late. He'd normally be at work already. Oliver hadn't seen him in the breakroom or bathroom either.

A knot formed in his chest, and the dull ache he'd felt the day before, after Benjy dumped him, returned in full force. Then he looked closer at Benjy's workstation, and the sinking, hollow feeling inside him seemed to expand. All of Benjy's personal items had been removed from the cubicle. His mini calendar no longer hung on the cubicle wall. There was no cup holder, and his Star Wars mousepad had been replaced by one with a blue company logo. Someone had cleaned out the cubicle. Benjy had moved to a new work location, or he'd….

He caught the attention of a supervisor as she walked by. "Laura, what happened to Benjy?"

"Benjamin Erickson? He transferred. He's still working with IT, but no longer in software programming. He's now in claims. Upstairs."

"Really? That was sudden."

"The posting for the position's been up for the past three weeks in the breakroom. Benjamin's the only one who applied for it. He came in early this morning and requested that the transfer happen as soon as possible."

Oliver sank into his seat, stunned.

Laura gave him a puzzled look. "He's just upstairs. It's not like he's moved to the other side of the country."

He turned away from her and stared at his computer monitor. "He might as well have," he muttered under his breath. "He might as well have moved to Siberia."

CHAPTER SIXTEEN

WHEN OLIVER walked through the rear entrance of the Rainbow Café, he immediately heard someone call his name. He looked across the room and saw Devon waving. Oliver smiled, waving back, then stopped at the counter to purchase a bottled water. As he made his way to the table where Devon was sitting, he hesitated, noticing Devon was not alone.

"Oliver!" Devon motioned for him to have a seat. "How cool you showed up."

Oliver pulled out the chair and sat down, waiting for an introduction.

"I'm Ryan." The young man sitting on the other side of Devon spoke. He seemed young, maybe even still a teenager, but he was cute, nonetheless. With his backward baseball cap, his clean-shaven face seemed boyish, maybe a little too perfect.

"I was just telling Ryan about you," Devon added. "But I wasn't sure you would show up."

"Am I interrupting?"

"No, no! Not at all. Ryan goes to our gym too. Seems like most of the gay members know each other."

"Really?" Oliver had never seen the kid, and even if he had, he wouldn't have suspected him to be gay. His all-American look sort of defied the gay stereotype.

"Not a morning person," Ryan explained. "You'll never see me there before midafternoon. In fact, I'm on my way there now."

"That explains it—why I've never seen you, I mean. I only go in the mornings."

"Well, if you ever decide to change things up, I wouldn't mind spotting for a guy like you." Ryan winked as Devon reached across the table to slap his arm.

"You're fucking shameless!"

"You're one to talk." Ryan grinned, flashing a perfect row of pearly whites. He pushed himself up from the chair he'd been straddling. "Anyway, I better get going. You two have fun, and don't do anything I wouldn't."

"That pretty much leaves us with a world of possibilities." Devon winked.

Ryan laughed, then nodded to Oliver before he took off.

"Was that guy flirting with me?" Oliver felt his cheeks flush with warmth. He looked at Devon, embarrassed.

"Of course he was." Devon laughed. "You better get used to it."

Oliver had never experienced flirting like that, and now it had seemingly happened three times in the same day. Maybe it was just a thing with the gym bunnies, something they did to be funny. So far he hadn't observed any of them getting fresh with one another, though. Instead, they seemed to just be hitting on him.

"I doubt I'll ever get used to it. You saw what I looked like a few months ago, back when I first started working out. Before that, I was even heavier. I'd already lost over sixty pounds at that point."

"Wow. You should be proud."

"Thanks. But my point is, nobody—not one person my entire life—ever said I was attractive."

Devon looked at him sympathetically. Pityingly.

"Well, that's not exactly true. One person did. Only one."

"Moms don't count." Devon laughed and reached over to grab Oliver's arm. "Just kidding, man."

He smiled obligingly. "Well, other than my mom, I mean. But you're right, she never would admit I was fat. Even after I started losing weight, she worried I'd starve myself."

"Dude, you look great now. And speaking of great, I'm having a picnic-slash-beach party over at my condo this weekend. Why don't you come?"

"Really? I might."

"What do you mean, you might?" Devon leaned in, mere inches from his face. "Say you'll come, *please*."

Oliver smiled again, then bit his bottom lip. He was supposed to be going with Benjy to Missouri for Sam's wedding, but after what had happened, Benjy probably wouldn't even want him to go. "All right."

"Awesome!" Devon slapped Oliver on the shoulder. "It'll be pretty much all people like us, so I'm sure you'll have plenty more dudes hitting on you."

"That's what I'm worried about."

"Well, just stick close to me. I promise, I won't let *any*one touch you."

Under the table Oliver felt Devon's other hand slip onto his thigh, sliding inward between his legs.

Oliver gulped and nodded. *That's what I'm* really *afraid of.*

SHIRLEEN SQUEALED gleefully, rushing around the counter into the waiting area where Oliver stood. Her enthusiasm and bearlike hug elicited a smile from Oliver as he responded by wrapping his arms around the bubbly, gregarious receptionist.

"Honey, I barely recognize you." She held him at arm's length, looking him up and down. "This isn't the same man who started coming here less than a year ago."

Not bothering with protocol, she ushered him into the examination area, calling out cheerfully for Dr. Brad. "Look who's here! Brad, you've got to see this!"

The doctor stepped into the hallway and stopped, smiling and shaking his head slowly. "Unbelievable. Oliver… I have no words." He too stepped up to Oliver and embraced him with a manly bro hug, slapping him proudly and firmly on the back repeatedly.

In spite of himself, Oliver grinned. The acclamation felt good—gratifying, if nothing else. And it seemed so sincere. The doctor wasted no time escorting Oliver to the scale, and this time Shirleen bore witness, standing on the other side of Oliver, watching him step onto the scale.

"One eighty-four!" She clapped her hands and patted Oliver's shoulder. "Oh, dear, another success story." Placing one hand on her heart, with the other she wiped a tear from her cheek.

Oliver's own emotions bubbled within him, though somewhat eclipsed by the inexplicable surrealism that consumed him. In fewer than fourteen months, he'd changed himself, found a new person inside him. For months, he'd dieted, walked in circles in his garage, resisted thousands of relentless temptations before he even mustered the courage to step foot in a gym. But once he did, everything about him changed. For the nine months that ensued, he'd risen every morning before dawn and forced himself through a grueling workout. No matter the weather, no matter how he felt, no matter the day of the week, the time of the year—he never missed a workout. And before his very eyes his body reshaped itself. The fat melted away and was replaced by lean, solid muscle.

"I have so much loose skin, though." Oliver looked from the doctor to the receptionist, holding up his left arm. He pulled down on the saggy skin beneath his bicep, stretching it a good three inches. "And my stomach is gross. I can't even take my shirt off. It just hangs there, so much excess, I have to tuck it into my waistband. And you don't even want to see my legs."

The doctor smiled. "Oh, Oliver, minor details! I know it's frustrating. You've worked hard, and you deserve to show off the fruits of your labor, but trust me, we can easily fix the loose skin."

Shirleen rubbed his back before dismissing herself, then headed back down the hall to her workstation at the desk while the doctor accompanied Oliver into the exam room. "Well, let's see specifically. Hop up on the table and take off your shirt."

Oliver recalled how hesitantly he'd disrobed in front of the drop-dead gorgeous doctor a few months ago. The man was now no less attractive, but Oliver didn't have a hundred fifty pounds of excess baggage on his frame anymore. He peeled off his dress shirt and slipped out of the arms of his one-piece compression garment, sliding it down to his waist.

As Oliver took his seat on the bench, the doctor ran his fingers over Oliver's pectorals, tugging against the skin, then slid lower on his torso, examining the abdominals. "Yeah, I think you're ready to consult a surgeon. Oliver, I'm impressed. You've built up a very solid core of muscle. Your abdominals are firm beneath this excess skin."

"Isn't there anything else I can do in the meantime... until the surgery?"

"Sorry." He smiled sympathetically. "Unfortunately, there's no such thing as a skin-tightening exercise. But it seems you're already doing everything you can. The compression garment is a good, temporary solution. Does it extend onto your thighs?" He reached down between Oliver's legs, feeling the spandex through the fabric of his pants.

"Yeah. Down to my knees, actually."

Brad took a step back and slid onto the stool behind him. With one hand on Oliver's knee, he looked into his face. "I can't speak for the surgeon, but I can tell you in most cases, they perform the excess skin removal in two stages."

"Two operations?" Oliver didn't want more than one surgery. He just wanted to get it over with.

"Upper and lower. They're painful, and you'll be laid up a few weeks for each one."

Oliver sighed. "I don't see how…."

"What about family? Do you have anyone you can stay with? I doubt it will be as long of a recuperation period as we might normally predict. You're very determined, very motivated. I mean, look at you. But still…."

"I honestly don't know if I can even afford it right now."

The doctor nodded. "It's going to take some planning. And, you know, there's nobody rushing you. Some people wait months, even years, after losing a lot of weight before they have the skin removal. Some elect never to remove it."

"I want it removed." Oliver scowled. "I didn't work this hard to get to a point where I'm still… uh… ashamed to take off my shirt. Look at this chest. Could you imagine me on a beach?"

Brad smiled. "Actually, yes. I can relate to every word. Remember, I've been through all this myself. And I'll even refer you to the same surgeon who did my skin removal. But I want to caution you about something, Oliver."

Oliver stared at him intently, expectantly.

"If you're not comfortable in your own skin before the surgery, you won't be afterward."

What was he talking about? Of course Oliver wasn't comfortable looking like this. His skin didn't even seem human. It grossed him out the way it hung down, sagged. He could stretch it and pull it away from his body, and its hideousness revolted him.

"Not even a year and a half ago, you were still a fat boy. You'd been obese most of your life, and in your mind—in a part of your psyche—you will always be imperfect. You'll always be less than others. Always be one milk shake away from backsliding and becoming an orca once again."

Did the doctor think about himself this way? His words rang true, though. Oliver felt exactly as Brad was describing. He'd never be hot like Ethan and Devon. He'd never quite fit in, with or without the fat, and probably with or without the loose skin.

"I can give you the referral today to a surgeon, but I'd urge you to consider at least one or two sessions with a counselor."

Oliver wanted to roll his eyes, shake his head—protest. He wasn't mentally ill. He just had some extra skin he needed removed. "But it's my choice? It's not mandatory for the surgery, is it?"

"No, of course it's not mandatory, but I strongly recommend you at least explore these feelings. It's important you're prepared. And even the surgeon will concur. Plus, you're just now at your weight-loss goal."

"Almost."

"I'd say four pounds is close enough. Oliver, you also need to continue your work with the nutritionist. You want to be able to healthily maintain."

He took a deep breath, releasing it with an audible sigh. "Will I ever just be normal? Will I ever get to a point where I'm not...."

"Obsessed? Again, this is why you need to talk to someone."

As he left the doctor's office, Oliver's emotions swirled within him, a bittersweet mix of gratification and discouragement. He'd arrived so excited, so eager to step on the scale and share the result of his progress, but now he felt he still had so far to go. And he now felt alone, no one to help him through what might prove to be the most challenging part of the journey. Amanda had her own life changes to tackle. And Benjy... there was no Benjy, not anymore. He'd severed Oliver from his life. Now they no longer even worked together.

The dull ache in his chest returned. What was the point bemoaning his losses? He slid behind the wheel of his SUV, the seat now at least a foot closer to the steering wheel than it used to be. He looked up at his reflection in the rearview mirror, now seeing only one chin and a narrow, high-cheekboned face that seemed more angular than round.

"Oliver," he said to himself. "You're a new person. You need a new life."

CHAPTER SEVENTEEN

OLIVER NEARLY dropped his phone, staring for a few seconds in disbelief. Benjy hadn't spoken to him since the day Oliver had left his apartment. Although he'd seen Benjy's car in the employee parking lot, he'd yet to run into him on the job. Benjy now worked on a separate floor, and so far they hadn't so much as crossed each other's paths in the employee breakroom. To Oliver it was obvious Benjy had made a concerted effort to avoid him.

His hand trembled just a bit as he pressed the screen of his phone to open the email. Then he sighed disappointedly as he read the words.

> *Oliver, I'm sending $242.18 to you via PayPal.*
> *This is a refund for the airline ticket you purchased to*
> *Missouri. In light of all that's happened, I'm sure you*
> *did not still plan to attend this weekend. The airline was*
> *unable to refund your credit card at this late date, so*
> *instead they issued me credit on a future flight. I'll just*
> *pay you back your money now, and in exchange, I'll hold*
> *on to the credit and use it myself. Thank you for agreeing*
> *to go with me and even paying for your own ticket. I*
> *shouldn't have allowed you to do that in the first place.*
> *Thanks again, Benjy.*

Resisting the urge to reply with snark, he simply backed out of the email to return to his in-box where, as promised, another email had appeared from PayPal. *Benjamin Erickson Sent You $242.18.* He didn't want Benjy's money. Feelings of sadness and anger battled inside him. Accepting the money just seemed so final. It strangely confirmed the reality he'd been trying to deny this past week. To make matters worse, he'd not only lost Benjy as a boyfriend, but also as a coworker and friend. Benjy had pointedly decided to completely cut Oliver out of his life.

And on a certain level, that pissed Oliver off. Granted, he had no right to dictate to Benjy what he should feel, and in all honesty, Benjy had probably done way more for Oliver than he'd ever returned, yet it still felt like a slap in the face. He closed out of the email program angrily and went to his text messaging app.

Hey, what's up? How about dinner tonight?

Without allowing himself time to rethink his impulsiveness, he clicked Send. A few seconds later, he had his reply from Ethan.

Sure, man, as long as it includes dessert.

A tingly sensation traveled from his chest, across his shoulders, as a surge of excited arousal ignited below his waist.

Can't wait. Meet at the café at 7.

Cool. Counting the minutes.

SLIDING INTO the passenger seat of Ethan's sports car, Oliver felt his heart race, which seemed only appropriate as Ethan peeled out of the parking lot. Not familiar with his "date's" personal taste, he asked Ethan to choose a restaurant.

"I know just the place. Ever go to the Radcliffe?"

"I thought that was a golf course or something."

Ethan shrugged. "Country club. My parents have a membership." He tilted his head slightly to the side, but Oliver wasn't entirely sure he was looking at him. With his dark, Tom Cruise sunglasses, his gaze remained concealed. "So, what happened the other day with you and Devon? Did you do anything?"

Oliver smoothed out his pant legs, wondering if the spandex compression suit underneath his clothes was as obvious as it felt. "We just talked for a while at the café. Another guy was with him, Ryan."

Ethan sighed in an exaggerated manner. "Figures. They're exes, ya know."

"Oh. No, I didn't know that."

"Well, the list of guys who *aren't* Devon's exes is much shorter than those who are. He's a bit—how shall I say? Trashy."

"He invited me to his condo this weekend."

"The beach-bash thing? Yeah, it should be a blast. You're going, right?"

He cleared his throat, holding on to the door handle as Ethan carelessly whipped around a curve.

"Jesus Christ!" Ethan screamed. "Would you *move!*" Annoyed by the vehicle in front of him, he slammed his palm into the steering wheel car horn. Apparently he wasn't one of those drivers who paid attention to speed limits. Or dangerous curves.

"I think so. I told him I'd go, and I don't want to go back on my word."

"Good. Trust me, you'll fit right in."

He wasn't so sure. What he'd seen so far didn't help him feel much like one of the gang. Ryan had been nice enough, and Devon was beginning to warm up to him. He doubted he'd ever mend fences with AJ or his boyfriend, Roger. "What do you do, by the way? I mean, we hardly know anything about each other. I know you're a musician...."

Ethan shrugged. "That's just kind of my latest thing. I'm still not sure what I'm going to do when I grow up." He laughed. "Although I'm twenty-seven. I have a bachelor's, but it's in English. Not sure what to do with that. Started on postgraduate work, then dropped out. My folks are telling me I should go back, but you're only young once, ya know. I don't want to waste all my twenties in college."

"Oh. So you don't have a day job?"

"Why bother?" He grinned. "My grandfather set me up with a trust fund. I could go my whole life without working, if I wanted."

Wow, Oliver wasn't sure he'd ever had a friend who was independently wealthy. It explained a lot, though. No wonder he was able to spend so much time hanging out at the gym and café, and going to clubs. But what about the rest of them? "Does Devon work?"

"Supposedly his father will eventually hand over the reins of his business, but I don't see it happening anytime soon. He lives in a condo just around the corner from mine. I think he's technically a vice president or board member or some shit of his dad's company. They sell computer software."

"Really?" Oliver's ears perked up a bit. "I'm a programmer."

"Talk to him about it. Maybe he could get you a position."

"Right now I work for an insurance company. The pay's okay, but…."

Ethan feigned a yawn, then laughed. He pulled off the main road and headed down the driveway of the country club. As Oliver sat beside him, he recalled their exchange earlier when they'd texted. He took in the golden, coppery color of Ethan's skin, the rippling muscles in his arms and chest, and he couldn't help but feel a bit insecure. Had he been standing, his knees might have buckled. As hard as he'd worked to lose weight and put on some muscle the past year, his body still didn't compare to Ethan's.

All the gym bunnies looked good, though, including Devon. He too had ripped abs, powerful legs, and broad, masculine shoulders. Oliver had always imagined worshiping guys like Devon and Ethan. For most of his teen years, he had viewed this type of guy as a god. Now here he sat in the passenger seat of such a man, and if he didn't screw things up, he could later find himself in Ethan's bed.

But was that what he really wanted? He wasn't sure how Ethan would react to seeing him naked. Oliver was now more fit than ever before in his life. Was there any way for them to be intimate with each other without Oliver having to dispense with the compression suit?

"Dude, you're doing it again. You're in outer space." Ethan, who'd pulled up to the front of the building and stopped in the circular drive, slapped Oliver on the shoulder. "We're here, man."

"Oh, right." He looked at Ethan, puzzled, wondering why he hadn't parked in the lot, when suddenly his door opened. A middle-aged man, wearing what looked like a butler's uniform, stood on the other side of the car door, holding it open. Another such employee had appeared on Ethan's side of the car. Ethan hopped out nonchalantly and removed his sunglasses.

"Good evening, Mr. Carville," the valet said with a nod. "Dinner for two this evening?"

He smiled and clasped the older gentleman's shoulder. "Yes, Arthur. Dinner with my friend Oliver. Just the two of us." He looked over the car at Oliver, who now stood beside the vehicle, and winked. Ethan handed his car keys to the maître d', who escorted Ethan around the car to join Oliver. The valet, the man who'd opened the door for Oliver, took the keys, and Ethan accompanied Oliver inside.

Oliver wondered if perhaps he wasn't underdressed for a swanky place like the Radcliffe, but even Ethan had worn informal attire. Though Oliver now didn't doubt his friend owned only name brands Oliver had never heard of, they both wore short-sleeved dress shirts and khaki-style pants. And as Oliver fell in behind Ethan as the maître d' led them to their table, Oliver looked down at Ethan's perfectly rounded ass.

His heartbeat quickened, and thoughts of what he'd like to do with Ethan flooded his consciousness. His cock awakened, plumping a bit in his khakis. Benjy had been the only guy to ever show even the remotest interest in Oliver, and he'd been the only person with whom Oliver had been intimate. But everything had changed, and oh so quickly. Now two unbelievably hot guys had all but bent over backward the past week trying to win his affection, and here he was on the verge of getting laid by one of them.

As they took their seats, Ethan casually blurted out an order for a bottle of wine, and when the young, strikingly handsome waiter handed Oliver his menu, the first observation Oliver made was the lack of prices. He read through the options, not as concerned about the cost as the caloric and fat content of each item.

"Order anything you want," Ethan said flippantly. "I guarantee you'll never blow your diet here…. I mean, if you're still even *on* a diet. They're not known for portion size."

"Oh." Oliver took a sip of his water, then smiled. "Actually, I'll probably always be on a diet. Maybe not formally, but I'll always be aware of fat and calories. I really don't want to go back to who I was before."

"I can hardly blame you," Ethan scoffed. "You were quite the sight, but look at you now." He waved his hand like Vanna White unveiling a word puzzle. "You just need to stay focused, and within a year or so, you might start to buff up like…." He cleared his throat as the waiter returned with the wine. After uncorking it, he offered Ethan the cork. He smelled it and handed it back without comment, and the waiter poured each of them a quarter-full glass. "I'm assuming you've started using supplements."

"Definitely." Oliver picked up his glass, not bothering to hold it in his palm and swirl the contents as Ethan so expertly continued to do. Oliver took a sip and set the crystal goblet back onto the table. "Protein mix, the stuff Adam recommended."

"You *do* realize you've already advanced beyond the point where Adam Wilcox can be of any assistance to you."

Oliver stared at him a moment, puzzled. "No, I didn't. What do you mean?"

Ethan rolled his eyes. "Adam's one of these… how shall I say it? He's a nice guy and all, but his whole life is that gym. He has a two-year degree from a community college and has always worked at the Fitness Warehouse. I went out with him a few times." He shuddered, then took a gulp of his wine. He leaned toward Oliver as if to disclose a delicate secret, then continued in a hushed voice. "Maybe five inches at the most, but I'd say that's being generous. Let's just say, the nice body hardly makes up for the lack of anything *substantive*, if you know what I mean."

Oliver felt his cheeks growing warm. God, he'd never bothered measuring himself. He wondered if Ethan would think something similar of him. Benjy sure hadn't been disappointed, but what did he know?

He looked up to see the waiter waiting to take their order. He turned to Oliver first, who ordered whitefish. "I need a big piece of meat—*red* meat," Ethan said. "Whatever cut you'd recommend, medium rare."

"Yes, sir." The waiter, a dark-haired twentysomething wearing a tuxedo, carried no order pad but seemed to just remember everything. He nodded. "Will there be anything else, gentlemen?"

"Other than your number?" Ethan raised his eyebrows as he took another sip of wine.

"That's very flattering, sir, but you know how they are here—quite strict when it comes to fraternizing with the members."

Ethan grinned. "While on duty, of course."

The young man seemed unfazed by the blatant flirtation and just smiled sweetly. "I'll make sure you both get a tasty dessert." He winked as he walked away, and Ethan stared directly at his ass for a good five seconds until he was out of sight.

Wow, the whole scene was crazy. *Beyond* crazy. Weren't Ethan and Oliver on a *date*? Maybe he'd misinterpreted the whole thing. Of course he had. He'd been the one to send Ethan the text. All this time Oliver had assumed things that weren't true.

Embarrassed, he looked down at the table.

"Hey, man, you okay? You know I was just teasing that kid, just messing around, right?"

Oliver looked up, offering a weak smile. "Sure."

"Hey, are you okay?" Ethan reached across the table and placed his hand on top of Oliver's, and for the first time since he could remember, Oliver felt small. Vulnerable. As a fat boy, he'd often felt ostracized, even put down. He'd grown cynical and defensive and at times angry. Sure, he'd suffered a lot of hurt. He'd felt crushed, demoralized, and even depressed. But he'd never felt vulnerable.

Did this feeling stem from an underlying sense of inferiority? How could he deny he'd always felt like less of a person than the perfect-looking guys like Ethan, but why did he still feel this way after losing so much weight? Was it because he still had so far to go? He didn't have Ethan's muscle mass. He didn't have his striking, man-boy face, his flawless golden skin tone. He didn't possess the double row of perfectly aligned teeth that gleamed with his every smile, the fastidiously coifed hair, sculpted without a single strand out of place.

No, it wasn't just Ethan's looks that laid bare Oliver's soul. It was Ethan's very countenance that intimidated him. How had it taken Oliver so long to realize? In their previous interactions, Ethan had seemed so interested in Oliver, and how could Oliver deny that he was flattered? His heartbeat took off like a locomotive every time he even allowed himself the possibility of being intimate with Ethan. But at what cost? Was it worth it to sacrifice his dignity, to allow himself to feel so belittled?

"I'm fine," he said, pulling back his hand and placing it in his lap. He squared his shoulders, straightening his posture in the chair. "I just think I got the wrong impression, and it's probably my own fault."

"What do you mean?" The same plastic smile, beautiful yet vapid, met Oliver's gaze as he looked across the table into Ethan's face.

"I mean… I know this is gonna sound silly, but I thought…."

"What?"

"I thought this was a date."

"It is, silly." Ethan's deep, bubbly laugh should have warmed Oliver's soul, should have reassured him. Instead it felt hollow. "I thought I made that clear. I don't bring just anyone to this place. Of course it's a date. If you're worried about me flirting a little with the waiter…." He waved his hand dismissively. "It's all in good fun. I'm not interested in that kid. I'm interested in you."

Oliver leaned back in his chair as another server approached, carrying salads. After sliding the oversized plate containing perhaps a couple ounces of greens and a single cherry tomato in front of him, the waitress offered crushed pepper. "Please." Oliver smiled at her.

Disinterested, Ethan continued as if he hadn't noticed the distraction. "I promise I'll make it up to you when we get back to my place."

"*Your* place?"

"You promised dessert. Remember?"

The waitress turned to Ethan as Oliver stared at her face, wondering how she maintained such a neutral expression. "For you, sir?"

He barely shook his head, not bothering to even acknowledge her. "Thank you," Oliver offered meekly, somewhat embarrassed by Ethan's dismissiveness. After the waitress had departed, he answered Ethan. "I wasn't sure you were serious about that."

"How about we enjoy our time together and see how it goes?"

Oliver picked up his fork, releasing a silent sigh of relief. "Okay." He smiled, and somehow felt smaller than he ever had in his life.

"And that right there is Devon's condo." Ethan pulled into the Lakeshore Estates and stopped briefly at the intersection to point to a particular condominium unit. "Mine's on the next block, around the corner."

Ethan's voice sounded distant to Oliver. With the elevation of his blood pressure combined with an annoying queasiness in his gut, he struggled to focus. It seemed he'd suddenly entered a fog—a surreal state where the impossible had become possible and fantasy became reality. How was he even here right now, and why?

Worse yet, he was trapped. Without his own vehicle, he'd have no escape were he to decide to leave. But dinner had gone okay. After Oliver overreacted to Ethan's flirting with the waiter, the rest of their meal went smoothly. And he wanted the intimacy. He wanted to touch and be touched, to experience a man like Ethan, even if only one time. For so many years he'd envied guys like this from afar, and now at last he found himself up close and personal. Hadn't he earned this privilege? Hadn't he worked damn hard to mold himself into a better person, one worthy of this honor?

Ethan's hand sliding onto his thigh, easing downward between his legs, triggered a jolt of excitement that raced through him. With one hand, he gripped the door handle on the passenger side of the car. With the other, he held on to the side of his seat, not daring to look over at Ethan but instead staring out the window, still as a statue.

"Here we are." Ethan pulled into the drive as the garage door opened. Oliver glanced over, his eyes trailing the length of Ethan's body. Starting at his knees, Oliver's gaze traveled upward to the man's waist, taking in the solid abs of his core, ascending farther. His polo shirt hugged his pumped, chiseled pectorals, and the short sleeves extended only partway down his muscular arms, ending midway across bulging biceps. Oliver's gaze trailed back to his neck, which bore not a single ounce of unwanted fat. He'd never gazed into a mirror and held back his head far enough to erase a double chin. Ethan's squared, masculine jawline outlined a perfect man-boy face, eyes as blue as the sky and lips soft, luscious pillows.

When Ethan leaned toward him, Oliver surrendered, closing his eyes as those perfect lips pressed against his own. He felt Ethan's hand brush softly against his cheek, and as Oliver tasted this other man's breath—crisp and minty from the after-dinner chocolate—he moaned softly. Responding to the kiss, his tongue explored Ethan's mouth, and Ethan's hand slid down onto Oliver's shoulder. Tilting his head to the side, he submitted to Ethan's guidance, allowing him control to ravage his mouth.

Now throbbing, Oliver gasped when at last they separated. Ethan stared into his eyes, smiling. "I suppose we should get out of the car, unless you want to get frisky right here in the garage."

His heart now beating like a bongo, Oliver simply nodded and unfastened his seat belt. Ethan did the same, and they exited the vehicle. Oliver stepped around the sports car within the spacious garage and followed Ethan to the entrance. He gazed once more upon Ethan's backside. His sturdy legs—the muscular contour of which could be identified even beneath his slacks—perfectly transitioned to the globes of a magnificent bubble butt. The man's broad shoulders and narrow waist formed a V-shaped torso, which unquestionably would be the envy of most any man, Oliver included. He watched patiently as Ethan stopped just inside the door and entered a code into his alarm system. He then turned to Oliver, inviting him forward with his outstretched hand. Oliver slid his own hand into Ethan's palm and moved closer.

Ethan pulled Oliver inside, closed the door behind him, and pressed Oliver against it as he kissed him once more. This time, one of his hands slid to Oliver's crotch and began massaging his bulge through the fabric of Oliver's pants. Excited, Oliver grabbed hold of Ethan, wrapping his arms completely around Ethan's upper body, marveling at the solid firmness of his muscular torso.

"Mmm." Ethan grinned as he reached for the tail of Oliver's polo.

"N-n-no. Please…." Panic surged through Oliver as he pushed Ethan away. "I mean, not yet."

"You're not being shy are you… all of a sudden?"

He shook his head and looked around. "Wh-where are we?"

"Utility room. Leads into the kitchen." Ethan laughed. "I get it. Of course you don't want to do it in the fucking mudroom on top of the washer and dryer." Oliver spotted the laundry facilities as Ethan spoke. "Although I have to admit, it's a nice fantasy." He leaned forward and kissed Oliver softly on the forehead. "C'mon. Let's go inside, and I'll show you around. I'll get us a drink."

As they entered the kitchen, Oliver looked around for appliances. The industrial-sized countertop stove sat against the opposite wall, and a pair of ovens stacked one over the other were built into the wall. There seemed to be no refrigerator, dishwasher, microwave, or any other appliance, though. A stainless steel double sink, gleaming spotless, was positioned adjacent to the stove on the neighboring wall. Ethan walked over to what looked like a large cabinet and pulled it open. *Aha, the refrigerator.* The bright light from the appliance's interior illuminated the dim kitchen as Ethan reached inside.

"Beer?"

"No, thanks. Water, if you have one."

He removed two bottles of water and handed one to Oliver. The kitchen darkened as he closed the refrigerator door. The light cast from the utility room provided a subdued ambiance, perhaps spooky—perhaps romantic. "Of course, with a kitchen this big, we could even do it right here. Right on the table."

Oliver chuckled nervously. "You're really revved up, raring to go." He twisted off the cap of his water and took a sip. "This is quite the kitchen."

"I can't stand clutter. I insisted all the appliances be built in. Out of sight, out of mind."

"Hm. Seems your plan was effective. If not for the stove, I wouldn't have known it was even a kitchen. You're a very tidy housekeeper." He pushed back a memory of Benjy that threatened to invade his mind.

"Not really. I have a housekeeper who comes twice a week—at least. Basically, whenever I need him."

"Oh, cool. That's convenient."

Ethan smiled coyly. There had to be more behind the story he wasn't saying. There was something about his tone when he said the word *need* that implied he was referring to more than cleaning. He turned and headed across the room, Oliver following. "In here is the dining room slash living room."

Oliver nearly gasped as Ethan flipped on the dining room overhead light. The total square footage of the combined rooms had to be more than Oliver's whole house. A partitioning wall and bar separated the two rooms, and the dining room table was enormous, easily able to accommodate twelve people. That still left plenty of space for the ornate bureau or china cabinet—whatever it was—that rested along the back wall, and a narrow serving table that ran along the opposite wall.

"Wow" was all Oliver could think to say.

"This room rarely is used except when the family shows up, which is hardly ever. But you never know. I just might start hosting dinner parties if I ever learn to cook."

Oliver shrugged and almost under his breath muttered, "Or just hire a personal chef."

Ethan heard him and laughed. "My housekeeper, Robbie, cooks for me. He's really good and promises to teach me some day, but right now I'm just too busy. Between working out and rehearsing for my one-man show...."

Strange how different Ethan actually was from Oliver's initial impression. Oliver had thought of him as an artist, and weren't they supposed to be struggling? Starving artists—that's what people always said. He was anything but.

"And this here's my living room." He led the way into the next area of the condo, which nearly took Oliver's breath away. On one side of the room, a grand piano majestically rested beneath the glow of well-positioned track lighting. Along one whole wall, a bookcase extended, and Oliver immediately stepped over to get a closer look. Ethan flipped on a light switch, and an overhead chandelier cast muted illumination along the oak shelving.

"Wow, you have a ton of books."

"I'm a collector." It made sense. He'd said he had an English degree. "The classics, mainly."

Oliver examined the gilded lettering on the rows of matching leather-bound titles. *Wuthering Heights. Moby Dick. Dracula. Pride and Prejudice. Frankenstein.* Oh God, wouldn't Benjy go nuts in a room like this? "Wow," he whispered, trailing his fingertips across the binding of one of the books.

Ethan laughed, dismissive of Oliver's awe, or perhaps too polite to make a big deal of it. "Do you want to watch a movie or something?" He motioned toward the big-screen TV on the far side of the room, mounted on the wall. "I have some *inspiring* films that just might set the mood perfectly."

"Uh, no.... I just can't get over this collection."

"I haven't even shown it to you yet. I have hundreds of porn...."

"No, I mean the books."

"Oh…."

"You know, I read *Wuthering Heights* back in high school. What's the main character's name again?"

Ethan stared at him blankly, slowly shaking his head.

"Heathcliff!" Oliver laughed. "God, it took me forever to finish that book. Talk about a soap opera."

"Are we going to talk about books, or are we going to…?" He stepped closer, placing one arm around either side of Oliver, grasping a shelf of the bookcase. Oliver, now trapped between Ethan's arms, looked up into Ethan's face. Only inches from him, Ethan smelled good enough to eat. His cologne, whatever it was, contained a hint of vanilla. Oliver inhaled as he gazed into Ethan's eyes.

"Ethan…," Oliver whispered.

Ethan leaned in and kissed him, at first gently, then gradually intensifying. Oliver moved his lips, opening and closing in coordination with Ethan's expert guidance. Ethan slid his hand beneath the tail of Oliver's shirt, across his back.

He pulled away slightly, looking directly into Oliver's eyes. "What are you wearing? Spandex?" He smiled.

Oliver nodded slightly, somewhat embarrassed. "It's… um… a compression garment. Full-body style."

"Mmm. I once dated a guy who had a Lycra fetish."

"It's not that…."

"Can I see you in it?" He took a small step back, now holding on to the tail of Oliver's shirt with both hands, ready to peel it over his head.

"I wear it because…."

Ethan stared expectantly, smiling.

"You know I lost a lot of weight."

Ethan nodded.

"Very quickly… or, um, *relatively* quickly. Anyway, I have loose skin. Eventually I'll have surgery."

Ethan's head tilted slightly to the side, but he continued to smile. He seemed uncertain what to think of Oliver's words.

Oliver held out his left arm. "See." At first the arm appeared fairly normal as he flexed his bicep, but when he reached over with his right and pulled against the skin, it sagged, stretching a good three inches below his arm.

"What the fuck." Ethan laughed.

"My legs are the worst and my abs. I have to wear the compression suit because, even though I have pretty much tightened my abdominals by working out, they just look like… well, hideous. They look like pizza dough or something."

"Pizza dough?" The smile began to fade, draining from Ethan's face. "It's cool." He shrugged. "You don't… you don't have to take off your clothes."

"I don't?"

"We can… ya know, do *other* things." He took hold of Oliver's wrist and pulled it downward to press it against his bulge. He reached up with his other hand, grasped Oliver's shoulder, and pressed downward. "Why don't you… ya know…."

Startled, Oliver pulled his hand away. "No, I *don't* know."

Smiling, Ethan raised his eyebrows. "But you promised dessert, right?"

"Ethan, are you telling me that you don't want to see me naked because… because of my loose skin?"

Ethan raised both hands in the air, his expression sobering a bit. "Sorry, man. I didn't mean to hurt your feelings. I just… I don't want to embarrass you or anything."

"I'm not embarrassed." Ironically, his face grew red hot. "I'm not embarrassed. I'm *pissed*! Why should I be embarrassed of my loose skin? I'm fucking *proud* of my loose skin. I'm very comfortable in it."

Ethan turned, took a step away, and then spun back around. "Are you crazy or something?"

"Huh?"

"You're acting like a crazy person."

Oliver's mouth opened, but no words came out. Stunned, he allowed the tingling sensation to travel along his extremities and down his spine. That's exactly what he'd said to Benjy.

"You know what?" His voice was barely a whisper. "I think I *am*. I was crazy to believe you. Crazy to come here with you." His voice grew louder. "Every little detail about you—your fancy sports car and luxury

condo, your designer clothes and gilded classic books you never read—
let me guess. You hired someone to do your coursework and complete
your theme papers in college—it's all bullshit.

"You have a great body, Ethan. It's perfect. Not an ounce of fat,
every muscle rippling. Perfect hair and teeth too. I've always dreamed of
being with a guy like you. I'd always dreamed of *being* you. But that's
all you have. You're nothing but pretense."

Ethan hardly seemed fazed by Oliver's outburst. Maybe he'd heard
the speech before. He stood with his arms crossed. "Are you done?"

"Very much so."

"Then leave."

Recalling suddenly that he had no car, he shook his head in
astonishment. "What's your address?"

"Huh?"

"Your fucking address! So I can call a cab."

Chapter Eighteen

As he sat on the curb at the end of the condominium entrance, awaiting the arrival of his cab, Oliver considered simply walking to Devon's condo. He'd promised to attend Devon's beach party this weekend, but Ethan would most likely be there. What would Devon think about what had happened tonight? Would he make excuses for his friend? Would he be equally shallow? Maybe he would. They were two peas in a pod, so to speak. According to Ethan, Devon was just another spoiled rich boy, inheritor of his family's wealth.

When the cab pulled in, a minivan with a plastic mounted sign on the roof that read TAXI, Oliver barely had the energy to hoist himself up to his feet. The driver, perhaps not much older than Oliver, smiled warmly as Oliver opened the side door and climbed inside.

"Hey, man, where ya headed?" The folds of the young man's neck formed a double, if not triple, chin. His chubby hands, fingers puffy like a Cabbage Patch, gripped the steering wheel. Oliver's heart cracked down the center. He smiled meekly and gave the driver his address.

As they drove to Oliver's house, he learned the cabbie's name was Leonard. He was twenty-three, working part-time as he completed his four-year degree. It seemed almost like looking into a mirror, the reflection being a former version of himself. Oliver judged Leonard to be approximately the same weight he had once been, and he recalled how his stomach used to press against the steering wheel as he sat behind the driver's seat. And like him, Leonard smiled a lot, appeared happy and unconcerned about his nearly two hundred pounds of excess baggage, but Oliver knew it was on his mind every second of every minute of every day.

What could he say? What words would make a difference in this stranger's life? Could he ever even begin to explain his journey? No, it wasn't something he could convey with words. Had someone tried to talk to Oliver back then—back when he was so overweight—and said they used to be fat but lost a lot of weight, Oliver wouldn't have been encouraged. He'd have been mortified. He'd have been reminded of his repeated failures. He might even have rationalized, made excuses for why he was different.

And who knows? Maybe this young man *was* different. Maybe he suffered a medical condition. Maybe he used to weigh eight hundred pounds and was already halfway on his journey. Maybe he didn't care at all but had accepted himself as overweight. How could one assume things about another?

But when the van at last pulled into Oliver's drive, he leaned forward, patted Leonard on the shoulder as he handed him a fifty, and told him to keep the change. Leonard turned to him, his eyes wide with surprise. "Are you sure, man?"

"Positive." He paused for a couple seconds. "Leonard, please take care of yourself."

"I will. You too, and… thank you. Thank you very much."

FRIDAY MORNING, the day after his disastrous "date" with Ethan, Oliver headed reluctantly to the gym. Though the possibility of a dreadful confrontation with Ethan loomed, he refused to allow fear to control him. His workout routines were too important, not because he envisioned himself one day possessing a body like Ethan or Devon, but because he cared about his health. He cared about his own well-being. He truly *liked* being thinner, not only because he looked and felt better, but also because he was worth the effort.

The first half of his night had been fitful. He'd tossed and turned, even sat up for a while on the edge of his bed, mulling over all that had happened. He'd decided to have a talk with Devon, which was another reason he hadn't foregone his morning workout routine. He'd politely decline his invitation to the party but not by spinning a lie. He at least owed it to his friend to be honest. He wasn't comfortable around Ethan and probably would not bring much joy to the party. He wasn't going to insert himself into a situation that could turn ugly, where a scene could ruin the event for others.

If Devon wanted to maintain their friendship, Oliver was fine with that. They might be able to find some common ground, and cultivating a new friendship could prove worth the effort. But that was as far as Oliver was interested in going with the gorgeous jock. Oliver didn't want a relationship with him, nor with any of the other buff gym bunnies. Oliver wanted Benjy.

After his workout, he'd go into work, and he'd find Benjy. He'd track him down and corner him if he had to. He'd force him to listen. The whole situation had been a mistake—no, a major fuckup on Oliver's part. He'd been insensitive and selfish. He'd told Benjy to quit acting like a crazy person, knowing he suffered a mental illness. He'd expected Benjy to face a challenge he wasn't yet ready to tackle. Instead of being supportive, Oliver had been demanding.

And the Facebook thing… that too was reprehensible. He never should have gone to meet Ethan at the café. He should have gone back to Benjy's to apologize, to work out an amenable plan for the day, and do something together Benjy was capable of handling.

As he pushed through the entrance doors to the gym, he resolved to stay focused, complete his workout first, and then find Devon. As he headed across the room toward the staircase, he heard someone call his name. He stopped in his tracks and turned. "Hey, Adam."

"Oliver, wow. I've been hoping to catch up with you."

"I know. I'm sorry." Somewhat winded from rushing, Oliver sighed. "You know how it is, but everything's going great. I'm using the protein supplements, right on track with my weight-loss goal. Probably should boost my resistance training a bit, but I'm taking it slow. I honestly don't want to get really bulky."

"Oliver, I said you're doing great." Adam laughed, and Oliver realized he was talking like a magpie. "I didn't want to talk about any of that. I have a new client, and I'm hoping maybe you'd be willing to talk to him, maybe eventually become his workout partner."

"Really?" Oliver smiled. "Why me?"

"Well…." He draped his arm around Oliver's shoulder, turning him toward the front counter. "My new client, Leonard, is exactly the same height and weight you were when you started."

Oliver's mouth dropped open as he stared in shocked disbelief. "Leonard! My taxi driver!"

Adam and Oliver walked over to the counter, and when Leonard looked up and spotted Oliver headed in his direction, a broad smile lit up his face. "You're my big tipper!" He pointed his finger, though not in an accusatory manner.

They shook hands, both laughing, and Oliver related his story. He told Leonard briefly how he'd been on his weight-loss journey for over a year now, and he'd pretty much achieved the goal he'd set out to accomplish. They chatted a couple more minutes, and Oliver answered questions about the process. They then agreed to meet later, after the weekend, when Leonard officially started his exercise routine.

Oliver was still smiling as he scurried down the staircase toward the locker room. He actually felt the extra bounce in his step, springing from the joy in his heart. Excitement and hope surged through him. He came to an abrupt halt just outside the door when he heard the cackle of laughter. He recognized the voices of AJ, Roger, Ethan, and Devon.

"Oh my God, you should have seen it. I about threw up." Ethan was talking. "When he pulled down the skin under his arm, it looked like a fucking...." Oliver stepped forward slightly, just enough to see around the corner and watch Ethan shudder. He took a step back and leaned against the wall as he continued listening. "Like a freakish sea creature or something. You know how some animals have webbed feet."

"Like frogs!" AJ blurted out.

"Yeah, like a frog or something. Then he had the fucking nerve to ask me if I wanted to see his stomach. He said his abs are like fucking pizza dough."

The foursome again burst into hysterical laughter.

"Of course it's like pizza dough," Devon added, barely able to talk through his gale of fitful laughter. "He was a fucking manatee a few months ago. The fat might be gone, but the skin's always going to be stretched out. Oh God! I just got a visual.... Ew! Please, God, no! Why can't I unsee this?"

"I think you two should just call it a draw," AJ said. "Do either one of you really *want* to have sex with *that*?"

"I was so fucking close, though! I had him in my house and everything. I could fucking be five hundred dollars richer right now, but hey, I forfeit. If you still want to try fucking him this weekend, Dev, have at it. It'll be worth the money to pay you to keep him away from me."

Suddenly Oliver was twelve years old again, in middle school. As he stood quietly against the wall, his face burning up, tears streamed down his cheeks. It had all been a ruse, a practical joke. They'd bet on him, wagering on which of them could fuck Oliver first. But not because he was any sort of prize. No, because he was the opposite.

His first impulse was to retreat, to turn tail and run as fast as he could out of that gym and never, ever come back. He looked straight ahead, staring at the opposite wall for moment as he blinked, then reached up to wipe away his tears. Squaring his shoulders and taking a deep breath, he turned and took a step into the archway of the locker-room door. He cleared his throat and stood there, staring straight at the foursome on the other side of the room.

"Oliver…." Devon's smile evaporated as did those of the other three. Devon took a step toward Oliver, who held up his arm, palm out.

"I heard everything you said."

"We were just—"

"Being the shallow, pretentious bitches you naturally are. Don't bother making excuses or apologizing. I'd love to tell you all off, point out the litany of ethical, social, and mental deficiencies you each have, but it's not worth my time. You wouldn't get it. But it's okay, you have each other. Sort of. As much as you ever will be capable of grasping the concept of a true friend.

"All I'm going to say is that I wish you well. Today for the first time in over a year, I'm skipping my workout routine. I have something more important to do. Two things, actually. I'm going upstairs to file a formal complaint about the four of you, requesting you be banned from the gym. I've read the antidiscrimination policy."

"You can't prove anything!" AJ shouted.

Oliver reached into his pocket and pulled out his phone. "I have the whole thing on video, asswipe." It was a bluff, but it seemed to work. Their four mouths dropped open.

"And when I'm done with the formal complaint, I'm going to go track down the only man who's ever truly loved me… and who I love just as much… if he'll take me back, that is."

He spun on his heels and marched out of the locker room, straight up the stairs and to the front desk, where he indeed filled out the complaint, citing the four of them for terms of service, ethical, and antidiscrimination violations.

He smiled as he headed out the door a half hour later and drove as fast as he could to work.

WHEN HE made it to the second floor, with which he wasn't all that familiar, Oliver glanced to his left and right. He spotted the supervisor and rushed over to her. "Laura, where's Benjy's cubicle?"

"Benjamin Erickson? You mean his office? It's right down the hall, but he's not in today."

"He's not?" He stared at her, shocked and crestfallen. "Um… why? If you don't mind…."

"Well, he took a personal day, and Monday he starts his vacation. He's flying to Missouri, I believe, to attend a wedding."

Fuck. Benjy must have changed his flight to arrive earlier and go to the wedding rehearsal dinner after all. He allowed his shoulders to sag. "Laura, I know this is short notice, but you know I've hardly ever missed work, only one call-in in… like two years or something. Can I take a personal day today? I'm supposed to start vacation on Monday too. We'd planned the trip together, Benjy and me."

"Well." She pursed her lips. "You're right, this is very short notice."

"I'm begging you. Please! I'll get on my knees…."

She shook her head. "That won't be necessary. Yes, go ahead. You're on vacation after today anyway. I'll notify HR."

"Oh, thank you!" He leaned in to offer a hug, extending his arms. When she didn't respond, he hugged anyway—briefly. He quickly released her, and she looked at him, baffled, then smiled. Then he spun around and raced back down the hallway and down the steps to the front door.

Chapter Nineteen

OLIVER COULDN'T get a flight until late afternoon. By the time he arrived at the Kansas City Airport, it was already dark. He had a copy of the wedding invitation Benjy had given him months earlier when they'd first talked about vacationing together. Benjy had booked them a room at the Westin, so in all likelihood, that's where he was. He might have changed his plans, though, and decided to stay with his friend Samantha or her family.

Oliver took a seat in the baggage claim area, waiting for his suitcase to drop down on the turnstile. He pulled out his phone and tried calling Benjy. Of course, he got the same exact message he'd received the five or six other times he'd tried calling that morning. The number was not in service. Had Benjy changed phones? If so, was it specifically to avoid calls from Oliver? If he'd just gotten himself a new phone, he'd probably have elected to keep his number.

Maybe that meant Benjy wouldn't even see Oliver, wouldn't talk to him at all. Oliver didn't want to make a scene. He didn't want to interfere in any way with the wedding. If he did something out of line, Benjy would never forgive him. He was going to have to walk on eggshells when, and if, he did find Benjy, and simply try to find a way to get him alone so they could talk.

He took a cab to the Westin, and once there, explained to the desk clerk that he'd originally booked a room with Benjamin Erickson. She courteously nodded, a plastic smile on her face the entire time, and checked the computer. "I'm sorry. We have no reservation under that name. It looks like the room was canceled."

Oliver sighed, disappointed. "Can I get a room of my own? Do you have any available?"

"Certainly." She asked him a few questions about his preferences, and finally he had his key card.

171

Once inside his room, he plugged in his laptop and googled directions to the church. Fortunately he wasn't far. Most likely, they had some sort of rehearsal tonight, since the wedding was the next day, unless they'd already had a rehearsal dinner earlier and Benjy was just going to follow the directions they gave him. As an attendant, he simply had to walk down the aisle and stand at the altar, then wait for the bride.

Oliver could only imagine the fear and anxiety that probably gripped Benjy at this very minute, and he chastised himself for not being with Benjy to help him through what was sure to be a stressful time for him. If only he'd called Benjy last night… then again, he probably wouldn't have been able to. Benjy must have changed phones at some previous time. Oliver should have just gone to Benjy's apartment and demanded he listen.

Should he take a cab over to the church to see if anyone was there or wait till morning? He decided to wait. He wouldn't be able to talk to Benjy in the middle of a rehearsal. Then again, would tomorrow be any better? He began to question whether or not he'd made the right decision in coming here. Maybe he'd have been wiser to wait for Benjy to return and talk to him back home.

Something inside him—intuition perhaps—had drawn him. He'd known in an instant he had to go after Benjy. Benjy would need him. Benjy would welcome him. That's what Oliver's heart had told him, but now his head was saying something different.

He changed into shorts and a tight tank top and headed downstairs to the fitness center the desk clerk had told him about. Relieved to find it empty that time of the night, he had the place to himself. He used the cardio equipment and some of the free weights, trying to make up for the fact he'd skipped his workout that morning. He finished off with some routine exercises—crunches, burpees, push-ups. As he at last rose to his feet, dripping with sweat, he grabbed a towel from the machine beside him and wiped his brow. He suddenly froze in place, terrified to move a single inch.

"Oliver, what are you doing here?" Benjy stood before him, cuter than fuck in his shorts and matching Under Armour T-shirt. As slender as he was, wearing a crisp, brand-new pair of sneakers, he looked like he was headed to high school phys ed.

"Benjy," Oliver whispered.

"I refunded your money, canceled your flight."

He nodded, taking a step closer to Benjy. "I bought another one."

"I see you did… but why?"

Oliver didn't detect hostility or defensiveness in his voice. Not even anger. It felt like a genuine question, something he really didn't understand and wanted to know.

"I came for *you*, Benjy. I love you, and no matter how hard I try, I can't stop."

Benjy gulped, not speaking, then nodded.

"How are you doing? How are you holding up?"

As he looked into Oliver's eyes, Benjy's shoulders began to tremble. His eyes filled with tears, and he opened his mouth to speak. It took a couple seconds, and then at last he managed to utter, "I'm not… holding up, I mean. I'm terrified."

Oliver stepped forward, refusing to wait another second for permission, and swept Benjy into his arms, pulling him against his much larger body. "Baby, I'm here. Don't be afraid."

Benjy's arms slipped around him, squeezing him tightly, and he buried his face against Oliver's shoulder, his body now vibrating against Oliver's. As he trembled, crying in Oliver's arms, Oliver rocked him back and forth, kissing his forehead and smoothing his hair with one hand.

"I'll go with you. I'll be there the whole time, and when you feel anxious, you can look at me. You can look at me and remember how proud I am of you for facing your fear. And when it's over, we'll celebrate. We'll talk about how smoothly it all went, how fucking sexy you looked in your tuxedo."

"Oh, Oliver! I'm so sorry! I'm sorry for what I did to you."

"Baby, no. You didn't do anything to me. I'm the one who's sorry. What was I thinking, saying that to you, calling you—I won't even say it again. I shouldn't have pushed you to do so much all at once. We could have talked it out. We could have taken small baby steps together."

"That's what my counselor says. I started seeing someone." He pulled back from Oliver and stared up into his face. "She wasn't even sure I should come to the wedding, but I couldn't cancel on Sam."

"I'm so glad. And you know what? I'm going to see a counselor too. I figured out I've got some issues of my own. I've got to learn to get comfortable in my own skin before I go get some of it chopped off."

"You look perfect. You don't need to chop any part of yourself off." The fierceness of his gaze spoke the truth. He meant every word. "But if you do feel you want a surgery, you know I support you."

"I know."

Oh my God. He spoke in the present tense. Does this mean...?

"Benjy, can I kiss you?"

"Right here?" He smiled the most beautiful, coy smile Oliver had ever seen. "Right here in front of the whole world?"

"Right here. Right now."

"What are you waiting for?"

Oliver grabbed hold of Benjy's face, framing it, and kissed him deep and passionate. He pulled back, just a little, and gazed into his gorgeous eyes. "Oh my God, you taste so wonderful."

Benjy bit his bottom lip. "I was going to work out, but...."

"I know another way to work out." Oliver raised his eyebrows.

Benjy grinned wickedly. "But you're already sweaty."

"I'll take a shower, then get sweaty again… and again… and again."

"Mm-hm."

Oliver wrapped his arm around Benjy's shoulder and guided him out the door, then grabbed his hand as he headed briskly toward the elevators. "Why weren't you listed at the desk? They said you canceled your reservation," he asked.

"Oh, Sam insisted on paying for my room. She had already booked one, so I had to cancel mine."

"I LIKE it." Benjy lay beside him, pressing his fingers gently into the skin on Oliver's belly. "It's soft and doughy like you said, but I can feel the hard muscle underneath."

"You're tickling me, you know."

Benjy laughed, and Oliver couldn't help but find it ironic. Benjy tickled him, and Benjy laughed, not Oliver.

"You don't think it's gross?"

"It's you. It's a part of the man I love." He leaned forward and kissed Oliver's abdomen, allowing one hand to travel downward and squeeze his cock lovingly. *Fuck.* They'd already made love twice, and Benjy still got him excited with a single touch.

"I don't think I have the energy for another round just yet." Benjy sighed. "But by the looks of it, I might have to give you head."

"No…." This time Oliver did laugh. "No, I'm fine. You just turn me on."

"Mmm-hmm. I love your big broad shoulders, your strong chest. I love when you tower over me, pin me to the mattress, and fuck me like a wild man."

"Benjy, stop it!" Oliver groaned. "Stop talking dirty to me."

"Never." He slid on top of Oliver's body and kissed him squarely on the lips. Oliver caressed his backside, hands gliding down his naked body to his buttocks. He cupped the perfectly rounded globes as he savored the feel of Benjy's svelte body atop his own. Benjy's hard-on pressed against Oliver's abdomen, and it too was rock solid again.

"I love you." He looked into Benjy's eyes.

"Even with all my imperfections?"

"Especially with them. I love you *because of* your imperfections. Baby, you're perfectly flawed… and so am I."

"You certainly are."

OLIVER SAT in the second row, right behind the bride's parents. God, Sam was amazingly sweet. He totally understood how she and Benjy had become such close friends. Really, the whole wedding party had been awesome, welcoming Oliver as a member of the family.

When Benjy walked down the aisle as an attendant of the bride, not the groom, he accompanied one of the groomsmen. Oliver wondered if it might be awkward, but to his surprise, their arms were linked, exactly as would be the case if one of them were a bridesmaid. They parted at the altar, and Benjy took his place on the bride's side between two female attendants.

Benjy looked spectacular, decked out in his tux, and as Oliver stared at him, he couldn't stop smiling. He also found it difficult to peel his eyes away, even when the wedding march began. Finally he turned to see the gorgeous bride. He glanced back at Benjy, who didn't seem a bit nervous. Benjy smiled as tears streamed down his cheeks. Fuck, he was going to make Oliver cry.

After the ceremony, Benjy quickly found Oliver and hugged him tightly. Oliver could tell he was relieved he'd made it through and happy with the outcome. "You should be proud of yourself," Oliver whispered. "I am…. I mean, I'm proud of *you*."

"I know. I don't want to make this about me, though. This is Sam's day."

"Of course, and that's why you should be proud. You didn't make it about you. You were perfect. You *still* are perfect, in each and every way."

Epilogue

OLIVER PULLED his SUV into the garage, careful not to hit the tricycle. Benjy must've had Dylan out playing again. The toddler loved to race up and down the sidewalk. At two, he certainly thought he was at least five. When Oliver stepped into the kitchen, he inhaled deeply. *Mmmm.* Benjy had already started cooking dinner. He was a much better cook; Oliver loved when it was his turn. With their busy schedules, and with having Dylan, they were careful to divide up the household responsibilities.

Benjy appeared in the archway of the kitchen, holding the little guy in his arms. Dylan's hair was wet, and he had a towel wrapped around him. "Someone decided it would be fun to make mud pies."

Oliver laughed. "Well, it doesn't smell like mud pie's for supper." He walked over, first kissing their son, then his husband. He took Dylan from Benjy, pulling him against his chest and hugging him.

"Daddy Owie!"

"Were you a good boy while Daddy was gone? Or did you drive Daddy Benjy crazy?"

"He was an angel, as usual."

"Just like his father," they said in unison, then laughed.

They'd gotten married a year after their reconciliation in Missouri. A year after that, Oliver finally made the decision not to have the skin surgery. Instead, they wanted to use their money to pay a surrogate to carry their child. Maybe someday Oliver would get the skin surgery, but he wasn't worried about it. He liked his body the way it was, and Benjy loved him exactly the way he was.

Oliver didn't go to the gym every day anymore. Three times a week now. He also remained active, and the two of them loved to bike. He no longer refused every dessert or weighed himself incessantly. He did have to consciously monitor his caloric intake, but not in the fastidious manner he once did.

Oliver donated time at the gym helping guys like Leonard. Leonard had made a lot of progress, far more slowly than had Oliver, but his effort was impressive nonetheless. He now was a regular at the gym, at least a hundred pounds lighter than he had been five years previously. And there'd been other guys.

The gym bunny foursome no longer frequented the Fitness Warehouse. They received one-year suspensions as a result of Oliver's complaint and elected not to return. It was no skin off Oliver's ass, and frankly, he felt their absence was a good riddance to bad rubbish.

His parents remained actively involved in Oliver's and Benjy's lives, and they spoiled their grandson worse than any grandparents in the history of the world. Oliver and Benjy visited them several times a year, particularly on holidays, and Benjy seemed to only get closer to Oliver's mom as the years passed.

Benjy's anxiety was now much more manageable. It hadn't magically gone away. It might never, just like Oliver's loose skin. It didn't matter, though. There were times Oliver had to make concessions. He had to be patient and understanding, even when it was difficult. But it was such a small sacrifice to make, and he was so proud of his husband and all the progress he'd made.

"You do realize next week will be four years." Benjy spoke in a flippant, nonchalant manner as he pulled a tray from the oven.

"Six," Oliver corrected.

Benjy scoffed, laughing as he placed one hand on his hip. "You think I don't remember our wedding anniversary? It will be four years on Saturday."

"But we met two years before that. Why doesn't that time count too?"

Benjy rolled his eyes as he stepped over to the table. "Put your son in the high chair."

Oliver kissed the little boy once more, then did as he was told, lowering Dylan into his seat. "Him's a big boy. He's getting so big and strong."

"And we love him exactly as he is. No matter what," Benjy said. He stepped over to Oliver and wrapped his arms around him, squeezing him tightly. Oliver kissed his husband softly on the lips, then pulled back slightly, gazing into his eyes.

"Because he's perfect," Oliver whispered.

"Absolutely perfect."

JEFF ERNO began writing in the early 1990s. Originally his work was posted on a free, amateur website, where it was eventually discovered and published. He writes gay-themed stories that span several subgenres including young adult, m/m romance, gay fiction, BDSM, and sci-fi.

Until recently, Erno worked as a retail store manager but now writes full-time. He currently resides in southern Michigan. He loves animals, particularly cats, and enjoys reading, movies, theater, country-western music, community service, political activism, and cake decorating.

Website: www.jefferno.com

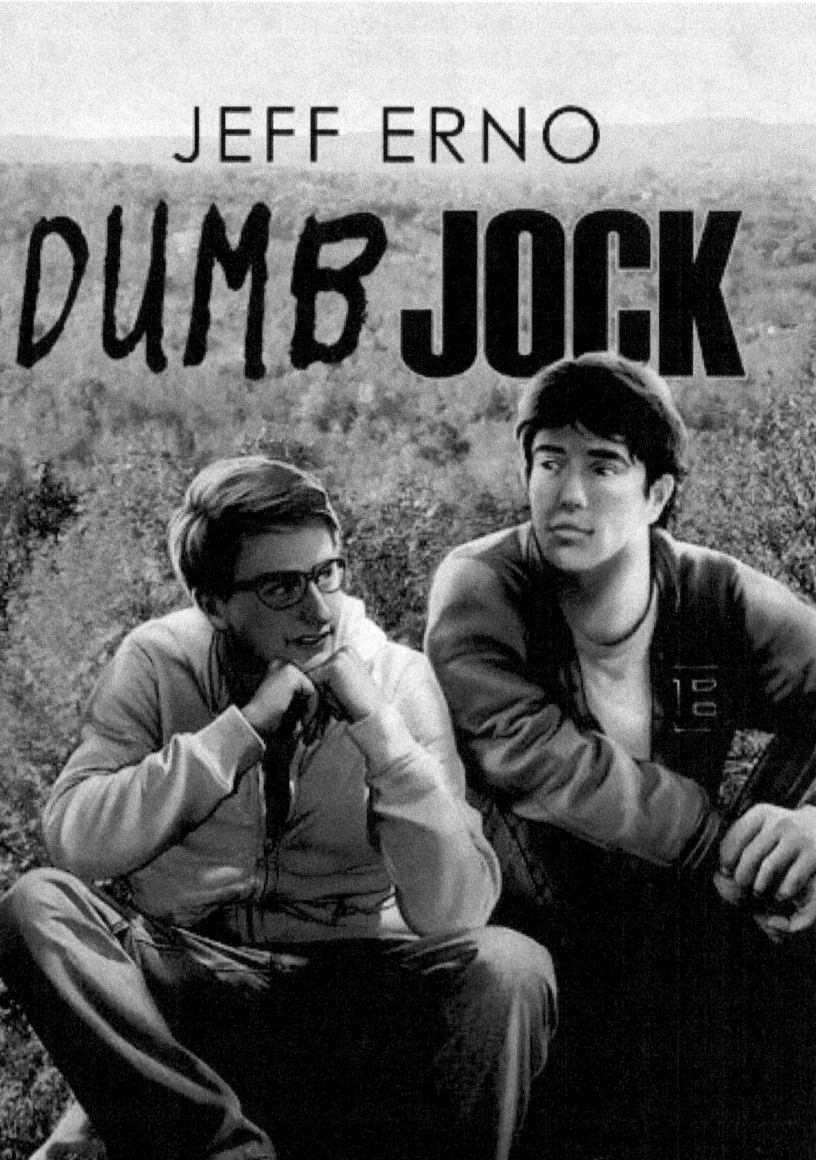

Dumb Jock: Book One

Jeff Irwin is short, timid, and studious. A bit of a social outcast, he lives quietly in the shadows of the popular kids at his school, his life ruled by his ever-present fear of rejection or failure.

Enter high school football hero Brett Willson and the chance for Jeff to embark upon the challenge of educating the world's dumbest jock.

But what develops between Brett and Jeff proves far more challenging than any tutoring session. In 1983, rural Michigan isn't ready to embrace love between two men, never mind two teenage boys. If they're going to make a go of it, Jeff will have to come out of his shell—and Brett will have to prove he's more than just a dumb jock.

www.dreamspinnerpress.com

THE
Left-Hand
PATH

JEFF ERNO

William Austin has always wanted to be a nurse, though he's no longer sure the gratification is worth the pain of losing a patient. For now, he's a nursing student and works two jobs—barista and private nurse. Will meets Blaine Coventry at the coffee shop, and when the altruistic young attorney offers him a job caring for his Uncle Elliot, Will accepts. Will finds that Elliot's stroke has left him unable to walk or talk, and Elliot's husband, James, says the goal is to keep Elliot comfortable until he passes. But Will starts rehabilitation, and his patient soon begins to make progress. When James resists, Will realizes something isn't right, and investigates. Then he discovers a chilling secret that threatens to forever change Will's life… or perhaps end it.

www.dreamspinnerpress.com

SECRETS
THE FULL NELSON

JEFF ERNO

Full Nelson: Book One

Detective Chris Nelson and his husband Ethan are about to go on a weekend getaway to celebrate their third wedding anniversary. Instead, a case comes in for Chris. The brutally murdered body of a swim coach at the local military academy was found in the pool. Seventeen-year-old cadet Alex has already confessed. It looks like an open and shut case.

However, when Chris interviews Alex and reviews the forensics, he becomes convinced Alex is innocent. Searching for the truth behind the actual murderer and why Alex would take the fall, Chris follows a trail through a series of students. He discovers they all experienced sexual abuse at the hands of the murdered swim coach. Digging deep, Chris finds further links between the school administration and the district attorney's office covering up the allegations. When he finally solves the case, it will blow the conspiracy wide open.

www.dreamspinnerpress.com

GLITTER
THE FULL NELSON

JEFF ERNO

Full Nelson: Book Two

When Detective Chris Nelson catches a police call at a gay bar, he finds a murdered drag queen in the alley behind the building. Andrew Brooks, the victim's co-worker at Bambi's, claims he found her. Because she is sprinkled in the same red glitter Andrew uses in his act, Nelson takes him in for questioning.

Forensics clear Andrew but reveal the victim was into hardcore kink. Following a trail of evidence, Nelson arrives at his next suspect: Andrew's brother. Todd Brooks is an avowed neo-Nazi racist homophobe, but Andrew is still devastated. After the near-mistake with Andrew, Nelson isn't ready to rush to judgment again. Taking his time, he digs deeper, intent on apprehending the actual murderer.

www.dreamspinnerpress.com

JEFF ERNO

TEACHER'S

THE FULL
NELSON

PET

Full Nelson: Book Three

Detective Chris Nelson faces another murder investigation. This time the victims are educators—a college professor and a high school teacher—and both are gay. Jared Bressman, the first victim, is found strangled in his apartment. A few days later, Stephen Hayes is found in his home, a victim of the same type of assault. Chris must piece together the clues to find a connection—if there is one—between the murders and stop the killer before he strikes again. Once he discovers that the killer also has a link to someone close to him, Chris races to beat the murderer to his final victim.

www.dreamspinnerpress.com